W9-BUK-645

TEXAS LEGENDS ★ BOOK 4

Texas Legends: Book One *Last Gun*
Book Two *Captain Jack*
Book Three *Rawhider*

Tascosa Gun

The Story
of Jim East

GENE SHELTON

A DOUBLE D WESTERN
DOUBLEDAY
New York London Toronto Sydney Auckland

A DOUBLE D WESTERN
PUBLISHED BY DOUBLEDAY
a division of Bantam Doubleday Dell Publishing Group, Inc.
666 Fifth Avenue, New York, New York 10103

DOUBLE D WESTERN, DOUBLEDAY,
and the portrayal of the letters DD
are trademarks of Doubleday, a division of
Bantam Doubleday Dell Publishing Group, Inc.

Library of Congress Cataloging-in-Publication Data

Shelton, Gene.
Tascosa Gun: the story of Jim East/by Gene Shelton.—1st ed.
p.   cm.—(Texas legends; bk. 4) (A Double D western)
1. East, Jim—Fiction. 2. Tascosa (Tex.)—History—Fiction.
I. Title. II. Series.
PS3569.H39364T37   1992
813'.54—dc20   92-15647
CIP

ISBN 0-385-41902-3
Printed in the United States of America
December 1992
First Edition

To my mother, Bea—

Who taught me to read and write at an early age and who was always able to squeeze the cost of a book from a tight budget, this work is dedicated in love and respect, and with thanks.

The book is also a salute to the people of the Texas Panhandle, some of the finest folks on the face of this planet.

—GENE SHELTON

FOREWORD

This is a work of fiction based on the life of James H. (Jim) East, who came to the Texas Panhandle as a working cowboy, joined Pat Garrett's posse in the pursuit and capture of Billy the Kid, and later became sheriff in one of the West's legendary frontier settlements—the brawling cattle town of Tascosa—during one of the most turbulent periods in the development of the Texas High Plains.

Many of the individuals portrayed in this work actually existed, but the reader should draw no conclusions as to their actual characters, motivations and actions on the basis of this story.

Every effort has been made, within the framework of the fiction novel, to portray as accurately as possible the actual dates, locations, and sequence of events that shaped the life of Jim East and his role in the history of the state of Texas.

ACKNOWLEDGMENTS

The author wishes to express his appreciation to the staff of the Panhandle-Plains Historical Museum and Society on the campus of West Texas State University in Canyon for their courteous assistance in providing many details critical to the development of this story.

Thanks also to the staff of the East Texas State University Library at Commerce for valuable assistance.

While no definitive biography of Jim East has been compiled, to this author's knowledge, a number of scholarly works contributed greatly to the research and preparation of this manuscript. Among those of significant value to the author were:

John L. McCarty, *Maverick Town; The Story of Old Tascosa*, University of Oklahoma Press; Pauline Durrett Robertson and R. L. Robertson, *Cowman's Country*, Paramount Publishing Company; Leon C. Metz, *Pat Garrett: The Story of a Western Lawman*, University of Oklahoma Press, and *The Shooters*, Mangan Books; Dulcie Sullivan, *The LS Brand*, University of Texas Press; and Jon Tuska, *Billy the Kid*, Greenwood Press.

And finally, heartfelt thanks to fellow members of the Western Writers of America, Inc., for their collective and individual encouragement, help and comradeship.

TEXAS LEGENDS ★ BOOK 4

ONE

LX Ranch, Texas Panhandle
November 1880

Jim East flipped the tie rope from the legs of the weanling calf and stepped aside. The heifer bawled once again, finally got her feet under her and bounded up, snorting. She ran toward the cedar thicket that flanked Frio Creek, tail curved over her back like a figure nine.

Jim kept a cautious eye on the calf's mother, a leggy brindle Longhorn wearing the LX brand. The cow stood at the edge of the brush, pawing the ground and shaking impressive horns at Jim from time to time. She was worried about her baby, but at least she wasn't on the prod. Many a cowboy working alone had caught a horn from an enraged mother cow.

"Take it easy, Mama," Jim said casually to the cow, "I didn't hurt her." Within a few weeks, he knew, the cow would kick the calf off the teat. When the weaning was complete she would lose interest in her offspring.

Jim watched as the calf raced up to its mother. The two disappeared into the brush. Jim's scowl deepened the lines in a square-jawed face browned by sun and wind. In his twenty-seven years, a dozen of them spent chasing cows from South Texas to railheads in Kansas and Colorado, Jim East had seen his share of "sleeper" stock.

That didn't stop him from getting mad about it.

The weanling was the fourth sleeper he had found this week. Somebody was stealing stock from the LX, and Jim rode for the brand. The cows might belong to Bates and Beales, the ranch owners, but Jim took the thefts as a personal insult. Any cowboy worth his pay took pride in the brand he rode for and protected it as if it were his own.

Jim stowed the tie rope, re-coiled his Plymouth Manila hemp lariat and secured it to the saddle. He paused for a moment and stared toward the brush where the calf and its mother had disappeared.

He had no real quarrel with legitimate mavericking. Catching and branding grown, unmarked stock was about the only way a man who worked for cowboy's wages of thirty dollars a month and grub could ever build a place of his own.

But sleepering wasn't the same. The calf had been earmarked with the LX overbit, a quarter-moon shape cut from the upper side of the ear. The cut was still fresh, not much more than a week old. The animal had been earmarked but not branded; when spring roundup time came the cattle would still be wearing their thick, shaggy winter hair. Odds were the cowboys working the herd would see the earmark and assume the calf wore the LX brand as well, so they would pass her by. Later, the man who had earmarked the calf would find her, brand her, alter the earmark with a new cut, and add the critter to his own spread.

The way Jim East saw it, sleepering was worse than outright theft. It was actually creating maverick stock. Something that took that much time, effort and patience had to be done by someone who knew the country and the cattle well. Possibly someone who rode for the LX itself. A true rustler would just steal the calf. It seemed less painful to lose stock to an honest thief than to a dishonest cowboy.

Jim reached into a pocket for the makings. He crouched on the downwind side of his sorrel cowhorse and dribbled tobacco into the brown paper. The north wind still held a bite of the early season norther. Patches of snow remained on the shady side of the scrub brush, Spanish dagger plants and stunted cedars sprinkled amid the knee-deep grass of the Texas Panhandle. Jim finished rolling the smoke, lit the quirly and pinched the head of the match until he was sure no heat or spark remained. The last thing the LX needed was a prairie fire to wipe out a section or more of winter graze. It looked like a long winter was taking shape.

He dragged the raw smoke into his lungs, held it for a couple of heartbeats, and exhaled through his nostrils. He didn't yet know who was behind the sleepering. It could be almost anyone who rode for the LX, and that included more than fifty hands during peak seasons. There were twice that many cowpunchers on the big nearby ranches and no shortage of nesters looking to build breeding herds the easy way.

Jim hoped he could find out who was responsible. He had to actually catch them at it or come up with other solid proof. You didn't call a man a rustler without being able to back it up. That was a good way to catch a bullet.

"If I do find out who you are," he muttered to the unseen stock thief, "you'll get your pick of a tall cottonwood tree, a lead slug or a jail cell. Man so lazy he'd steal instead of work doesn't deserve more than that."

Jim finished the smoke, ground the butt beneath a boot heel and mounted the sorrel. He glanced at the low, cold sun a handspan above the western horizon. He had just about enough time to make it back to the dugout line camp on the banks of Palo Duro Creek before dark.

Jim topped out of the Frio Creek breaks onto the windswept, rolling plains, and abruptly pulled his sorrel to a stop. A horseman moved toward him at a brisk trot two hundred yards away. Jim's hand instinctively dropped to the scabbard of the Winchester slung behind his right leg, then fell away as he recognized the rider. His frown dissolved into a grin. The rider on the gray was the last man Jim would ever suspect of stealing stock.

He crossed his forearms over the saddle horn and waited as the rider drew near. Then he waved a greeting to Tom Emory, a top hand on the neighboring LIT Ranch. Tom was a few years younger than Jim and had the lanky narrow-hipped build of a bronc rider. His blue eyes sparkled with the mischievous glint of a young colt most of the time, but when he quit grinning any thinking man paid attention. Tom Emory could handle a rifle or a handgun as well as he handled horses and cattle. Jim East and Tom Emory had taken a liking to each other at first sight on Jim's first big roundup after he signed on with the LX more than a year ago. The friendship had grown with the passing months until either man would trust the other to hold his horse and watch his wife and be sure his friend wouldn't get the instructions backward.

"Wasting the boss's time and money again, Jim?" Tom asked by way of greeting as he reined up alongside. A wide grin lifted the corners of his shaggy mustache and crinkled laugh lines at the corners of his dark blue eyes.

"You're one to talk, Tom," Jim said. "I'll lay a dime against a dollar you haven't hit a day's work in the last two months."

Tom chuckled aloud. "Ah, the glamorous life of a cowboy," he said. "Nothing to do but ride along, admire your shadow on horseback, court the señoritas, get drunk and shoot up the town every Saturday night."

Jim answered with a wry smile. Nothing could be further from the truth and both of them knew it. Other hands bitched constantly about the back-breaking work. Jim East and Tom Emory just did it.

Jim noticed that Tom's grin had faded. "Problem, Tom?"

"Maybe. Major Littlefield told me there's a war council brewing at LX headquarters. Sent me as a rep."

Jim's frown returned. When Major George Washington Littlefield smelled a war, a man could look for the gunsmoke. "What's up?"

Tom shook his head. "Not sure. But I think maybe it's got something to do with the Pecos River cow thieves over in New Mexico. They hit the LIT pretty hard this year."

"We lost more than our share, too," Jim said, a hard edge on his voice.

Tom pulled a twist of tobacco from his pocket, gnawed off a chew and settled it into a cheek. "So did Torrey's outfit. And the LS. The Major's kind of upset about people stealing livestock. Especially when they steal his."

"We going after them?"

Tom Emory turned his head downwind and spat. "Looks like it, Jim. The Major says the cattlemen's association wants to put an end to it and get our stock back. The two of us got invited to help with that little chore. Bill Moore sent word to the LIT that he wants you in on the parley. Said he'd send somebody else up here to ride drift in your place."

Jim's scowl deepened. He didn't completely trust LX foreman Bill Moore. There was something about the man that didn't set right, and it wasn't just the yarns that he'd killed a couple of men before drifting into the Texas Panhandle. Jim reached for his tobacco sack and glanced at the lowering sun.

"Guess we'll find out soon enough, Tom," he said. "Meantime, we'll overnight at my palatial estate on Palo Duro Creek." He reined his sorrel back toward the one-room dugout grubbed from a rocky hill overlooking the creek. The dugout came complete with its own set of scorpions and centipedes, but it was warm and dry. He winked at Tom riding alongside. "Had to let the servants have the weekend off. You'll have to make do with my cooking tonight."

Tom's gray gelding backed its ears at Jim's horse and tried to take a nip at the sorrel's neck. Tom yanked on the reins, barked a curse, and rammed a spur into the gray's side. The horse got the message and calmed down in a hurry.

"How's Hattie?" Tom asked.

Jim felt the corners of his mouth lift in a smile at the mention of his wife's name. "Aside from the fact that she's thirty miles away, doing fine," he said.

"Damn me for a sore-pawed badger if I can see what a woman like Hattie finds in a broken-down saddle bum like you, Jim East," Tom said.

Jim chuckled. "She knows quality when she sees it." The two men rode in silence for a time.

Jim's thoughts stayed with Hattie. He had made three cattle drives from the chaparral country in South Texas to Kansas railheads and learned something from every drive. On the first trip he'd learned how to handle Longhorns—just leave them alone as long as they're headed in the right direction. He used that same philosophy in dealing with men, and it worked just as well as it did on cows. He'd also learned on that first trip north that a Texas cowboy was a lot better off if he stayed out of the saloons, whorehouses and gambling dens at railhead. A ringing headache and a flat wallet had taught him that lesson.

On the second drive he had kept his spending to clothes and supplies, stayed out of the rougher parts of town, saved a little of his pay—and met Hattie Boulding. Memories of her soft Virginia drawl, the lively sparkle in her eyes, and her quick, bubbly laughter rode with him all the way back to Texas.

When he started the third trip he was determined to find the girl again, marry her and bring her back to Texas. He fretted all the way to Dodge City about how to ask her and what he'd do if she turned him down. He was more than a little surprised when she said yes. Sometimes he still had trouble believing it. She could have had any man in four states, a man with money and breeding and a better education, and more of a future. She picked a Texas cowboy. That was the kick in the pants Jim East needed to get serious about the future. He landed the job with the LX, rented a small three-room adobe house in Tascosa and settled Hattie into her new home. There wasn't a decent place on the ranch for a married couple, so Hattie had accepted the arrangement. Jim got one weekend a month off except in the busy times, and on those two days they enjoyed what other couples spent a lifetime trying to find. They had been able to save a few dollars a month from Jim's paycheck. Soon, he figured, he would start drawing top hand wages. That was another ten a month. Then maybe wagon boss and another ten. Eventually they would have enough saved to start something of their own—a ranch, maybe, or a freight line. Or buy into a business in town.

Jim had confidence in himself because Hattie had faith in him. That meant he could do nearly anything. There were lots of opportunities in a part of the country growing as fast as the Texas Panhandle . . .

"Jim," Tom finally said, breaking his friend's reverie, "you run across any sleeper stock over here lately?"

"Four in the last week. Turned one loose just a few minutes before you rode up. You?"

"Yeah. Half a dozen in the last ten days."

"Any sign as to who might have done it?"

Tom shook his head. "Nothing you could count on. But I'm beginning to get some suspicions. Does it seem funny to you that the sleepers start showing up just after Bill Moore takes a three-man crew through checking drift brands?"

"It is a tad curious," Jim said, "now that you mention it."

Pellets of sleet pecked against the stubbled faces of Jim East and Tom Emory as they paused to scrape the mud and ice slush from boots on a garden hoe blade nailed to the porch at LX Ranch headquarters.

"Looks like we're in for one bitch of a blue whistler," Tom said.

Jim glanced at the low gray sky overhead and nodded. He swung the door open and instinctively ducked as he stepped inside. They didn't make doors quite tall enough for a man who stood six-two and packed a hundred ninety pounds, most of it muscle from years of wrestling broncs and Longhorns. A gust of frigid air trailed in behind the two riders and stirred the tobacco smoke that hung blue against the ceiling. A potbellied stove glowed faint red in the center of the big room. To Jim the heat felt oppressive, the air tight and close, after the long ride in the cold outside. His fingers and toes began to ache as they warmed.

Five men sat around the pine table in the center of the room. Jim's brows arched in surprise. *Tom was right,* he thought. *This is a war party if I've ever seen one; some of the toughest men and best guns in two states here.*

Bill Moore held down the chair at the table's end. At Moore's left were Frank Stewart, range detective for the newly formed Panhandle Cattleman's Association, and Charlie Siringo, the lanky LX rider who was as good with a gun and a horse as he was bad with the cards. Luis Bausman of the LIT, a solid, broad-shouldered man whose perpetual scowl hid a hearty sense of humor and an eye for the absurdities of life, sat at Moore's right. Sprawled in a chair at Bausman's side was the six-foot-five, pale-eyed Pat Garrett, sheriff of Lincoln County, New Mexico. Garrett clutched a fat cigar in long, thin fingers.

"Coffee's hot, Jim, Tom," Moore said. "Grab a cup and warm your gizzards. I reckon you two know Sheriff Garrett?"

"We've met," Jim said as he stripped off his gloves and offered a hand. Garrett's grip was firm. "Good to see you again, Sheriff."

Garrett merely nodded, the cold expression in his eyes unchanged as he silently greeted the two cowhands.

Jim slipped out of his coat and vest, unbuckled his gunbelt, draped the equipment over a peg on the wall and topped off the peg with his hat.

"Everything all right up on the Palo Duro Creek range?" Moore asked.

Jim nodded. "Pretty fair, considering. Not much drift yet. Few head from the VP and Rafter I outfits, no more than usual. This little doodlebug of a snowstorm won't hurt us much. The stock's in good shape. Plenty of grass and it hasn't got cold enough yet to freeze the waterholes."

"I'm sending Dink Edwards out to take your place. Think he can handle it?"

"I don't see why not. He's young, but making a good hand." Jim rubbed a thumb across his thick brown mustache. It came away damp from ice melt. "Come the first big blizzard you might want to get Dink some help up there. Palo Duro Creek country catches a lot of drift from up in Kansas and Colorado during the bad ones." Jim plucked two coffee cups from a shelf, filled them, handed one to Tom and blew across the lip of his own mug to cool the thick black liquid before pulling back a chair.

Moore grunted in satisfaction at Jim's report. "Okay. Might as well get us some snakes stomped here." Moore pulled a Bull Durham sack from his pocket and rolled a cigarette, fired it with a sulphur match and squinted through the smoke at the men around the table.

"We've got us some big stud hosses to cut, men," he said. "Frank will fill you in on what's going on."

The association detective leaned forward, his elbows on the table. Frank Stewart, Jim thought, always looked like a man with a bellyache. Jim didn't remember ever hearing Stewart laugh. "I just got back from White Oaks over in New Mexico," Stewart said. "Traced several head of LIT cattle to a butcher over there. I figure he's whittled up quite a few Littlefield beeves, some LS stock and most likely plenty of others, too."

Stewart drummed his fingertips on the table and frowned in disgust. "I couldn't hang the bastard because he had a bill of sale, but the brands had damn sure been altered. I convinced him he'd be a sight healthier if we had a little parley about where the cattle really came from. Seems young William Bonney overstayed his welcome in Tascosa, then took some Panhandle stock with him when he left a while back."

Jim sipped at his coffee. "No big surprise there," he said. "Billy can't seem to break his bad habits."

"This time we're going to break 'em for him," Stewart said. "Sheriff Garrett here's come to ask our help. Pat?"

Garrett shifted his weight on the hard wooden chair, apparently trying to find some place to put legs that seemed even longer than they were, which was long enough to begin with, Jim noticed. Garrett's pant legs were a good four inches short of reaching his ankles.

"There aren't many men in New Mexico I can trust, boys," Garrett said. "Billy the Kid's got too many friends there. I need a handful of hard-nosed, tough men who don't call the Kid friend and aren't scared to buck him. Men who can stick on a trail through the worst kind of weather and don't mind dropping a hammer on a man if it's necessary. Seemed to me the Tascosa country was the best place to shop around for men like that."

Jim shook his head cautiously. "I don't know, Garrett. I'm a dollar-a-day cowpuncher, not a manhunter. I hate it as bad as any man when somebody steals stock from the brand I ride for, and I'll throw down on them if I catch them at it. But I'm not a gunhand."

"Jim," Moore interrupted, "this job isn't to nail Billy the Kid. It's to get our stock back. We know there are several hundred head of Panhandle cattle in eastern New Mexico. All we've been asked to do is get an outfit together, go get what's ours and trail them back home." The foreman stubbed out his smoke. "All the big ranches— us, the LIT, the LS, Torrey's TS Connected—are sending men to do that. I'd like for you to go along with the LX crew."

Jim sighed inwardly. When Moore said he'd like for someone to do something it was an order, not wishful thinking. "Whatever you say."

Moore grunted in satisfaction. "Good. I'm putting Charlie Siringo in charge of our outfit. We'll have Charlie, you, Cal Polk, Lon Chambers and Lee Hall to look after LX interests. You'll leave as soon as we can get everything organized. We'll lay in a few days' worth of chuck. Charlie can buy more supplies along the way." The LX foreman turned to Tom. "Major Littlefield told me he's asked you to head up the LIT crew, Tom," he said.

Tom nodded, his gaze steady on Moore's face. Jim thought he detected a challenge in Tom's eyes, but if Moore saw it he said nothing.

Pat Garrett dragged at his cigar and gazed at the ceiling. "I'll ride on ahead and pick up a few of my own men. We'll rendezvous at Anton Chico and start hunting Panhandle cattle."

Garrett unfolded himself from the chair, shook hands around, and gathered up his hat and coat. He paused at the door and glanced back. His gaze caught Jim East's. "Better bring along an extra set of longhandles," Garrett said. "Gets colder than a banker's heart in New Mexico in winter. See you boys at Chico." He ducked under the low doorframe and stepped into the biting wind outside.

One by one the others filtered from the overheated room, bound for the more familiar comforts of the LX bunkhouse. Jim sipped at his coffee and made no effort to follow.

"Something on your mind, Jim?"

Jim's gaze met the foreman's stare. "We've got more than just rustlers, Bill," he said. "We've got some sleepering going on up on the Palo Duro. Over on the LIT, too. I found four head in the past few days. Tom tells me he found a half dozen long yearlings sleepered."

Jim watched Moore's eyes closely for any visible reaction. There was none. The LX manager merely nodded. "Not surprising. I'll ask the rest of the boys to keep an eye out. Anything else, Jim?"

Jim checked the urge to tell Moore he didn't agree with his choice of leader for the outfit. Jim East liked Charlie Siringo well enough personally, but he didn't trust him as far as he could throw a grown buffalo when it came to handling money. But Siringo was Moore's favorite, and Moore was the boss.

"No. I reckon that's it." He rose and started for the door, then turned. "I suppose you'll get word to Hattie that I'll be gone for a while?"

Moore half smiled. "You tell her yourself. Take a couple days off and go see Hattie." The slight grin faded. "Jim, I want those cows back. That's why I'm sending my best men on this hunt. I'll spend every dime the LX can spare if I have to. We've got to let the Kid and the rest of those Pecos River thieves know what to expect if they steal our stock. And if you get a chance at the Kid, take the little buck-toothed sonofabitch down," Moore said. "I want to be damn sure he's stolen his last LX cow."

Jim shrugged into his heavy coat and turned to the foreman. "Bill, I'll bust my butt to bring our cows back. I won't set out to gun any man. But if the Kid gets in our way, we'll handle him."

Moore nodded. "That's good enough for me."

Jim donned his gear and stepped outside. Miniature buckshot pellets of sleet ticked against his hat and stung his exposed cheeks. The wind had picked up. Jim East had ridden the Texas Panhandle range long enough to know that a bitter cold spell and most likely a full-bore blizzard were in the making.

He made his way toward the bunkhouse. He wanted to go straight to the barn, saddle up and ride to Hattie. But he figured he'd best take the time for a bath and shave before heading to Tascosa. He didn't want Hattie to have to hug somebody who smelled like a he-goat at breeding time.

After he'd cleaned up, Jim would catch the blaze-faced bay for the ride into town. The bay was Jim's personal mount, a solid horse with a smooth, ground-eating foxtrot and the eager nature of a hound dog anxious to please.

The LX cowboys had a tendency to refer to horses by their specialty, like "cuttin' hoss," "ropin' hoss," and "drive hoss."

They called the bay "Old Jim's courtin' hoss."

Tascosa

Jim East reined the bay to a stop on the bank of the Canadian River and studied the crossing below. The river's main channel ran shallow here, probably less than knee deep to Courtin' Hoss. The only ice visible was a thin fringe on shallow pools separate from the main river course. The crossing looked solid and secure enough.

Jim had crossed here many times. His first trail drive to Kansas had forded at this spot on the way to Dodge City. He knew the river ford's history as well as he knew his own.

The ford had been in use for hundreds of years before the town called Tascosa sprouted on the north side of the Canadian, nestled in a grove of trees at a curve of the riverbed. It was the only reliable passage across the often treacherous quicksands of the ever-changing river for miles in any direction. The ford was one of the more favorable quirks of nature. A wide, grassy valley flowed from the open plains of the vast Llano Estacado to the south; across the river a similar but smaller valley climbed toward the rolling grasslands of northern Texas and on to Kansas. The north valley provided a natural trail, a gradual slope upward to the plains beyond. It was an almost level path in contrast to the steep hills and bluffs of the river breaks that spread for a dozen or more miles along the reddish ribbon of water. It was through the two valleys that cattlemen moved their herds up the Dodge City Trail to market.

Before the big ranches came, the valleys and the natural ford of the river had welcomed huge herds of migrating buffalo. Red-, brown-, and white-skinned hunters followed the trails hammered into the red earth by the hooves of millions of the shaggy brutes.

The bend in the river, with its clear spring waters, its surrounding hills that offered protection from bitter winter winds, and its groves of trees had seen the passing of the *carretas* of Comancheros bearing goods for trade with the Plains tribes who only a few years ago had been pushed from the Panhandle into Indian Territory to the north and east.

The Mexican sheepmen had come, settling in the meadows called "plazas" along the Canadian. Their flocks flourished until the Anglo cattlemen came. The cowmen bought up most of the plazas. The ones they couldn't buy they took at the point of a gun. There were still many Mexican families in Tascosa and along the river, but few sheep remained. The cattlemen hated sheep worse than they hated droughts, blizzards or even rustlers.

Jim's bay splashed through the deepest part of the main river channel, climbed the sandy bank on the north side, and lifted into an easy foxtrot toward the settlement ahead.

Tascosa seemed to have grown more each time he came home, Jim thought. New adobe homes sprouted among the cottonwoods and elms. The settlement now boasted more than a hundred permanent residents, most of them making their living from the heavy demands of the cattle trade.

The wide and sandy streets led past almost thirty residences, two general stores, a blacksmith shop, two livery stables, a hotel, two restaurants, an assortment of small shops offering everything from fresh-baked bread to saddles and bridles, and three saloons. There was even talk about building a church and school.

Main Street's east end led to Lower Tascosa, commonly called Hogtown, where the more adventuresome cowboys could satisfy their cravings for women, liquor, and gambling. North of Hogtown along a spring-fed creek were the homes of several Mexican families, a couple of orchards and hay meadows, and a wagon yard where freight carriers from simple carts to big eight-horse-hitch

Conestogas and Studebakers parked between trips to and from Dodge City, Fort Worth and Mobeetie.

Jim East had been to and through a lot of frontier towns from South Texas to northern railheads. Tascosa was his favorite. He had come to look upon the collection of adobe buildings as his town, a place where he planned to put down some roots and stay awhile.

Jim reined in at Mickey McCormick's livery stable on Main Street and called a greeting. There was no answer. Jim knew the little Irishman wouldn't be hard to find when it was time to pay the bay's board bill. All a man had to do was look for a faro game and Mickey would be there.

He shucked off the saddle, found a stall for the bay and shouldered his rifle. Good weapons had a tendency to disappear when left unattended in Tascosa. Jim supposed that was part of the price paid for growth and progress. His footsteps quickened along with his heartbeat as he strode the fifty yards to the rented adobe at the northwest corner of Main and McMasters.

A wisp of smoke drifted from the stone fireplace and flattened itself against the north wind. Jim paused for a moment at the door, savoring the scent of baking bread. He tapped on the wooden doorframe.

He heard Hattie's footsteps and then the door swung open. She stood and gazed at him for a moment. Dark brown hair burnished with tints of auburn brushed her shoulders and rippled in the breeze. Rivulets of sweat painted dark streaks on the bodice of her simple white cotton house dress. Hattie East wasn't a beautiful woman in the classic sense, but she wasn't hard to look at. She was about five-foot-three, slender in the right places and just full enough in the others. Laughter lay just beneath the surface of her large brown eyes framed by small crow's-foot wrinkles. Her features were almost plain until she smiled, and then the whole room brightened up. Jim had never met anyone who could be down in the dumps around Hattie. She was the kind of person who never saw the storm clouds but never missed a rainbow.

"Well, look at this," she said, a twinkle in the brown eyes, "another saddle tramp looking for a handout."

Jim swept the hat from his head. "Reckon you can spare a cup of coffee and a stale biscuit, ma'am? I could chop some wood or something . . ."

Hattie stepped aside and waved him in, closed the door and then hurled herself into his arms. "I just got through chopping wood, cowboy," she said, "but we'll think of something else." She raised onto her tiptoes and kissed him. "It's about time you came home, Jim East. I thought you must have found some rancher's wife or dance hall girl."

Jim tightened his embrace and grinned at her. "No need to steal bacon when there's steak at home, girl," he said. "God, Hattie, I've missed you."

"I missed you more, cowboy," Hattie said. She leaned back and looked up at Jim, tears of happiness pooling in her lower lids. She reluctantly released him from her embrace. "Don't get me too distracted, Jim East," she said, "or you'll make me burn the bread." She turned toward the Dutch oven resting on a bed of coals in the fireplace. "How long can you stay this time?"

"A couple of days." Jim shrugged out of his coat and draped it over a peg, then settled into a cane-bottomed chair at the crude table. He hesitated for a moment, like a man about to dive into the water of a cold spring, then decided to go ahead and jump. "It may be a long time before I get to come home again. A little business over in New Mexico."

Hattie glanced up from her work. Disappointment flickered briefly in her brown eyes. "How long, Jim?"

"I don't know." He drew in a deep breath and told her the whole story. She listened attentively, then nodded as Jim finished. She came to him and took his hand.

"At least we've got a couple of days, cowboy," she said. "We might as well make the most of them . . ."

Jim East had never known two days could go by so fast. Hattie stood at his stirrup, shivering in the cold. He leaned down to kiss her one last time before heading back to the LX. He tasted the salt of tears on her lips.

"Take care of yourself out there, Jim," Hattie said.

"I will, girl. And one of these days I'll be home to stay." He had to touch spurs to the bay before his own voice cracked under the strain of emotion. Riding away from Hattie always hurt, like a fingernail bent back to the quick inside his chest. A grown man wasn't supposed to let a thing like that show in public.

He glanced over his shoulder and waved as he kneed Courtin' Hoss down McMasters Street toward the river crossing. The north wind seemed to have grown a few more fangs in the last two days. *It's going to be a long, cold ride to New Mexico,* he thought.

TWO

Anton Chico, New Mexico
December 1880

Jim East didn't believe in wasting good cuss words, but Tom Emory had no such compunction. When the easygoing LIT man got mad, he got mad all over. Like now.

The growl in Jim's belly and the empty buckboard in front of the adobe left him tempted to give Tom a hand in dusting Charlie Siringo's ears with the barrel of a pistol. Siringo had taken the buckboard to Las Vegas to buy grub and ammunition for the men and grain for the horses. It would save time to do it that way, Siringo had said. *We should have sent somebody with him,* Jim thought in disgust. *Charlie never could buck a monte dealer.*

"What the hell do you mean, there's no supplies?" Tom's tone was a mixture of disbelief and growing rage.

Siringo stared back at Tom, his expression unworried and unrepentant on the lean and angular face. Siringo shrugged. "It ain't my fault the games were rigged," he said.

Tom balled a fist. Jim glanced at his friend and saw the veins in Tom's temples bulge in fury. Jim put a hand on Tom's shoulder. "Damn you for a fool, Charlie!" Tom all but shouted. "You ride out of here with better than four hundred dollars in expense money in your pockets, gamble it all away and come back here with no grub? I'm half a mind to yank you off that buckboard and kick your ass 'til you look like you're wearin' a brown necktie!"

"Easy, Tom," Jim said. "We didn't ride all this way to wind up killing each other."

Jim saw wariness flicker in Siringo's eyes. It was obvious the rangy LX cowboy wanted no part of a mad Tom Emory. Siringo— and Jim—feared Tom might not know when to stop kicking. Jim knew Charlie Siringo wasn't about to pull a gun on a friend. Besides, there was a better than even chance that Siringo would be the one to catch lead and Charlie knew that, too.

"No use gettin' all worked up over it, Tom," Siringo said. "What's done's done. Ain't no sense in two old pards like us tanglin' over a little nonsensical thing like this."

"Nonsensical! Dammit, Charlie, you haven't been the one living on beans and weevily flour around here the last few days!"

Jim tightened his grip on Tom's shoulder. The wiry muscles were rock-hard with rage. Jim became aware that the other cowboys from the Panhandle outfits had gathered around, dark stares pinned on Siringo's face. They weren't all that far from a hanging, Jim sensed. Maybe Siringo deserved it, but not from his own crew.

"Let it drop, Tom," Jim said, his tone firm. "We can't get the money back. Charlie, you screwed up. We all do, sometimes. But not this bad." He pinned a steady stare on Siringo's face. "I've half a mind to turn Tom loose on you. Maybe even help him out myself."

Jim felt Tom's muscles relax, heard the lanky LIT man's snort of disgust, and sensed the danger had passed. For now. "Charlie," Jim said, "you better step real damn light around this camp for a while—and if I catch you with anything more than a piece of stale sowbelly in your hand, I'll personally flatten you like last summer's cowpatties."

Jim led Tom away from the buckboard. He turned his back to Siringo and faced the half circle of riders who had gathered around. "Well, boys," he said, "it looks like we're going to have to tighten our belts and postpone a few meals. We'll be in White Oaks in a couple of days. Garrett should be there a day or so after that. Maybe he'll bring some grub with him." He turned to toss one last glare at Siringo before striding away. "Charlie, you damn well better learn how to play cards before you decide to start gambling with our supper again."

Jim stalked back into the rough adobe that served as the Tascosa posse's temporary headquarters. *Nothing to do now but wait for Garrett and listen to our guts groan,* he thought.

White Oaks, New Mexico

Pat Garrett leaned against a wall in the Texans' quarters and surveyed the crew assembled in the small, close room. The posse had to be thinned down some.

Garrett had made sense when he told Jim that ten men or less would have a lot better chance at catching the Kid and getting their stock back than a mob like this. Garrett had already picked out the men he wanted. They were the toughest of the lot.

Word had already spread through the Pecos country that a posse was hunting the Kid. The locals had already put a name to the hunters. They called them "the Tascosa Guns." The story went that as soon as the news had reached the Kid's gang, several of his men decided the fire was getting too hot and pulled out for a cooler climate.

Garrett pulled a thick cigar from a pocket and twirled it between his fingers. "The Kid isn't the only one in New Mexico with spies, boys," he said. "I've got information on where we can find him. He's trailing a herd of stolen stock up by Fort Sumner. When we catch up with him, there'll be a fight. You can count on that."

The lawman struck a match on the seat of his pants and fired the cigar, turning it over the flame until the end glowed red. "Stewart's riding with me. So's Barney Mason here."

Jim studied Mason's swarthy, broad face. He didn't fully trust Mason. There were those who said Barney had ridden with the Kid before he married Garrett's sister, and that Mason was scared to the bone of the little buck-toothed gunman they were about to chase. Jim shrugged the thought away. Maybe Garrett could keep him in line. If not, there'd be at least one LX man keeping a close watch on Barney Mason.

Garrett shook out the match just before the flame reached his fingers and flipped the charred stick into the fireplace. "We'll pick up a few more New Mexico men along the way." He sucked at the cigar and cocked an eye at Jim East. "Jim, I'd like you to ride with us."

Jim nodded. "I gave the boss my word I'd do whatever it took to get our stock back."

Garrett nodded in satisfaction. "That makes three. Okay, let's see who else . . ."

Fifteen minutes later Garrett had his posse: himself, Frank Stewart, Barney Mason, Jim East, Lon Chambers, Lee Hall, Tom Emory, Luis Bausman and George Williams. Men who were seasoned to the hardships of the trail and were good hands with rifles and pistols.

Cal Polk, the likeable and eager young red-haired LX hand who was a favorite among the Texans, begged to go along; Jim breathed a silent sigh of relief when Garrett turned him down. Cal was too short on years and experience to risk on a cold and dangerous trail.

Jim wasn't surprised when Charlie Siringo declined to join the group. It was more important, Siringo argued, that he stay in White Oaks and organize a winter camp for the men who stayed behind to hunt stolen stock along the southern Pecos. Jim knew the main thing behind Siringo's decision was that Charlie didn't take kindly to long rides and cold camps. Jim didn't question Siringo's guts. The man was no coward. Charlie just liked his creature comforts. Jim had the feeling Garrett knew that, too. Garrett hadn't seemed overly anxious when he invited Siringo to come along. More likely, Jim mused, the lawman had asked Siringo just because Charlie was supposed to be the leader of the LX crew. *I'd lay a month's wages against a dime,* Jim thought, *that when Siringo tells this story it'll be a lot different than the way it really happened.*

"All right, boys," Garrett said, "we saddle up at first light. We've got nearly a hundred miles to cover to Puerto de Luna. We don't stop until we get there. We'll lay over a couple of days while I pick up some of my men and set a trap for the Kid. After that we won't slow down a hell of a lot for another forty-some miles until we hit Fort Sumner."

Fort Sumner

Jim East had to try three times before he was able to loosen the latigo strap of his saddle in the growing gloom of Pete Maxwell's stable. He had lost the feeling in his hands three hours ago in the final stage of the long ride from Puerto de Luna through two feet of snow into the teeth of a sub-zero wind. He knew his fingers were still there. He could see them. He just couldn't make them work. It was as if they were carved from wood instead of flesh and bone.

Finally the tongue of the buckle slipped free of the latigo. He pulled the saddle from the sorrel's back, wrestled it onto a nearby rack, and turned to stroke the sorrel's neck. The horse stood with its head down, nostrils flared and flanks gaunt, exhausted from bucking the snow and drifts on half rations. Jim felt the cowboy's sympathy for a game horse that kept going when it had to fight hard on every step just to get one foot in front of the other. He also battled a pang of guilt at abusing the animal, but there was nothing he could have done.

The other riders in the Panhandle posse spoke seldom, and then in soft voices, as they stripped saddles from worn-down mounts. Jim found a grain sack in the feed bin, scooped a double handful of corn into a morral and slipped the feed sack over the horse's head.

Jim glanced up and frowned as Pat Garrett rode into the stable and dismounted. Garrett tossed the reins to Barney Mason. "Take care of this horse for me, Barney," Garrett said. "I've got to take a piss. The rest of you boys get over to the old hospital and get a fire going." Garrett strode toward a vacant stall. Jim followed. *Now's the time to get some answers,* he thought. *It may be a while until I can catch Garrett alone again.*

Jim waited as the lawman relieved himself and started fumbling with his fly. "Pat, something's been bothering me," Jim said. "I didn't want to bring it up in front of the others."

Garrett arched an eyebrow. "What kind of bee you got in your britches, Jim?"

"You told us the Kid was trailing a herd. Dammit, we both know nobody drives cattle in this kind of weather. You're the man with the spies. I'd like to know where this herd is."

Garrett stared at Jim, his gaze cold and without expression. "What are you driving at, East?"

"Just this, Sheriff," Jim said, his tone as icy as Garrett's. "I came out here to get back our stolen stock. I'm beginning to get the idea that maybe you have something else in mind."

"Such as?"

"Using us to catch the Kid. I think it's been eating at your gut for months that you haven't been able to get him. I don't like to be used by any man out to settle personal scores."

Garrett glared, but made no effort to deny the charge. "You pulling out on me, Jim?"

Jim shook his head. "I signed on for the whole roundup, Pat. I don't quit a job once I start. I just wanted you to know there's some things about this I don't like all that much."

Anger flared in Garrett's pale eyes. Jim braced himself for the showdown. Then Garrett abruptly sighed and smiled. The grin seemed forced. "Oh, what the hell, Jim," Garrett said. "The Kid's got that herd stashed somewhere. When we catch him I'll make him say where. Then everybody will be happy. Trust me on this. There's no future in us arguing about it out here in the cold. Let's get on up to the hospital. The boys will have a fire going good by now."

For an instant Jim thought of bringing up the topic of the reward money. He had seen the notice in the Las Vegas newspaper, a brief one-paragraph statement that the governor had put up five hundred dollars for the capture of Billy the Kid. Garrett damn well knew it, but he had made no mention of splitting up the money if they caught the Kid. Jim shrugged the idea away. He wasn't out here for reward money in the first place. He sighed. "All right, Pat. Like I said, I'm in for the whole ride." *But I'm not so damn sure I trust you all that much,* he thought. He followed Garrett from the stable.

A half hour later Jim sat cross-legged on his blanket beside the fireplace in the old adobe hospital at the edge of the plaza on the Fort Sumner–Portales road. He was beginning to feel warm for the first time since Puerto de Luna. *A hell of a way for a cowboy to spend the week before Christmas,* Jim mused, *waiting to ambush a man I don't even know.* The wind still moaned outside, but at least the snow had stopped. The skies had cleared. A half moon bathed the plaza, its white light made more intense by the glare from the snow. The moonlight deepened the shadows until they were the color of printer's ink.

Lon Chambers had the watch, standing outside in the bitter cold. Jim could hear Chambers stamp his boots from time to time, trying to jar some warmth back into numb feet as he stared down the trail toward Portales.

Several members of the posse had broken out a deck and started a poker game. Garrett sat in, watched in obvious disgust as Tom Emory raked in a small pot, then reached for the cards.

"Pat, are you sure the Kid's coming this way?" one of the players asked.

Garrett shifted his cigar to the other side of his mouth and riffled the cards. "He'll be here. My spies got word to him that we've pulled out for Roswell. I hear the Kid was right happy to hear the news. Whooped and hollered about how it would save him the trouble of whipping us in a fight, taking our horses and driving us on foot down the Pecos like a herd of cows. Five-card stud." Garrett dealt the first round of cards. "Billy'll be here. He'll be wanting to celebrate."

There was one other bit of bait to lure the Kid into the trap at the hospital building. The Mexican wife of Charlie Bowdre, one of the men who had stayed with the Kid when news of the Tascosa posse spread, had living quarters in a room at the back of the hospital. She was now confined to her bedroom under threat of dire consequences if she tried to shout a warning.

"Do you trust this spy of yours? He wouldn't sell us out, would he?"

Garrett half smiled. "He won't sell us out. He's more scared of me than he is of the Kid. Queen's high."

Jim pondered the conversation. He might not like what Garrett was up to, but he wouldn't bet against Garrett where the Kid was concerned. Garrett was shrewd. He understood the Kid's thinking, knew his friends and the countryside.

Jim felt his eyelids grow heavy. The murmur of conversation among the card players was soothing to his ears. He felt himself drifting toward sleep when a gust of cold air breezed into the room.

Lon Chambers stuck his head in the door. "Somebody's coming," he said.

Garrett tossed his cards down and reached for his rifle. "Nobody but the men we're after would be riding this time of night, boys," he said. Garrett jacked a round into the chamber of his Winchester. "Grab your guns. You know what to do. Let them ride in close. Nobody says anything until my signal. Somebody douse that lantern."

The room went dark as Jim rolled from his blanket, threw on his heavy buffalo hide coat and picked up his rifle. Moments later the trap was ready to be sprung.

Jim huddled against the crumbling adobe wall of a low corral beside the building and stared toward the approaching riders. Tom Emory stood an arm's length away, already sighting down the barrel of his Winchester. Jim counted six horsemen, hunched in their saddles against the cold and strung out single file. He glanced toward the front of the hospital. Garrett stood in the deep shadows, barely visible, a dangling harness further obscuring his tall form. Lon Chambers waited beside Garrett, rifle in hand. Barney Mason and the others were concealed behind the adobe corral or waiting at the back of the building to cut off any escape in that direction.

Garrett's spy had named the men riding with the Kid—Charlie Bowdre, Tom O'Folliard, Dave Rudabaugh, Tom Pickett and Billy Wilson. Jim knew none of them by sight, but Garrett knew them all. He had said the best way to spot the Kid was by the big Mexican sombrero he wore. Rudabaugh, Garrett added, would be easier to smell than to see. The man had a strong aversion to water. The story was he hadn't bathed since the age of ten.

Jim felt the steady thump of his heart against his ribs as he watched the file of riders grow closer. One of the men reined his horse about and rode toward the back of the strung-out column. Jim couldn't be sure in the moonlight, but he thought the rider who turned back was wearing a big hat. Jim slipped the glove from his shooting hand and immediately felt the bite of the cold on his fingers. He cupped his fingers against his mouth and blew on them. The warmth of his breath took away some of the sting.

The lead horseman was almost in the hospital courtyard now, headed straight for the doorway beside which Garrett and Chambers waited. Like the others, he rode with his head down, the brim of his hat blocking most of the wind from his face. The horse stopped almost under the front porch of the building barely an arm's length from Garrett.

Jim lifted his rifle, thumbed back the hammer and waited. He picked his target, a slightly built man a few yards behind the lead horseman.

"Halt!" Garrett yelled, "Throw up your hands!"

The command jolted the rider bolt upright in the saddle. The horseman's hand stabbed toward the revolver at his hip. Jim saw tongues of fire flash from the muzzles of two rifles as Garrett and Chambers both fired. The horseman's body jerked; he cried out in surprise and shock. He almost fell from the saddle as his horse bolted, then righted himself.

Jim squeezed the trigger of his Winchester as the second rider wheeled his horse away from the hospital. The rifle slammed against his shoulder. Jim knew the slug had gone wild. Another muzzle flash lanced from the porch, then a ragged volley of gunshots sounded from the concealed Texans. Jim levered a fresh cartridge into the Winchester, lined the sights as best he could and squeezed the trigger. He heard the solid whack of lead against flesh, like the slap of a hand on a side of beef. The muzzle flash of his second shot wiped out what little night vision Jim had left. He couldn't be sure what his slug had hit.

The outlaws rammed spurs into their frightened horses. The animals floundered a moment in the deep snow, then regained their footing, hit the trail they had broken only moments earlier, and raced back the way they had come. The firing from the posse gradually faded as the horsemen fled beyond rifle range. Jim blinked as his night vision slowly returned. He wasn't surprised that none of the other outlaws had gone down. Shooting in moonlight at moving targets was no way for a man to make a living.

One of the horses continued to crowhop and lunge in the snow, then gradually stopped as the rider regained control. Jim recognized the man as the one who had ridden almost into Garrett's lap. The rider reined back toward the posse, slumped over the saddle horn. Jim heard the man's groans of pain as he approached. Garrett stepped from the deep shadows and slowly lowered his rifle.

"God, please—don't shoot any more!" The wounded man's call was weak, the words shaky. "I'm dying, Garrett! You hit me hard."

"Put up your hands!" Garrett called back.

The wounded man made no attempt to comply. One hand gripped the reins, the other pressed against his chest. Garrett stepped from the porch, rifle at the ready, Lon Chambers at his side. One by one the members of the posse approached the wounded man.

"It ain't the Kid," Jim heard one man say.

"It's Tom O'Folliard," Garrett replied, his voice calm. "Ease him down from that horse, boys. Watch him close. He might still have a trick or two left in him."

Barney Mason was one of the first to reach the wounded man. He pulled him from his mount—a bit roughly, Jim thought, considering the man's obvious condition—and with the aid of a second posse member half carried, half dragged O'Folliard inside.

"Put him on my blanket," Jim said.

Mason dumped O'Folliard onto the blanket, yanked open the wounded man's coat and stared for a moment at the wound. Mason glanced up at his brother-in-law and grinned. "Nailed him solid, Pat. He hasn't got a chance." Mason leaned back over the moaning O'Folliard. "Take your medicine, old boy," he said, his tone mocking. "Take it like a man."

Jim stepped around one of the possemen and stared down at Tom O'Folliard. He was surprised at what he saw. The wounded man seemed little more than a boy, clean-shaven, his smooth features twisted in agony, slender body half curled against the raging pain. Tears misted the pale blue-gray eyes. A thick shock of light brown hair still showed the impression where his hat band had been.

"Oh, God," O'Folliard gasped. "It's awful cold in here, Garrett."

Garrett stared into the pain-glazed eyes. "Tom, your time is short," Garrett said, his tone soft.

O'Folliard stared at the ceiling for a moment, his breath shallow and labored. "The sooner the better, then," he gasped. "It will stop the pain—" He cried out as a fresh wave of agony ripped through his body.

One by one the men turned away from O'Folliard. Jim remained, kneeling at the wounded man's side. A rifle slug had ripped into O'Folliard's chest, narrowly missed the heart, and shredded a lung. *God, what a way to die,* Jim thought; *lungshot, drowning in his own blood, surrounded by enemies. But he picked the trail he rode, and now it's ended.* Jim shucked his coat, folded it, and placed it beneath O'Folliard's head as a pillow.

Jim tossed a quick, disgusted glance at the other members of the posse. The whole bunch, except for Tom Emory, had gone back to their card game. To the gamblers it was as if the dying man on Jim's blanket was nothing more than a coyote. Tom stood and stared into the fire, unwilling to look the dying man in the eye. Tom's face was pale. Jim suspected his own might be a bit white as well. It wasn't an easy thing to watch a man die.

"Jacks bet a dime," Barney Mason said. "Damn shame we missed the Kid."

"Call," Garrett answered. "We'll get him."

O'Folliard stirred and moaned. He muttered something, his voice weak. Jim leaned closer. "Water, for God's sake," O'Folliard groaned. "Water."

Jim brought a dipper of water from the pail on a shelf near the stove. He lifted the wounded man's head and let him drink, but pulled the dipper away after a moment. "Easy, Tom," he said. "Not too much."

O'Folliard's eyes wavered in and out of focus. "Damn that—sonofabitch Garrett—to hell," he muttered. "Shoot a man down cold from out of the dark." Jim lowered Tom O'Folliard's head back onto the blanket. There was nothing else he could do.

Jim kept his vigil at O'Folliard's side for almost a half hour. The outlaw's breathing turned bubbly. Pink froth formed at the corners of his mouth.

"Goddamn you, Garrett," O'Folliard said, his voice suddenly gaining strength, "I'll see you in hell."

Garrett didn't even look up from his cards. "I wouldn't talk that way, Tom," Garrett said. "You're going to die in a few minutes."

"Ah, go to hell, you long-legged sonofabitch," O'Folliard muttered. Then his eyes glazed over. The young outlaw shuddered once and died.

Jim pulled his coat from beneath the dead man's head, covered the body with a ragged blanket, and stood. "He's dead, Garrett," Jim said. "What do we do now?"

"Call the bet," Garrett said before glancing at Jim. "We'll bury him tomorrow. Plenty of room for one more in the Fort Sumner graveyard." Garrett watched as the four of clubs fell and wrecked his possible flush. He grimaced and folded the hand. "If I know the Kid, he'll be headed back for Wilcox's ranch a few miles out of town by now. We'll sit tight, wait for word that he's left Wilcox's, and then track him down. Shouldn't be any problem in this snow."

Jim East stared in silence at Garrett for several heartbeats. *That is one of the coldest men I've ever met,* he thought.

THREE

Fort Sumner
December 1880

Jim East stood with hat in hand, his head bared to the crackling cold, as the first shovel of mixed ice and dirt fell on Tom O'Folliard's crude pine coffin.

There were few mourners at the scene. Garrett and Mason were there, along with most of the members of the Tascosa posse. Luis Bausman and George Williams of the LIT were not among the group; they were searching for the trail of the Kid and his band. Jim doubted they would have much luck. During the night the wind had kicked up again and drifted the snow. The Kid's tracks would be covered.

Jim glanced at Barney Mason and frowned in disgust. A smirk twisted the swarthy Mason's face as he watched the burial. The man hadn't even removed his hat in a show of respect for the dead. Any man, even a smooth-faced kid who rode the outlaw trail, deserved that much. Jim checked the urge to walk over to Mason, yank the man's hat off and jam it into his gut. *I'm going to have trouble with that one,* Jim thought, *and I can't say I'll regret it.*

Jim dismissed Garrett's brother-in-law with a mental shrug and studied the faces of the handful of strangers in the burial party. Most were Mexican laborers hired to hack O'Folliard's grave from the frozen ground. Apparently many of those who had called Tom a friend had decided to stay away, afraid of Garrett and his posse of Tascosa gunmen.

The graveside funeral had been brief to the point of abruptness. Bitter cold had a tendency to rush certain formalities. Jim wondered idly what the weather would be like when his time came.

The posse began to drift away from the grave, headed for the warmth of the old hospital. Jim fell into step beside Tom Emory. The LIT rider's shoulders were hunched against the cold, his chin jammed down into the collar of the heavy coat he wore. Neither man spoke. There was something about a funeral that made a man ponder his own life—and his certain departure from it, sooner or later. The end could come from a bullet, Jim mused, but there were a lot of ways a cowboy could die besides getting shot. A horse could fall on him, an unseen rattlesnake could strike, he could hang up in a stirrup or rope and get dragged to death. Or he could be set afoot, lost in a howling blizzard or a screaming sandstorm in the middle of nowhere miles from shelter or water. He could be gored by a mad mama cow, or get his neck or back broken when a bronc bucked him off. Nearly anything could happen and you never knew when it might come. Anybody who said it was an easy life either had never tried it or was a damned liar, or both.

The two friends reached the hospital porch before Tom finally broke the silence. "He deserves a marker," Tom said softly. "Maybe he was a thief, maybe even a killer. But from the stories I've heard and what I saw for myself, Tom O'Folliard had sand."

Jim stamped the snow from his boots and reached for the door. "Just a kid," he said. "It's a shame he picked the wrong bunch to ride with."

Minutes later Garrett, Mason and a couple of others had resumed their poker game. Jim stood by the fireplace, rubbing warmth back into his hands, and noticed that Garrett was a better lawman than gambler. Garrett's stack of coins grew smaller with each deal.

At Jim's side Tom Emory scratched chipped fingernails against the heavy stubble of his reddish-blond beard. "Damn, I could use a bath and a shave," Tom said.

"We're all beginning to smell a bit ripe," Jim answered, "but I wouldn't be in too big a hurry to part with the face hair if I were you. In this kind of cold every little bit helps."

Jim had almost gotten warm again when Bausman and Williams reined up at the hospital, their scout completed. Bausman clomped into the room. Flakes of wind-whipped ground snow sparkled on his coat and ice frosted his beard.

"Lost the trail a couple miles out, Garrett," Bausman grumbled. "Looks like they were headed east."

Garrett nodded without looking up from his cards. "Probably headed back to Wilcox's place," he said. "Jack bets a quarter."

"Found a dead horse about a mile from here," Bausman said as he shrugged out of his coat and headed for the fire. "One of us got a slug in the critter last night, I guess."

Jim winced inwardly at the news. He remembered hearing the whack of lead on flesh after his second shot. He hated the thought that his bullet had killed a horse. Nothing the Kid's bunch had done was the horse's fault.

"What did the horse look like?" Garrett asked.

"Big bay, stockin' feet in back. Roman nose."

"Sounds like Rudabaugh's mount," Garrett said.

Jim almost groaned aloud at that news. From what he had learned of the Kid's bunch, Rudabaugh was the meanest. He had killed a lawman in Las Vegas while breaking a buddy out of jail—shot him six times just because the deputy was a little slow getting out the cell keys. And Jim's slug had missed Rudabaugh so far it killed the horse. He wouldn't allow himself the excuse that he was firing by moonlight at a moving target. *Mighty poor bit of shooting on my part*, he scolded himself.

"So what do we do now, Pat?" Mason asked. "We can't kill 'em if we can't find 'em."

Garrett glanced at Mason. "I want this bunch alive if possible, Barney, but if they want to make a fight of it we'll oblige them." Garrett glared at his next card, winced in disgust and folded his hand. "For now we set and wait. When the Kid makes a move, I'll know it soon enough."

Jim sat down on his blanket, already beginning to feel the effects of boredom. Waiting wasn't his strong suit. He watched through a broken windowpane as the gray sky slowly cleared and gave way to a bright sun. The glare of sunlight on snow hurt his eyes.

The sun was almost overhead when a horseman rode in at a slow walk, reined in and called for Garrett.

The lawman tossed down his cards, walked outside and spoke for several minutes with the rider. Jim strode to a window overlooking the porch. The horseman, a grizzled man with a full beard and a paunch that stretched the limits of his heavy coat, talked rapidly, gloved hands snapping in excited gestures. He kept looking over his shoulder as if he feared someone might be watching.

The conference ended and the man reined his horse away. Garrett came back into the room, his jaw set. "That was Wilcox," he said. "The Kid was at his place, all right. Wilcox says Billy and his bunch are headed for an abandoned shack on the Taiban up by Stinking Springs."

Barney Mason rose to his feet and reached for his rifle. "Let's go get the bastards," he said.

Garrett waved a hand. "Don't be in such a rush, Barney. If we ride up on them in daylight they'll empty a couple of saddles for us. Say what you want about the Kid and his men, but they can shoot fair enough." Garrett settled back into his place at the poker game. "We move out at moonrise, ride all night, and be waiting for them when the sun comes up."

Taiban Arroyo

Jim East hunched deeper into his buffalo coat in the bone-breaking cold as the first pale light of dawn crept across the eastern New Mexico plains. The long ride had taken its toll on men and horses, but Jim felt the weariness fade with the coming of day and the likelihood of a fight.

He lay face down in the snow at the lip of a shallow draw along the Taiban and studied the one-room house less than twenty yards away. It was made of rock, with only one door and one window. Both openings faced the arroyo where the posse waited.

Garrett lay in the center of the group, his rifle already cocked. Jim was next to Garrett, with Lee Hall at Jim's left. Tom Emory and Lon Chambers held down Garrett's right flank; Frank Stewart, Luis Bausman and George Williams held the horses a few yards away in the bottom of the arroyo.

Three horses stood hipshot, tied to exposed rafters that projected from the front of the house. There was no sign of life inside the building, no smoke from the crumbling chimney of the abandoned sheep camp.

"Wilcox said Billy was riding that race mare of his," Garrett half whispered at Jim's side. "She isn't tied out front. The Kid must have taken her inside with him."

Garrett stared toward the cabin. "Odds are they won't give up as long as the Kid's alive. If Billy shows himself it's my intention to kill him. Then the rest will come out peaceful enough."

Jim snapped his head to glare at the lawman. "Garrett, you said we were going to take them alive. Now you say you're going to just bushwhack a man?"

Garrett returned Jim's cold stare. "East, you're starting to sound like an old maid schoolmarm." Disgust tinged Garrett's words. "I'm getting a little tired of arguing with you, and I'm beginning to wonder whose side you're on. I brought you up here because next to me, you're the best rifle shot in the bunch. If you've got no stomach for shooting, go back and hold the horses."

Jim felt the flare of anger and humiliation in his cheeks. "Don't push me, Garrett, or the war'll start out here." His voice was low and cold. "I told you I don't like being used. I'll stay. I'll shoot any man I have to, but I don't like killing when it isn't necessary."

Jim thought Garrett was going to push the issue. Instead, the lawman merely shrugged. "Just back me up on this one, East, and we'll let our differences slide." He turned to the other members of the posse. "When the dance starts, you boys open on them when I shoot."

Jim hoped it wouldn't come to that. The men in the house were trapped. It would be easy enough to wait them out. If the outlaws had any common sense at all they'd give up without a fight. But then, he reminded himself, nobody had ever credited William Bonney, alias Kid Antrim, alias Billy the Kid, with being long on horse sense. *Maybe Garrett's way is quickest,* he thought, *but that doesn't mean I have to like it.*

The sky slowly brightened as the posse waited in silence. Then the door of the rock house swung open and a slightly built man wearing a broad-brimmed Mexican sombrero stepped outside, a sack of grain in hand.

Jim eased the hammer of his Winchester to full cock and glanced at Garrett. The lawman had drawn a bead on the man with the grain sack.

"Throw up your hands!" Garrett yelled. "You're under arrest!"

The man with the feed bag looked up, startled, then dropped the sack and reached for a pistol at his belt. Garrett's Winchester cracked. The man staggered; a slug from Lee Hall's rifle knocked him back a half step. Jim's finger tightened on the trigger and the Winchester thumped against his shoulder. Through the cloud of powder smoke at the rifle muzzle Jim saw the puff of dust from the outlaw's coat as his slug tore into the man's chest. The impact of the bullet drove the man back into the wall beside the door. He started to slide down the wall, then lurched to his feet and staggered through the doorway, slugs kicking rock fragments from the wall beside his head.

The firing stopped. Jim jacked a fresh round into the chamber of his rifle. The action was stiff from the bitter cold. Jim's ears rang from the concussion of muzzle blasts.

The voice from inside carried well in the thin air. "Charlie, you're done for," the voice said. "Go out and see if you can't get one of the sonsofbitches before you die!"

At his side Jim heard Garrett mutter a soft curse. "Dammit, that wasn't the Kid we shot. It was Charlie Bowdre. That was the Kid doing the talking just then."

The door of the rock house swung open. Charlie Bowdre stood in the doorway, a pistol in his hand. Jim could see the splash of blood over the young gunman's coat. Bowdre staggered toward the waiting men. Jim eased the pressure of his finger from the rifle trigger. There was no need to shoot again; Bowdre was obviously all but dead on his feet, too weak to even lift his handgun.

No one in the posse fired or even spoke as Bowdre stumbled forward. The outlaw staggered to the lip of the arroyo, almost within arm's length of Jim and Lee Hall. The youthful face was twisted in agony, the eyes staring at Jim as if pleading for help.

Bowdre stood weaving, trying to keep his balance. "I wish—I wish—" The voice sounded distant, weak. Bowdre took another step, then tumbled forward. His body fell across Lee Hall's shoulder. The LX rider heaved Bowdre aside and lifted the pistol from his fingers.

"He's dead, Garrett," Hall said.

Garrett gave no sign that he had heard. Jim studied Bowdre's lifeless face, within easy arm's reach of his own. The eyes were open, staring toward the brightening sky. *I guess we'll never know what it was he wished,* Jim thought.

"Come on out, Billy," Garrett called. "You're surrounded. You might as well give up."

"Not likely, Pat." The reply came from inside the rock house. "It's warm in here. Why don't you boys come on in for coffee?"

"Don't want any, Billy. Makes me nervous and I don't shoot as well. We're comfortable enough out here."

Garrett glanced at Jim. The three horses tethered to the projecting rafters of the old rock house, spooked by the gunfire, snorted and danced nervously as they fought the ropes. The animals' rumps swung from side to side as they tried to break loose. "If the Kid gets a chance, he'll make a run for it on that race mare. Maybe I better shut the door on him."

Before Jim could ask what the lawman had in mind, Garrett leveled his rifle. One of the tethered horses swung about so that its body was in front of the door. Garrett pulled the trigger. The horse dropped in its tracks. Its feet crabbed at the snow as it died. The body of the horse blocked the Kid's escape. There was no way he could mount his mare and get her through the doorway in a sprint to freedom.

"Hey, Garrett! What the hell did you do that for?" the Kid yelled.

"Just putting you boys afoot, Billy," Garrett answered as he levered another round into the chamber. He took careful aim and fired. The former buffalo hunter hadn't lost his shooting eye. The slug clipped the rope holding one of the remaining horses. Jim drew a fine bead and shot through the second rope. The two terrified animals spun and raced away, hooves throwing up chunks of frozen soil and clods of snow.

The echoes of the rifle fire bounced along Taiban arroyo. A red stain spread from beneath the dead horse's ear onto the snow.

"Garrett, you're one mean sonofabitch, shooting a horse like that," the Kid yelled. "Reckon you can hit anything smaller? Like a man shooting back at you?"

"One way to find out, Billy. Come on out."

There was no answer from inside.

Another hour dragged past. Charlie Bowdre's body stiffened in the snow. Blood from the bullet wounds formed a blackish, frozen crust on the dead man's chest.

"Hey, Pat," the Kid called, "how's Tom O'Folliard?"

"We buried him at Sumner, Billy," Garrett yelled back. "How come he was up front instead of you?"

"Needed a chew. Rode back to borrow some from Billy Wilson. Lucky for me but bad luck for old Tom."

"You're running out of luck now, Billy. Why don't you give it up and come on out?"

There was no reply.

The siege dragged on in silence for another half hour. There was no more firing from either side. The sun lay hard and cold, low in the southern sky. It brought no warmth to the men huddled in the snow on the Taiban. It would be just as cold to the men in the house, Jim thought. The wind had shifted and now blew across the flat, barren plains from behind the posse toward the open door and window of the abandoned shack.

"How you boys doing in there?" Garrett finally called.

"Pretty good." The Kid sounded cheerful enough. "But we have no wood to get breakfast."

"Come on out and get some, Billy," Garrett yelled back. "Be a little sociable."

"Can't do it, Pat. Business is too confining right now. Haven't got the time to run around."

Garrett stared toward the shack for several moments. "Didn't you fellows forget something? Like setting us afoot and driving us down the Pecos? Seems I heard that was part of your program yesterday."

There was no answer from within.

Jim East waited and watched, his fingers and toes numb from the unrelenting cold. He heard his belly growl and glanced at the sun. It was almost one o'clock; the men in the posse hadn't eaten for better than twenty hours. Jim scooped a handful of snow from behind a nearby rock and shoved it into his mouth. The cold made his teeth hurt, but as the snow melted it quenched his thirst and, for a moment, quieted the rumbles in his gut.

A rifle shot from the window kicked snow and sand from the lip of the arroyo onto Jim's hat. He poked his rifle barrel between two small rocks and fired. The slug nicked the windowsill and spanged into the interior of the house.

The posse and the outlaws settled in to the grim game of waiting each other out. From time to time a gunshot rattled the scrub brush of the arroyo or bellowed smoke from the door or window. None of the slugs hit flesh. The besiegers were well concealed in the arroyo, and the rock walls protected the besieged.

At midafternoon, Garrett cupped a hand to an ear during one of the extended lulls in the firing. "Listen close," he said to Jim. "I hear something."

Jim cocked his head. A moment later he heard the sound, a pecking at the back wall of the rock house.

"They're trying to knock a hole out back there," Garrett said. "Jim, you and Hall slip back up the arroyo a ways. Get behind the house and see if a few shots might discourage that."

Jim backed from his position until he was able to stand. The movement brought some life back to his fingers and toes. Lee Hall stood beside him, stamping his feet and blowing on bare fingers. Hall's hands were bluish-white in the first stage of frostbite. Jim handed him his rabbit fur–lined gloves and gestured toward a turn in the arroyo ahead.

Fifteen minutes later Jim and Hall knelt at the lip of the Taiban a stone's throw from the back of the house. The tapping noise was louder now, carried on the drift of the wind.

Jim cocked his Winchester and hammered a slug into the back wall. Stone chips flew as the lead ricocheted and whined off into the distance. Hall's rifle barked twice. The pecking noise stopped. "Guess they decided remodeling the place with a back door isn't all that healthy," Hall said with a wry chuckle.

The two held their position for a couple of hours and sent an occasional shot toward the back wall as a reminder. The men inside apparently had given up on that idea.

Jim heard Hall's stomach growl.

"Damn me if I don't think I could eat that dead horse down there right now," Hall said. "Only thing holds me back is a man could eat some lead first."

In the near distance Jim saw a rider appear, leading a string of three pack animals. He recognized the rider as the rancher, Wilcox.

A short time later Garrett sent two other men to relieve Jim and Lee Hall. Barney Mason had a fire going in the arroyo. The smell of sizzling steak, potatoes and coffee set Jim's mouth to watering. He realized the wind would carry the scent to the men in the rock house. Jim had a feeling the siege on the Taiban would end soon, and hopefully without more bloodshed. Hunger and thirst could break a man's resolve the same as a bullet.

Jim turned to Hall as the two neared the campfire. "Lee, we better keep an eye on Barney Mason. I've got a feeling Mason wants the Kid dead even if Billy decides to give up."

Hall nodded in silent agreement. The two filled tin plates and squatted by the cooking fire. Within a quarter hour the edge was off their hunger. The food, fire and hot coffee chased away the worst of the cold. Jim almost felt content for the first time since he had ridden away from LX headquarters back in the Panhandle.

"East, Hall," Garrett's call came from above, "get up here! It looks like this dance is about over."

Jim clambered to the lip of the arroyo and flopped into the snow, rifle at the ready.

A dirty handkerchief fluttered from the window of the rock house.

"We wanna talk, Garrett," a raspy voice called.

"That's Rudabaugh," Garrett muttered. "Watch him. He's a tricky one." He raised his voice and yelled to the cabin. "Come on out! Keep your hands empty!"

Rudabaugh eased his way over the dead horse, hands held high. "We've talked it over," Rudabaugh said. "We'll lay down our guns and give up, but you're gonna have to give us your word you won't shoot."

"You have my word," Garrett called. Jim noticed that the sheriff did not rise to his feet in a show of trust. That would expose him to a possible shot from the house. Jim didn't blame Garrett. Any man who trusted the Kid and his bunch was a fool first and probably dead second.

"You got to take us to jail in Santa Fe, not Las Vegas," Rudabaugh said. "Them Vegas folks don't like me just a whole helluva lot."

Garrett scratched a long finger against a stubbled jawline. "Agreed," he said. He turned to the Tascosa riders. "Watch out," Garrett warned, "I wouldn't trust these boys as far as I can throw a chuck wagon."

Jim watched as Rudabaugh stepped back inside the house. He glanced at Barney Mason. Anticipation and what appeared to be a spark of fear put a glitter in Mason's eyes. Jim turned his attention back to the door of the shack. One by one the fugitives came out, hands raised. There were no guns in sight. Rudabaugh came first. Garrett ticked off the names as the others emerged—Tom Pickett, Billy Wilson, and finally Billy the Kid, leading his race mare. The Kid had trouble getting the mare to jump over the dead horse, but finally managed to coax her into it. The group stopped and waited as the posse strode toward them.

Jim paid less attention to the outlaws than he did to Garrett's brother-in-law. Barney Mason carried his Winchester in both hands, the hammer drawn to full cock.

Mason started to raise the weapon. Jim whirled, his own rifle pointed dead at Mason's chest. On Mason's other side Lee Hall's rifle muzzle almost touched Mason's ear.

"Pull that trigger and we'll kill you," Jim snapped.

Mason's face twisted in confusion. His eyes went wide as he stared at the bore of Jim's rifle. "Better let me kill the little sonofabitch now, East," Mason said. "He's slippery. He may get away."

"You won't be around to find out if you don't drop that gun," Jim said. His tone was cold and matter-of-fact.

Mason stared at Jim for a moment, then grudgingly lowered the rifle.

The Kid chuckled softly. "Looks like they got the drop on you, Barney. You're smart, you'll let it slide." The Kid's tone turned derisive. "Barney, you never had the guts to throw down on me before. I don't think you better try it again."

Lee Hall plucked the rifle from Mason's hand. Garrett had made no move to stop his brother-in-law.

Jim dismissed Mason from his mind and studied the Kid with interest. It was the first time he had seen the young gunman up close. What struck Jim the most was the Kid's youthful appearance. He looked to be less than twenty, his sandy mustache little more than light fuzz on his upper lip. He was slender, about a hundred forty pounds on a five-foot-eight frame, with clear blue eyes that still held a glint of humor despite the circumstances. Sandy hair fell from beneath the broad brim of Billy's sombrero and brushed against his narrow shoulders. A slight smile tugged at his lips, baring front teeth that protruded beyond the line of his upper jaw. To Jim East, William H. Bonney looked anything but the gunman and cold-blooded killer he had been made out to be.

The Kid returned Jim's gaze. "Obliged to you, friend," the Kid said. "Old Barney there would have killed me for sure if you hadn't stopped him."

Jim nodded an acknowledgment of the young outlaw's comment. "Never held with shooting an unarmed prisoner," he said.

The Kid turned to Garrett. "Pat, can you spare some of that beef and coffee? I'm hungry as a Bosque Redondo Apache after a hard winter."

"Later, Billy," Garrett said. "We'll get you fed at the Wilcox place. Barney, take one of the boys and get Charlie Bowdre's body bundled up. We'll take him to his wife at Fort Sumner. The rest of you tie up the prisoners. Make it tight so they won't get loose. Wilcox brought some spare horses for them."

Jim used his own tie rope to bind the Kid. Tom Emory did the same with Rudabaugh while others tied Pickett and Wilson. Tom's nose wrinkled in distaste as he pulled the rope tight. Jim understood why. Garrett had described Rudabaugh right. The closest the man had been to water must have been the last time he rode horseback across a creek. Rudabaugh's body odor would have stopped a Union Pacific mainliner dead on the rails, Jim thought.

Within a quarter hour the trussed prisoners were boosted onto horseback. The posse fanned out around them in guard formation as they started the ride back to the Wilcox ranch. Jim hunched deeper into his coat as he rode. The sun was dropping toward the western horizon and the cold grew longer teeth as night neared.

Finally, the lights of the Wilcox ranch house glowed gold in the darkness. By ten o'clock the prisoners had been fed. They ate like starving wolves. The outlaws didn't seem to mind the ripe smell of Rudabaugh's unwashed body, which seemed to grow ranker in the small confines of the warm room, but Jim wanted to escape the scent. It was like sitting in an outhouse that had never seen the touch of lime. But someone had to stand guard, and he and Lee Hall had drawn first watch. Garrett gave orders to shoot the prisoners if they tried to cause trouble, then assigned the other men to sleeping quarters in other parts of the ranch house or the barn behind the home.

Billy tried a couple of times to crack a joke or draw his guards into conversation, but he failed, and finally dropped off to sleep.

Rudabaugh hadn't said a word since his capture. He snored loudly at his spot before the fire.

Jim stayed alert and watchful, his hand on the receiver of his Winchester as he studied the outlaw captives. They looked completely harmless—except for Rudabaugh—as they slept. Jim found himself wondering how many robberies, rustlings and killings had been credited to the Kid and his bunch that should have been tallied to somebody else. *I expect we'll never know for sure,* he mused. He settled in to await the end of his shift, blinked against the grainy feeling of exhaustion in his eyelids, and suddenly remembered that tonight was Christmas Eve.

The realization triggered a tightness in his chest. He tried not to think of the little rented adobe in Tascosa, and Hattie, but the images wouldn't go away. He couldn't keep the sights and smells out of his mind—the sharp scent of the small juniper Hattie would have cut for a Christmas tree and decorated with paper chains and popcorn, the butcher paper–wrapped packages under the tree, the odor of fruitcakes and fresh bread baking in the Dutch oven on the fireplace. And Hattie, sitting before the fire in her nightdress, her face scrubbed, brown hair smelling of rose or lilac water as if her husband could walk in the door at any moment. Jim knew she was probably even more lonely than he was. He wanted desperately to be there, to stroke the smooth curves of her cheeks, watch her eyes glitter with happiness, feel the warmth of her body and bathe away his worries in the comfort of just being close to her.

Jim finally managed to force the thoughts away. He knew Hattie would keep Christmas warm for him until this job was finished, even if it took until spring. She knew how to welcome a man home after a long, cold and dangerous trail. He sighed heavily. Tomorrow would come soon enough, and with it the ride back to Fort Sumner, the first stop on the trail back to Tascosa and home.

FOUR

Fort Sumner
December 1880

Jim East stood guard, rifle at the ready, as the Fort Sumner black-smith drove the final rivet into the shackles that bound Billy the Kid and Dave Rudabaugh to each other.

Tom Pickett and Billy Wilson, already in irons, sat nearby. They hadn't spoken a word since their surrender on the Taiban.

The Kid looked up at Jim and grinned as if he had no worry in the world at the moment. Jim didn't smile back. He and Billy had reached the stage where they called each other by their first names, but that didn't mean Jim had to trust the likeable young outlaw. Even if he had been inclined to trust the Kid, he couldn't put an ounce of faith in the man Billy was chained to.

Dave Rudabaugh sat scowling on the hard wooden bench in Beaver Smith's general store and muttered curses as the blacksmith gathered up his tools. Jim was certain now that Rudabaugh was a ruthless and dangerous man. He had no conscience, no remorse, and his word of honor was worth about as much as bird droppings on a pump handle.

The Kid had asked for a basin of water, a sliver of soap and a razor, and made a serious attempt to clean himself as best he could. Rudabaugh showed no such inclination. In fact, it seemed to Jim that the scraggly outlaw actually recoiled in horror at the sight of soap and water.

The Kid watched the blacksmith scurry out the door, then stomped his boot and giggled at the clank of chains.

"Don't know what you're laughin' at, you buck-toothed little fart," Beaver Smith growled from behind the counter. "Be a rope around your neck for sure 'fore first grass."

Jim glanced at the store owner. He was getting a little tired of the old man's constant badgering of the prisoners. "Leave them alone, Smith," he said.

"Leave 'em alone, hell!" Smith snorted. "This bunch has been helpin' theirselves to anything they want in my store for months and they ain't paid for nothin' yet. 'Charge it,' they says. I'm half a mind to take it out'n their hides."

Jim pinned a steady glare on the old man's face. "You really want to do that, I'll call that blacksmith back in here and cut them loose. Then you can have at it."

Smith's swarthy face flushed in anger, but Jim could see the fear just beneath the surface of the old man's chestnut-colored eyes. Smith's untrimmed beard twitched as he grumbled something and turned away.

Jim dismissed Smith from his mind as Pat Garrett strode into the store, Lee Hall trailing behind. "We'll stand guard for a spell, Jim," Garrett said. "I want you and Bausman to take Charlie Bowdre's body over to his wife." Garrett shook his head. "It's a shame about Charlie. I liked the kid. Talked to him just a few weeks ago and he sounded like he wanted to quit the outlaw business."

Jim shouldered his rifle and strode outside. Bowdre's body lay board-stiff, wrapped to the neck in a blanket in a wagon borrowed from Wilcox. Bausman waited by the wagon, taking the final drag from a smoke.

Jim stowed his rifle under the wagon seat, waited until the stocky Bausman climbed aboard, and clucked the horses into motion.

Ten minutes later Jim and Bausman swung down from the wagon in front of the old hospital building where Bowdre's wife lived. Bausman knocked on the door and called out. There was no answer. "Maybe she's not home," Bausman said with a shrug. "Guess we'll just have to leave old Charlie here and send word with the Messkins to find her."

Jim and Bausman wrestled the awkward bundle from the wagon, Jim holding the dead man's shoulders while Bausman handled the feet. Charlie Bowdre seemed a lot heavier in death than he had looked in life, Jim thought as he bumped the unlatched door open with a hip. Jim stepped through the doorway—and something slammed into the side of his head. He staggered, lost his grip on Bowdre's body. The dead man fell to the floor with a solid thump.

The unexpected blow jarred Jim's eyes out of focus, but he sensed a movement, threw up a hand, and took a solid and painful whack on his forearm.

"Hey! Hold it!" Bausman yelled. He lunged past Jim and grabbed at the hazy figure. Jim's Spanish wasn't all that good, but he picked up enough words from all the yelling and screeching to realize he wasn't being invited to any Sunday social.

His vision gradually cleared. Bausman stood before him, a powerful arm wrapped around a woman's waist. He held her off the floor as she kicked at his shins and screamed curses. Bausman's free hand gripped the staff of the branding iron Charlie Bowdre's widow had used to whack Jim alongside the head.

"You all right, Jim?" Bausman's booming voice carried over the steady stream of Mexican curses.

Jim rubbed a hand above his ear and felt a knot begin to form. There was no blood. It seemed to Jim that half his head had been knocked askew.

"I'm all right, Luis," he said. "I guess she's got a right to be a little upset. Let her go."

Bausman did.

It looked for a moment like that was a mistake.

Bowdre's wife lunged again at Jim, swinging the branding iron. Jim ducked, grabbed the iron and wrenched it from her hand as Bausman all but tackled the woman from behind.

Jim glanced at Charlie Bowdre's frozen body dumped unceremoniously face down on the floor, then at the woman Bausman held. "Missus Bowdre, I'm truly sorry about Charlie," he said in his stumbling Spanish. He became aware of a ringing in his ears and the start of a real wosshopper of a headache. He stooped to retrieve the hat knocked from his head by the iron, then cocked an eyebrow at Bausman.

"Luis," he said as he tossed the branding iron into a far corner of the room, "I think we better try to get out of here before somebody gets hurt. Like you and me."

"Ready when you are, Jim." A grin creased Bausman's broad face.

"Let's go!"

Bausman shoved the woman aside. Both men sprinted for the door. The unending string of Mexican profanity followed. Jim vaulted into the wagon, picked up the reins and had whipped the team into a run by the time the back of Bausman's britches hit the wagon seat. Jim glanced back over his shoulder as he pulled the horses into a tight turn and headed back up the road toward town.

Charlie Bowdre's widow had given up the chase. Jim caught a glimpse of her through the hospital doorway as the wagon sped past. She had flung herself onto her husband's body, wailing and screaming in grief.

A hundred yards later Jim eased the horses back to a trot. A low chuckle from beside him grew to a full-blown howl of glee. Jim glanced at Luis Bausman. The bulky LIT rider was bent over at the waist, laughing so hard he could hardly breathe. Despite the ache in his head, Jim felt a grin spread over his own face.

"God—Jim—" Bausman gasped between peals of laughter, "you shoulda—seen your face—when she whopped you upside the—head with that brandin' iron—"

Jim chuckled aloud. "Guess it was quite a sight, at that," he said. Finally he couldn't hold it back any longer. He threw his head back and laughed along with Bausman.

Jim had regained his composure by the time they reached Beaver Smith's store. Bausman was reduced to high-pitched chuckles; tears streamed down his face as Jim reined in the team. "Guess it—wouldn't of been so funny if—" Bausman hiccuped a brief chortle —"if she'd had her a ten-gauge smoothbore 'stead of a branding iron."

Jim swung down from the wagon. His head hurt from the impact of the iron and his jaws ached from grinning. He knew it would be a long time before he heard the last of this. He looked up at Bausman. "I don't guess you'd keep this quiet if I asked, Luis?"

Bausman howled again. "No way, Mary Ann," he finally managed to stammer. "Too good a yarn to waste. God, you shoulda seen—"

Jim sighed and strode into the store, Bausman chuckling behind him.

"What's so funny, Jim?" the Kid asked.

The question sent Bausman into another gale of glee. Jim told the story himself. Everybody in the store was doubled over in mirth by the time he had finished—at least everyone except Rudabaugh.

• • • •

Billy the Kid handed his empty dinner plate back to Jim East, stretched out on the dirt floor and sighed, contented.

"Don't get too comfortable, Billy," Pat Garrett said. "We'll be moving out for Las Vegas soon."

Jim East saw the color drain from Dave Rudabaugh's face. For a moment it looked as if he might speak, but his expression quickly subsided back to its normal scowl.

Garrett looked up as an aging Navajo woman strode into the room. Jim picked up enough of the conversation to realize the woman had come to ask Garrett to allow the Kid to visit a sweetheart before being hauled off to prison and possibly to the hangman. The girl's name was Paulita Maxwell. She was the daughter of a prominent Fort Sumner family.

Garrett listened to the plea, then shrugged. "Guess it wouldn't hurt anything," he said. The lawman turned to Jim. "Jim, you and Hall take the Kid over to say his goodbyes."

"Has she got a branding iron?" Jim asked.

Bausman started howling again. Garrett chuckled. "Keep a close eye on the Kid and Rudabaugh. Keep them shackled together, and don't give them a chance to escape. Shoot them if they try anything, and don't let it drag on too long. We move out in an hour."

Jim strode along the frozen street, threading his way through patches of ice and snowdrifts at the Kid's side as they walked toward the Maxwell residence. Lee Hall flanked Dave Rudabaugh. The two prisoners had to march in lockstep to keep from tripping each other up.

The Kid suddenly came to an abrupt halt, his face pale and eyes wide in fear as he stared down at his feet.

"What is it, Billy?" Jim asked.

"A bad sign." The Kid pointed with manacled hands toward Rudabaugh's leg irons. The shackle had come loose from the dirty outlaw's ankle. Jim glanced at the parted chain, then studied the Kid's face. The boy was obviously frightened. Jim had heard the Kid was superstitious, but he didn't expect to see the young face twisted in terror over such an insignificant event.

"It's just a bad rivet, Billy," Jim said.

"No." The Kid's eyes darted about as if some monster were poised to pounce from a deserted adobe. "That's a terrible bad sign. It means I'll die and Dave will go free."

Jim saw there was no point in arguing. "Come on, Billy. We'll get the leg iron fixed later. You haven't much time to see your sweetheart."

The two Tascosa riders stood guard as the Kid and Paulita embraced in the parlor of the sprawling Maxwell home. Tears of despair streamed down the young girl's face. Jim thought he saw moisture at the corner of the Kid's eyes as well. The embrace dragged on, punctuated by passionate kisses, until finally Jim had to grab Billy's arm and pull him from the girl's grasp.

"Come on, Billy," Jim said, his voice soft. "You've already had more time with her than I've had with my own wife in the last few months."

Jim had to almost physically drag the Kid away. Jim glanced back once and saw Paulita leaning against the doorway of the house, her face buried in her hands.

"I'll see her again, Jim," the Kid said, "if I don't get killed first. That broken leg iron . . ." His voice trailed away.

The Kid didn't speak again until they had reached Beaver Smith's store. Then he turned to Jim. "Jim, you've treated me right. I want you to have my rifle." The Kid cocked an eyebrow at Garrett. "That all right with you, Pat?"

Garrett shrugged. "Doesn't matter to me." He picked up the Kid's Winchester and tossed it to Jim.

"Just a goddamn minute!" Beaver Smith's howl of outrage almost rattled the rafters of the low-roofed store. "As much money as them bastards owes me, I got a right to take anythin' I want from 'em, and I got a claim on that there rifle!"

Jim looked at the Kid, felt his own face flush in anger, and then all but hurled the weapon at Smith. "Take it!" he snapped. "Put it toward what they owe you—and then shut the hell up!" Jim brought his temper under control with an almost physical effort. "Smith," he said, his voice tight and cold now, "I figure that rifle is worth maybe a hundred dollars. You want to dispute that amount?"

Beaver Smith started to sputter an answer, then saw the expression in Jim East's eyes. The storekeeper was the first to drop his gaze. "I reckon that's about right," he muttered, "considerin' whose gun it was." Smith turned away and strode toward the back of the store.

Jim watched him go. The flare of anger slowly faded. "Sorry about the gun, Billy," Jim said, "but I just can't stand a whiner. Thanks for offering it to me, anyway."

The Kid shrugged. "It's just an old Winchester." Then he grinned. "Worth it just to see somebody climb old Beaver's tree."

"Smith had a point, Billy," Jim said. "A man's got to pay his debts."

"Yeah," the Kid said, "I reckon that's what's got me a little worried right now."

By midafternoon all the prisoners were loaded into a wagon drawn by four mules. Lee Hall had the reins. Jim and Tom Emory rode in the wagon as guards, with Frank Stewart, Barney Mason and Pat Garrett serving as outriders. The lawman had given the Kid's race mare to Stewart as compensation for his services. Jim noted that Garrett pointedly did not mention distributing shares of the five hundred dollar reward with any of the Texans. Jim didn't dwell on the oversight long. He was there to do a job for the LX, not to collect bounty. Still, a few dollars would have helped buy that house in Tascosa for Hattie.

"Pat, where we going to overnight?" The Kid asked.

Garrett, riding alongside the wagon, shook his head. "We don't. We'll ride out the night. That'll put us in Puerto de Luna by morning. We'll rest up there and then head on into Las Vegas."

Las Vegas

"Well, Jim," Tom Emory said, "it looks like ol' Pat has gone and stepped in it this time."

Jim East stared through the smoke-smudged window of the passenger train at the restless mob outside. "So it appears," he said, "and I think he might have splattered some of it on us in the process."

The engine chuffed at idle at the Las Vegas station. The lynch mob had already pulled the engineer and brakeman from the cab. "You know how to drive a train, Tom?"

Tom lowered a window and spat a stream of tobacco juice outside. The brown glob barely missed a Mexican holding an old Colt percussion pistol. "Nope. Hell, it's all I can do to drive a horse."

Jim glanced around the passenger coach. There were a half dozen men, two women, three manacled prisoners, Tom Emory and himself trapped in the coach by the would-be lynch mob outside. The women's faces were pale and anxious and a few of the men fretted nervously on the unpadded seats.

Garrett had made a mistake. He had dismissed all members of the posse but Jim and Tom, then tried to sneak the prisoners from the jail to the train without anyone finding out about it. *Trying to do something on the quiet in a little New Mexico town's like trying to walk on water,* Jim thought, *and as far as I know there's not but one man in history been able to do that. His name wasn't Garrett.*

The rumble of voices from the crowd damped the soft chuff of steam from the locomotive two cars ahead. Jim studied the faces of the prisoners. Dave Rudabaugh wore his usual scowl, but the swarthy, bearded face seemed a touch paler than usual. Jim saw the glitter of pure fear in Rudabaugh's eyes. He knew he was the one the crowd wanted. He had killed a jailer here. The deputy had been a Mexican. The faces in the crowd outside were all brown.

The Kid leaned back in his seat, relaxed, a slight smile touching the corners of his mouth. He didn't look the least bit worried, Jim noted, even if he was headed for a hemp necktie if that crowd managed to break in.

Under pressure from the local law Garrett had admitted he had no warrants or claims on Billy Wilson. The young outlaw now sat in the dank, cold cell of the Las Vegas jail. The third prisoner, Tom Pickett, sat slumped in his seat, eyes darting nervously around the coach. He was one scared young man, Jim thought.

At the front of the coach Garrett stood, his hand on the Colt at his belt. The door swung open and the Mexican sheriff of Las Vegas, a big man with a florid face and a Smith & Wesson New Russian Model pistol holstered on a broad hip, stepped into the car.

"We want the outlaws. Especially the one called Dave Rudabaugh," the sheriff demanded. Dark eyes snapped in the scowling face. "Give up the prisoners and the people outside will let you go, Garrett. If you don't, I can't stop this crowd." The man spoke in Spanish, but Jim was able to follow the rapid-fire words well enough to know trouble wasn't but a pull of a trigger away.

Garrett studied the sheriff in silence for a moment. The rumble of the crowd outside grew louder, muffled only slightly by the gusty wind.

Garrett shook his head. "You can't have them. I promised these men safe passage to Santa Fe. I'm not going back on my word and turn them over to some lynch mob."

The sheriff's hand dropped to the big pistol at his hip. "Then I guess we'll just take them, Garrett," he said.

"I don't think so." Garrett whipped his own Colt from its holster and rammed the muzzle into the sheriff's belly.

The Mexican lawman swallowed hard and lifted his hand clear of the Smith & Wesson. The weight of a metal star on a man's chest wasn't nearly as heavy as the poke of a forty-five muzzle in the gut. "Get off my train," Garrett said. There was an edge to his voice now. "I'm moving these prisoners and I'll kill any man who stands in my way."

"You can't move the train," the sheriff sputtered. "We have the engineer and brakeman. You have no choice but to give us the prisoners."

"No. If I have to, I'll hand every prisoner a gun and tell them to do their best to kill the whole damn mob." Garrett's words carried well throughout the passenger car.

"Give me a gun," the Kid called out. "If I had my Winchester I'd whip the whole lot of them!"

"Shut up, Billy," Jim said. "This whole thing could blow up any minute. Don't make it worse than it is or you may get strung up along with your friend Dave."

The sheriff backed away, hands held palm-out. He almost tripped and fell as he went backward through the door. "I can't stop them, Garrett," Jim heard him say as the door started to close.

"Then we'll stop them," Garrett replied. The lean marshal holstered his handgun and turned to face the passengers in the car. "Everybody better get off here. We're going to have a fight and I don't want any innocent people hurt."

Three of the men and both the women practically jumped from their seats and bolted for the door. They jostled each other on the way out. Jim reached out, clamped a hand on the Kid's shoulder and jammed him back down into the seat. "I don't think Pat meant you, Billy. Stick around for a while. Let's see how this turns out."

Garrett raised an eyebrow at Jim. "East, you and Emory have done your job. I can't order you to stay and face a lynch mob. You can go if you like."

Jim shook his head emphatically. "I didn't ride all those miles, starve half to death, nearly freeze and almost get my butt shot off to turn these men over to a dishonest lynching." He cracked open the action of his Winchester, checked to make sure there was a round chambered, and looked at Garrett. "I'll stay. The job isn't done yet."

"Me, too," Emory said. "Maybe Billy and the boys deserve hanging, sure enough. But it ought to be an honest hanging. With a judge and jury, not some bunch of mad Mexicans." Emory nodded toward Rudabaugh. "Personally, I'd just as soon give 'em old Dave here. But I reckon he's part of the roundup and I ain't one to split a herd."

Garrett nodded in satisfaction, then turned to the remaining three men. "How about you fellows? This isn't your fight."

One of the men, a grizzled and weathered old-timer with a to-bacco-stained beard, shifted his chew from one cheek to the other and shook his head. "I paid my fare to Santa Fe. Reckon I'll stay on." He cradled an ancient trap-door Springfield rifle in his arms. His companion, a few years younger but just as weather-worn, nod-ded. "Me, too. Me and my partner here fought Apaches and griz-zlies from Arizona to Montana. We ain't scared of a few Messkins."

Garrett shifted his gaze to the third man, who pulled back his heavy coat to display a Colt Lightning forty-one caliber revolver in a shoulder holster. "Name's J. F. Morley," he said. "Post office inspector. There's mail on this train. I'll stick."

"Much obliged to you gentlemen," Garrett said. He turned and walked back to the front of the coach.

Jim lowered the smudged window at his side, winced at the blast of frigid air, and listened to the angry rumble of the crowd outside. Two rows ahead, Tom Emory also stared out an open window.

"Tom, you see that big Mexican in the red mackinaw? The one holding that double shotgun with bores big enough to put a groundhog in?"

"I see him, Jim."

"If they work up enough mad and enough guts to rush us," Jim said, "I'll take care of him. You pick out another target. No use both of us wasting lead on the same man."

Morley lowered his own window, leaned out and glanced around. "Rifle barrels sticking out from the woodpile yonder," he said. "No sign of the engineer or brakeman." Morley drew back inside and snorted in disgust. "No wonder the damn trains are never on time. Can't get good help these days."

The rumble of the crowd outside grew louder, more angry.

"Get set, boys," Garrett said. "Looks like they're going to come at us any minute." He pulled his revolver.

Jim centered the sights of his rifle on the chest of the man with the shotgun.

The crowd started forward, then suddenly stopped. Some of the men at the rear turned, pointed, and jabbered in excitement.

Garrett peered out a window. "Three white men coming up behind them," he said. "I know a couple of those boys. Jim McIntyre and George Close. They're carrying more artillery than the First Illinois."

Jim chanced a glance of his own. The three Anglos stood fanned out in the street, six feet apart, each man with a rifle or shotgun at the ready and revolvers buckled outside their heavy coats. The Mexican mob milled about, confused. Jim knew the reason for the sudden reluctance. With the white men at their rear and several guns in the coach with the prisoners, they faced some heavy losses if they charged the train.

Jim took his finger off the trigger. There was no predicting what a mob would do. A gang of men was as unpredictable as a herd of brush-wild South Texas Longhorns. But until they got things sorted out, there wasn't any reason to shoot the man with the smoothbore.

Morley strode to Garrett's side. "Sheriff," he said, "before I started working for the post office I was an engineer with the Chicago and Northwestern. While all this yammering's going on, I could slip out, work my way to the cab, yank the throttle open and get us the hell out of here."

Garrett thought for a moment, then nodded. "Might be worth the risk if you can pull it off, Mister Morley."

The postal inspector cracked the door, peered outside and slipped from the coach.

Ten minutes later the milling crowd scattered with yelps of surprise as a cloud of steam burst from the locomotive boiler and the whistle screamed. The drive wheels screeched against iron rails, spinning as they tried to find traction on the cold, slick iron. Then the wheels bit and the locomotive lurched forward. The jolt of slack yanked from couplings rocked Jim back in his seat.

By the time the mob realized what was happening the train was gaining speed. Jim heaved a sigh of relief as the coach rumbled from the station. Through the window he saw the expressions on brown faces change from confusion to anger and disappointment.

As the train passed the three heavily armed Anglos standing in the street behind the mob, Pat Garrett yelled through an open window, "Thanks, boys!"

One of the trio waved a hand casually and yelled back, "Glad to help, Pat."

Jim glanced at Tom Emory. A broad grin creased the LIT cowboy's stubbled face. "Morley must have the throttle jammed through the boiler," Jim said.

"Yeah. I just hope he remembers where the brakes are when we hit Santa Fe."

Billy the Kid's soft chuckle brought stares from both Tascosa men.

"Something tickle your fancy, Billy?" Jim asked.

"Just thinking. Looked like old Dave here was gonna crap his pants when that crowd started at us."

Tom wrinkled his nose. "How the hell could you have told the difference?" he asked.

Santa Fe

Jim East leaned against the rough adobe wall of the Santa Fe jail as a deputy turned the key on Billy the Kid, Dave Rudabaugh and Tom Pickett.

The gang the Las Vegas and Santa Fe newspapers had dubbed "The Forty Thieves" was out of business.

The Kid turned to Jim, his face solemn. "I won't hang, Jim. I'll die—you remember how those shackles broke—but I won't hang." He glanced around the barren dirt-floored cell. "God," he said, "this is an awful place to put a man in."

Jim shrugged. "Jails weren't built by the same folks who design hotels, Billy. It wasn't supposed to be a nice place." Jim waved a hand in farewell, turned and walked into the office at the front of the jail.

Pat Garrett and Tom Emory waited at the sheriff's desk. Garrett tucked a signed receipt for delivery of the prisoners into a pocket, then turned to Jim and Tom.

"Thanks for all you and your Tascosa men have done, boys," Garrett said. He handed Jim two railroad tickets. "Your job is finished here. You and Tom take the train back to Vegas, fetch your horses, and rejoin your outfits at White Oaks. You've done your part in the Pecos War, as the newspapers are calling this affair."

"Wasn't much of a war, Pat," Tom said. "I suppose we'll be seeing you again?"

Garrett half smiled. "Most likely. I'm kind of fond of that Tascosa country."

Jim and Tom strode from the jail into the teeth of a new storm. The north wind ripped at their coats and swirled fat flakes of wet snow around their ears.

"Reckon spring will ever get here?" Tom had to shout to be heard over the screech of the wind.

"I'm beginning to wonder, Tom," Jim yelled back. "Let's step on out. I don't want to miss that train."

FIVE

LX Ranch
March 1881

Jim East lounged in the saddle and tried to let the warmth of the early spring sun wash the lingering memories of the brutal winter from his mind.

It wasn't an easy thing to do.

Jim had lost count of the number of cattle carcasses and scattered bones he had ridden past on his way back from New Mexico. Only the strongest stock survived the bitter, icy blasts that came in waves from beyond the Colorado Rockies. The weak did not. Baby calves froze at birth before they even had a chance to stand and nurse; some were pulled down by packs of marauding coyotes. Older cows weakened by age dropped and died at the edge of frozen water holes, the strength to keep moving drained from bodies that were almost skeletons.

Twice he had ridden past cattle bearing the Double Bit brand. The livestock had drifted more than three hundred miles from their home range in central Colorado, turning their tails to the storms and moving south until the weather broke or death caught up with them.

Many of the survivors were little more than racks of bone covered by loose, shaggy hides. Jim counted a half dozen brands from Kansas, Colorado and the northern Texas Panhandle. The spring roundup was going to be a man-killer this year, he thought. LX and LIT cattle would be scattered all the way to central Texas. It would take a dozen wagon crews of ten to twenty men each more than six weeks to complete the gather, another two weeks for sorting and branding, and at least another week to trail them back to their home ranges.

It was that job that had summoned him from the Tascosa cowboys' winter camp in White Oak. The letter from Bill Moore had
reached him in late February, along with a dozen letters in Hattie's
fine, flowing script.

Jim read Hattie's letters again and again until he had them com-
mitted to memory. Moore's letter was brief and to the point, but it
was the key to the shackles that kept Jim East away from home.
Moore wanted him as wagon boss of one of the spring roundup
crews. Moore's letter had several meanings to Jim East. First, he
would get to see Hattie again. Second, he could get back to the
work he liked best, punching cows. And third, as long as he headed
a wagon crew he would draw an extra twenty dollars a month in
wages. That would help toward buying the house in Tascosa.

Tom Emory had received a similar summons from his boss and
had ridden with Jim from White Oaks until they hit LIT range.
Charlie Siringo and the rest of the Tascosa crews remained at
White Oaks to hunt the Lower Pecos Valley for Panhandle cattle
stolen or drifted into New Mexico.

The sorrel horse between Jim's knees had regained some
strength with rest and grain during the stay at White Oaks, but the
gelding was still drawn and lean. No amount of grain or even prairie hay would put meat back on a horse's bones the way green grass
would. The sorrel was still a bit weak from near-starvation—and,
Jim hated to admit, the abuse he had put the animal through during the hunt for Billy the Kid. But the sorrel now kept trying to
break into a trot, the idea of home pouring strength into its worn
muscles.

Jim's gaze swept the rolling hills as he rode. On the sunny slopes
of creeks and steeper hills, sprigs of fresh green grass poked cautiously toward the blue sky overhead. The legacy of a long winter
and heavy snows was not all bad. The moisture it left behind would
nourish the land for weeks, maybe even months. The Panhandle
range would have its best early season graze in years. Shallow
springs that dried up in times of scant rainfall would be recharged
by the snow melt. There would be plenty of water for the stock. It
seemed to Jim that nature had a way of making something good
come out of her meanest temper fits.

He was within forty miles of Tascosa and Hattie now. The
thought helped the sun chase the last of the chill from his bones.

Christmas in the spring was going to be a little strange, he thought, but a cowboy's life tended to get that way a lot of times.

Jim pulled the sorrel to an abrupt stop. Lost in his thoughts of Hattie, he had almost missed the distant sound. He waited, his head cocked to the gentle southern breeze. A moment later he heard the sound again—the bawling of a small herd of cattle, and above that the higher squall of a yearling in distress.

The sounds came from a small box canyon a half mile away. The canyon opened into the northern branch of the Prairie Dog Town Fork of the Red River. Jim hesitated for a moment, torn between his urge to get home and his cowboy's instinct to investigate anything out of the ordinary on the range. The sounds from the canyon were not those normally made by free range cattle. It could be a drift crew at work, he thought. Or it could be something else.

The cattleman's instinct won out. He reined the sorrel toward the canyon.

As he neared the rim of the cedar-studded canyon he caught the distinct scent of burning hair. Whoever was there was definitely using a hot iron.

Jim pulled the sorrel to a stop fifty feet back of the canyon rim, looped the reins around the limb of a low cedar, and shucked his rifle from the saddle boot. If this wasn't a drift crew it might not be healthy to walk in unarmed. He climbed the final few strides to the top of the canyon wall, near a cluster of sandstone rocks. Jim eased himself behind the boulders and peered between them into the canyon below.

A yearling heifer was tied down on the sandy canyon floor. One man, his back to Jim, was burning a brand onto the heifer's hip. A man on horseback was coiling his rope, ready to ride back into the herd of a dozen or so cattle bunched against the steep walls of the dead end canyon. Both men carried pistols at their waists. The mounted man had a carbine stuffed into a saddle boot.

The man afoot finished burning the brand, untied the heifer and shooed her toward the herd. Jim recognized the man as he turned. It was young Dink Edwards from the LX, the man who had replaced Jim riding drift when Jim was sent to New Mexico.

Jim's jaw muscles clenched as the mounted man began to shake out a loop. He didn't recognize the man on horseback.

The freshly branded heifer passed within a few yards of Jim's position in the rocks. The still-smoking brand on her hip was a Spade Diamond. It took only four quick strokes of the iron to change an LX into a Spade Diamond.

Jim studied the other cattle milling in the canyon below. He spotted one pure maverick and two mother cows wearing the LX brand. The others had fresh Spade Diamonds on their hips.

As Jim watched, the mounted man whipped a flat loop under the heels of a mother cow, jerked the slack and rammed spurs to his horse. The rope horse whirled and lunged. The rope snapped taut and yanked the cow's hind feet from beneath her. She fell, bawling, onto her side. The roper dragged his catch toward the branding fire, his big roan horse straining against the weight of the downed cow.

Jim eared his Winchester to full cock. He had two rustlers dead to rights. The only trick now was to bring them in—and stay alive in the process. His best edge was that these two men were going to be mighty busy for the next few minutes trying to burn a brand on a full-grown Longhorn.

He inched his way through the boulders and found a narrow game trail that twisted down to the canyon floor through the jumble of rocks and wind-twisted cedars. The men below had their hands full with the big mother cow; Dink Edwards twisted her horns, holding her down while the roper dismounted and reached for an L-shaped running iron heating in the fire.

The cow bellowed in pain and outrage as the hot iron seared her hip.

Jim stepped to the edge of the clearing and raised his rifle.

"Hold it right there!" he yelled.

The two men started at the unexpected sound of a man's voice. Edwards snapped his head around to stare in Jim's direction. His grip on the cow slipped; she slung her head. One of the heavy horns thumped into Dink's ribs and sent him sprawling. The roper dropped the branding iron and swung to face Jim, his hand slapping the butt of his holstered Colt.

"Don't try it!" Jim called. The man's hand came up with the pistol swinging toward Jim.

Jim squeezed the trigger and the Winchester thumped against his shoulder. The forty-four–forty slug hammered the rustler in the chest, staggered him back a step. Jim levered in a fresh round and snapped a second shot; the man's pistol fell as he spun and dropped face down in the dirt. The gunshots spooked the rustler's horse. The roan bucked and lunged, the rope parted with a crack, and the horse whirled and raced away, empty stirrups flopping. Jim worked the Winchester action again and shifted the muzzle toward Dink Edwards. The young man clambered to his feet, dusty and dazed from the solid crack of the cow's horn to his ribs.

Edwards stood, his face pale and eyes wide at the sight of the rifle pointed at his chest. He glanced at the downed man, then back at Jim.

"For God's sake, East! You killed him!"

"He didn't give me any choice." Jim's tone was cold and flat. "He played his top card and lost. Now it's your turn, Dink. Fold or call." He kept his gaze locked on Dink's eyes. The look in a man's eyes told more than his words did. Jim saw the dazed expression fade from the gray eyes, replaced by a flicker of anticipation and challenge. Dink's right hand dangled near the butt of the Colt at his hip, fingers curled.

"Think it over, Dink. You may be fast with that sixgun, but nobody's fast enough to beat a man holding a cocked rifle."

A shadow of doubt flickered in Dink's eyes. "What are you going to do now, East?"

"Depends on you, Dink. Reach for the pistol and I'll blow your guts through your backbone. I don't want to kill you, but I will if I have to."

"And if I give up, you'll hang me?"

"No. You have my word on that. I'll turn you over to Moore and let him decide."

Jim saw the sudden wash of relief in Edwards's eyes. *Curious,* Jim thought; *rustlers usually don't want to face the men they steal from.* "Unbuckle the gunbelt, Dink. Left hand. Let her drop and step back."

Edwards fumbled with the buckle a moment and the rig dropped at his feet. He stepped back and lifted his hands.

Jim cocked his head toward the dead man. "Who was he?"

"Name was Cochran. From up in the Cimarron Strip country. This whole thing was his idea, Jim. Not mine."

Jim kept his eyes on Dink as he stooped, hefted the gunbelt and draped it over his shoulder. "I'll let somebody else decide that." He sighed. "Dink, you disappoint the hell out of me. You had the makings of a top hand. I never figured you for a thief."

Dink Edwards shrugged. "Easy money. What now, Jim?"

"We mount up, catch Cochran's horse and take him and these cattle to headquarters." Jim lowered the rifle. "Dink, I give you my solemn promise that if you so much as twitch or even think about making a run for it, I'll kill you. Understood?"

Edwards nodded. He seemed mighty calm for a man caught with his spoon in another man's stew, Jim thought. He motioned with the rifle muzzle. "Come on. We've got some cattle and a dead man to move."

LX Headquarters

Jim East watched as Bill Moore stepped from the porch and stared toward the small herd and the two horsemen approaching.

Jim led the roan. Cochran's body was tied face-down across the saddle. Dink Edwards rode alongside Jim, helping haze the cattle toward the corrals behind the house. Jim kneed his gaunt sorrel toward the LX foreman.

"What happened?" Moore asked as Jim pulled his mount to a stop.

Jim gave Moore a quick version of the confrontation in the box canyon. Moore listened without comment, then grunted. He strode to the dead man, grabbed his hair and lifted the head. He studied the face for a moment, then let the lifeless face flop. "Never saw that one around here before."

"Dink says his name's Cochran. From up in the Strip."

Several cowpunchers gathered around. A couple of the younger ones turned pale at the sight of the dead man. Three of the seasoned hands took a casual glance at the body, then mounted up and finished the job of penning the cattle.

Jim stepped from the saddle and motioned with the rifle muzzle for Dink to dismount. The horse wrangler gathered in the reins of the three horses, promised to take care of the mounts and then to load the body in a spring wagon.

Moore turned to Dink. Jim thought he saw more worry than

anger in the foreman's gaze. Edwards looked calm and cool, confident.

Moore studied the young rider for a moment, then snorted in disgust and turned away. "Damn a man who'd steal from his own brand," he grumbled.

"What are you going to do with these two?" Jim asked.

Moore shrugged. "Should hang Edwards to a barn rafter. But I guess he deserves a trial. I'll personally take him to the lockup in Mobeetie."

Jim frowned. Mobeetie was better than a hundred thirty miles downriver. "Why Mobeetie? We're a county now, with a sheriff and a jail right up the road in Tascosa."

"Tascosa jail's a joke," the LX foreman growled. "That little adobe shack wouldn't hold a ten-year-old chicken thief. He won't get out of the Mobeetie hoosegow." Moore turned to a couple of cowhands standing by. "You boys skin out one of those beeves," he said. "We'll need proof the brand's been changed."

Jim knew the changed brand would carry more weight in court than his testimony. It was almost a dead lock on a rustling case; the new brand obscured the old one on the hair side, but the old brand scar showed through on the skin side. "Might as well butcher one of those yearlings," Moore added. "At least we can eat what we don't need for evidence."

The foreman gestured to the ranch's burly blacksmith. "Slim, take this little pissant"—he jabbed a thumb toward Dink Edwards —"and chain him in the springhouse. He tries to get away, put a slug in him."

"How about the dead one?" Jim asked.

"We'll take him into Tascosa and get the judge to hold an inquest, then bury the thieving bastard somewhere, I guess." Moore dismissed the rustling episode with a shrug. "Come on inside, Jim. I've got coffee on. We might even find something a little stronger."

"Didn't know there was anything stronger than LX coffee," Jim said. He followed the wiry foreman into the house.

Moore dug a bottle and two glasses from the bottom drawer of his desk, splashed a couple of fingers of whiskey into each and handed one to Jim.

"You boys did a fine job out there in New Mexico, Jim," Moore said. "Garrett sent me a long letter from Santa Fe telling all about it, and some stories he cut out of the Santa Fe and Las Vegas papers. Seems like you boys are legends out there. They're talking about how the Tascosa men brought law and order to the Pecos River."

Jim shrugged. "I don't know about that. We didn't get what we went after. Didn't find any LX cattle, just picked up a few rustlers along the way."

Moore smiled, but the light in his eyes was cool. "No matter. You and the boys made this outfit proud. Ready to get back to work now?"

Jim nodded, a wry smile on his lips. "It'll be fun to chase cows again for a change. Haven't met one yet who carried a Winchester."

Moore spent the next few minutes briefing Jim on ranch affairs. The LX was still losing stock to cow thieves, but the remaining cattle and horses had come through the harsh winter in reasonably good shape. The winter herd kill was probably less than twelve percent, Moore said—not bad considering that other outfits had lost one cow out of every four.

"We did have us one hell of a drift," Moore summed up. "We've got cattle scattered from here to down past the Caprock. Stock's drifted onto our range from all the way up in Wyoming. Going to be a tough job getting them all rounded up and sorted out."

"That's what us cowboys get the big money for, boss," Jim said. He took a sip of the bourbon. It was good Kentucky sour mash. It went down smooth and set off a warm glow in his belly.

"Jim, I want you to take a wagon crew down to the Pease River country," Moore said. "We'll have a lot of stock down that way. You'll get wagon boss wages, of course."

Jim nodded in agreement but winced inside. The Pease River watershed was brushy, wild and rugged. It was also more than two hundred miles from home. "What about Edwards? Won't I be needed to testify at his trial?"

"You can give a sworn statement to the sheriff in Tascosa. Besides, you might even be back before the trial comes up." The LX foreman downed the last of his whiskey, and tilted the bottle toward Jim. Jim shook his head. One drink was generally his limit.

"I'll make sure you have plenty of help down on the Pease," Moore added. "You can pick your own crew. That'll give you ten top hands. Every little rancher around will send at least one rep each, and the big spreads will have a wagon apiece there."

Jim pushed back his chair and stood. He hated to ask favors of anyone. Especially Bill Moore. Then he swallowed his pride and dove in. "Think you can spare me for a couple of days first? It's been a while since I've seen Hattie."

Moore grinned, stood and clapped Jim on the shoulder. "Sure. I reckon the outfit owes you a little time off. We won't pull the wagon out for another couple of weeks. Take four or five days, get reacquainted with your wife and put some meat back on your bones. You look like death warmed over."

Jim nodded and reached for his hat, anxious to be back in the saddle. He started for the door, then turned as Moore called his name.

"I've been sending your pay to Hattie while you were gone like you asked," Moore said. He reached for the rawhide box where the LX kept its spare cash. "Bates and Beales said you've earned a bonus. An extra month's wages."

Moore reached into the box, counted out thirty dollars and handed the cash to Jim. "I reckon you've got it coming. I'm putting in another ten for catching those rustlers on the way back."

"Thanks." Jim tucked the money into a shirt pocket, more than a little surprised. Bates and Beales were fair men where their hands were concerned, but they weren't known to be especially free when it came to handing out bonuses. "Anything else?"

"Nope. We'll see you in a few days. We'll form up the crews on the LS outfit's flat south of Tascosa before moving out. That'll give you an extra night or two at home."

"Sounds good to me," Jim said.

He strode from the ranch house, tugged his hat on, and headed to the bunkhouse for a bath and a shave. He became aware of a flutter in his gut and grinned to himself. All through the Pecos War business he'd been reasonably calm and relaxed, even if he had been colder than a Montana blizzard. Now he felt his nerves begin to twitch in anticipation, and the chill in his fingers wasn't from the cold.

After nearly five months away from home, Jim East was going courting again.

Tascosa

Death was no stranger in Tascosa. Accidents and disease had claimed a dozen lives, more than half of them children, in a town with no doctor. But a fatal shooting still drew a crowd, Jim East noticed as he glanced at the faces surrounding the wagon.

Most of the adult men, a few women, and what seemed to be every kid over the age of ten were gathered about the LX spring wagon that bore the body of the rustler named Cochran. Hattie East stood at Jim's side, her face pale, a hand clamped beneath his upper arm. Jim had asked her not to come with him for the inquest, but she had insisted. Now he was grateful for her presence and her support, unspoken but still something he could feel in her touch.

Sheriff Cape Willingham flipped aside the blanket covering the body. Jim felt a shudder ripple through Hattie. She turned her face away from the bloody corpse in the wagon, but she kept her firm grip on his arm.

"I'll be damned," Willingham said. "I think that's Bud Cochran. Got a wanted notice on him somewhere. He killed a store owner in a ten-dollar holdup in Kansas about a year back, best I can recall. I'll know for sure after I check out the description with the law in Kansas."

At Willingham's side, Oldham County Judge Jim McMasters leaned over the sideboard of the wagon to examine the body. Several tousled-haired and dirty-faced youngsters pushed closer for a look, eyes wide in awe and wonder. Many of them had seen dead people before. Few had seen an outlaw who had been killed in a gunfight.

Willingham, a former teamster and stage driver and now the first duly elected sheriff of the new county, growled at the youngsters and glared at them through wide-set hazel eyes. The kids tried to sneak one last glance at the corpse before the sheriff's cold stare and firm tone of voice shooed them away.

Judge McMasters leaned forward to study the bullet holes, then tossed the blanket back over the body. McMasters and Willingham had already heard the story of the shooting from Jim, who had arrived a half day before the LX wagon that bore Cochran's body turned onto Main Street. They also had read Dink Edwards's brief account of the shooting, a childlike scribble that confirmed Cochran had drawn his weapon. Edwards had made no reference to his own part in the incident. The young rustler would by now be on his way to Mobeetie, escorted by Bill Moore and the burly blacksmith called Slim.

"Sheriff, if you've nothing to add, I'd say the evidence is consistent with the statements of Mister East and young Edwards," McMasters said. "I see no need for a more formal inquest."

Willingham grunted in agreement.

"The findings of this inquest are that the deceased met his end at the hands of James H. East, duly employed by the LX Ranch, and that Mister East's actions were justified in the defense of his own life and the protection of his employer's property." McMasters glanced at Jim. "You're free to go, Mister East. There will be no charges filed." The judge turned to the driver of the LX wagon. "Take the body to the back room of the Exchange Saloon. We'll give him a decent burial. The LX Ranch has agreed to absorb the funeral expense."

Jim nodded his thanks to the two county officials, then let Hattie lead him toward home.

Later, Jim sat by an open window and sipped at a cup of coffee. The early spring breeze whispered past the flour-sack curtains Hattie had made and stroked a cool, comforting hand along Jim's cheek.

Hattie looked up from the fireplace where a stew bubbled in an iron pot over the coals. She dabbed a few beads of sweat from her forehead. "Jim, is something bothering you?"

Jim heard the concern in her words and saw the worried tenderness in the deep brown eyes. He forced a smile. "I'm fine, Hattie," he said. "It's just that I keep seeing that rustler's face. Charlie Bowdre's, too. I keep thinking maybe I could have done something different and those two might still be alive. It kind of leaves a hollow feeling inside. A life is something you can't put back after you take it."

Hattie rose from her perch on the hearth, straightened her dress and strode to him. She sat on his lap and put her arms around his neck. "Jim East, you stop that kind of talk," Hattie half scolded. "You didn't have a choice where those men were concerned. I don't like the idea of killing any more than you do. But if it's a choice between men like that and you, I know how I'd call it."

Jim reached up and ran his fingers through her hair. It smelled of rose water.

"I know it's hard, Jim," Hattie said, her voice soft and gentle. "But you're no killer. I've seen you stop in the middle of the street to pick a grass burr from a puppy's foot. I've seen you somehow manage to find a penny for a poor child staring at the hard candy in Rhinehart's store. I've seen you put blisters on your hands to help a newcomer dig a well or break land for a garden."

She snuggled closer against him. "You won't admit it, Jim East, but inside you're one of the most gentle men I've ever met." Hattie lifted her head and kissed him lightly on the corner of his mouth. "Before we married you told me this was rough country out here. Now I'll remind you of the same. The Panhandle needs men like you. It's no place for cowards or crybabies. Out here we need strong men. Men with compassion for others but who aren't afraid to fight for what's right. You did what you had to do. There's no rule that says you have to like it. I wouldn't have you if you *did* like it."

Jim lifted a hand and stroked her cheek. "Hattie, I guess you know me better than I know myself. Thanks for understanding."

"Are you going to the funeral?"

"I owe the man that much."

Tascosa was a young community, but already it had established its customs. The whole town turned out for a funeral, paying its respects to the dead regardless of their status in life. Stores closed, saloons emptied, and a long line of silently respectful men and women stood as Cochran's funeral cortege drew to the top of the rocky hill just west of Tascosa. If mass attendance had become a custom, so had the location of the deceased's final resting place.

The law-abiding and more affluent families of Tascosa laid their dead in the plot of land town founder Casimiro Romero had set aside on a grassy mesa on the hill east of town. Relatives of the respectable dead didn't want their cemetery tainted by those from the other side of the law.

The rocky hill to the west, overlooking the bend of the Canadian, held only a few graves. Jim East stood, hat in hand, as the rustler known as Cochran was buried in a distant corner of the small plot of land with the same respect due a man of honor.

The cemetery was called Boot Hill.

SIX

Pease River
May 1881

Jim East landed hard on his butt, bounced once on the hoof-torn grass, and watched as the dun gelding that had just dumped him bucked toward the LX chuck wagon, empty stirrups flapping over the saddle like the wings of a big bird in flight.

Jim looked up, a wry smile on his face, at the young cowboy astride a mouse-colored half mustang a few feet away. Charley Emory, Tom's younger brother, struggled to hide a grin.

"Dammit, Charley, I thought the wagon boss was supposed to get the gentle string," Jim groused, aware of the flush of embarrassment in his cheeks.

Charley Emory shifted his chew to the other cheek, spat, and winked at the sitting man. "You did. Besides, I thought any wagon boss worth his salt was supposed to be able to ride a bronc once in a while. You hurt?"

Jim stood and brushed the Pease River dirt from his backside. He knew he was going to have an impressive bruise on his butt. He shook his head, glanced around and spotted his hat three strides away. He'd lost the hat on the dun's first jump, both stirrups on the second and his seat on the third. "Hell, Charley," he said, "I just had to get off to get my hat. Catch that idiot horse for me and we'll try it again."

The LX rider grinned and touched spurs to his horse. Jim watched the chase until Charley's fast mustang caught up with the still-pitching dun. Jim lifted his Colt Peacemaker from its holster and examined the weapon. It had caught a little dust, but it wasn't damaged. He blew the dirt from the cylinder and holstered the pistol as Charley led the dun back to him and handed him the reins.

Jim stood for a moment and stared at the powerful, deep-chested dun. The horse's nostrils were distended, the whites of his eyes showing, ears pricked forward. "Sandy," Jim said to the dun, "you know damn well you can't do that twice in a row." He toed the stirrup and swung aboard.

The dun fell apart again, the first jump high and twisting to the right, the second short and choppy with a half-spin to the left. But this time Jim had the dun's rhythm. He rammed his spurs into the dun's shoulders and raked the rowels back to the cinch on each jump, his free hand braced against the saddle horn. Jim felt the dun's enthusiasm for pitching fade under the spur rowels. He sensed that Sandy now knew he had hit his best licks and the rider was still in the saddle. The horse lined out, crow-hopped a few times, then quit after thirty yards. Jim reined him toward the herd in the distance. The horse had his daily buck out of his system. Sandy would settle down to the day's work now.

Jim grinned back at the joshing he took from the other LX hands on the way to the herd. He heard the tone of respect under the wisecracks. Not many men had been able to ride the dun called Sandy to a standstill. And Jim had worked with cowboys long enough to know that when they joshed a man it was a sign of friendship, of acceptance. If the crew ever stopped ragging him— and each other—the outfit was headed for trouble.

Some wagon bosses kept their men in line with sharp tongues and threats. Jim didn't work that way. He led his men not with orders but with his own actions. Cowboys respected a boss who wasn't afraid to get his own britches dirty and his knuckles skinned, who took his share of the hard jobs, and who—when he wanted something done—asked a hand to do it instead of ordering him to do it. Jim knew that was one reason his men worked harder and better with less bellyaching than most other crews.

Two drift crew chuck wagons were set up in a grassy flat below a bend in the South Pease, their latest camp in a long string of stops. They moved the herd upriver a few miles every other day to keep from overgrazing the land and fouling the water.

The drift gather had gone about as well as could be expected, Jim thought. Now they were down to their last working of the

South Pease country. A few more days on this final herd and they
could start the long drive back north to home. More than eight
hundred head of Longhorns, Durhams and other breeds milled
and bawled on the flat. Jim was confident that they had found most
of the drift that could be located. The big gathers of two hundred
to three hundred cattle a day had dwindled to only a handful despite the efforts of more than twenty men on horseback. Jim's ten-
man LX crew had linked up with a Diamond Tail chuck wagon.
Three ranchers whose outfits were too small to afford to run their
own roundups had joined the gather.

Jim waved to one of the Diamond Tail hands who had been
riding nighthawk, keeping the cattle from scattering or drifting
through the dark hours. The nighthawks filtered back toward the
wagons for a meal and a few hours' rest before hitting the saddle
again.

Jim studied the herd as he had every day since they had run the
first two Longhorns out of the canyons and thickets along the Red
River well to the northwest. There were at least a dozen brands,
ranging from the big LX, LIT and LS outfits to the Bar M of Alton
Moseley, who ran only a hundred head on his section-and-a-half of
grass in the eastern Texas Panhandle. Here and there a milk cow
that had strayed from some farmer's pasture mingled with the
wilder stock.

The men worked well together. The routine established in the
first few days was now honed to a fine edge. The cowboys held their
horses to a slow walk as they approached and surrounded the herd.
The cattle were more accustomed to men on horseback now, but
still jittery early in the day. The mother cows and their calves
stayed together during the night; they would get separated if the
herd spooked, and the tedious wait while they mothered up again
would delay the day's work of sorting, cutting and branding.

The exciting life of a cowboy, Jim thought as he reined Sandy into
place a few yards from the edge of the herd. *Dust, heat, thirst, bruised
butts, scraped knuckles, and rope burns on the good days. Worse than that
on the bad. I can't figure out why a man would do this. Or why I like it so
much.* He motioned to Charley, then toward the herd. Charley Emory was a taller version of his brother, lean and rangy, a natural
horseman. He was new to the Panhandle country, but Jim had
hired him on the spot. His judgment of the man's ability had

proved right. Charley was the best herd man and roper in the
outfit. The little mustang he rode was a top cutter.

Jim eased the big dun into the herd and soon found a Bar M cow
nursing an early spring calf. He slipped behind the pair and slowly
worked them toward the edge of the herd. The dun's ears dropped
back against the thick neck. Jim knew the horse had the pair spotted and knew what was expected. All Jim had to do was go along
for the ride. It never ceased to amaze him how smooth and quiet a
good cutting horse could handle stock in a herd.

The dun edged the cow and calf from the herd toward Moseley
and his son, who were mounted and waiting a hundred yards south
of the main gather. A short distance away Charley Emory pointed
another cow-calf pair in the same direction.

Jim saw the glint of relief in Moseley's eyes as he and Charley
turned the cuts over to the rancher and his son. The LX could lose
five hundred head and never miss them on the profit sheet. Moseley couldn't afford to lose a single cow without feeling the ache in
his pocketbook.

Jim reined the dun back toward the herd. The long sunup-to-
sundown routine had begun. Roundup days meant hours under a
hot sun. Mother them up, brand and earmark, castrate the bull
calves, sort the stock owned by smaller ranches for the drive to
spreads closer to the Pease country. Change horses at least twice,
feel the ache of exhaustion build in legs and knee joints and shoulders. And at day's end savor the relaxed feeling of work done well.

At sundown they turned the herd over to the nighthawks and
headed back to the wagon for a supper of beef, beans, potatoes
when they had them and canned corn when they didn't, along with
sourdough bread, coffee, and tins of peaches or tomatoes. Despite
the grueling day's work the cowpunchers still joked, laughed, and
joshed each other until time to shake out the bedrolls. *Not such a bad
life,* Jim thought, *at least not for the young bucks who had never learned a
real trade and didn't expect to leave their widows rich women.*

He was spreading his own bedroll in the twilight when a familiar
figure rode up to the picket line where the night horses were kept.
Jim stood as Tom Emory dismounted, exchanged greetings and a
few words with his brother, then picketed his horse and started
toward the camp. Jim met him halfway, hand extended.

"Well, Tom," Jim said, "what brings the LIT's top hand over to this neck of the woods? Get out of riding with a roundup crew this year?"

"Sort of," Tom said, flashing the familiar quick grin. "Major Littlefield wanted me to do a little scouting around, see if I could turn up a rustler or two. Was on my way to the Yellow House country and thought it'd be neighborly to drop by and say howdy. It ain't but a couple hundred miles from there to here." The grin faded. "I think we better talk some, Jim."

"Sounds serious. And when you get serious, I start looking for something to booger at. Time for chuck and coffee first?"

"Nothing stronger?"

"Sorry," Jim said. "Nothing in the wagon but a quart we're saving in case somebody gets hurt, and it may be gone by now if the cook's found it. Closest town to here's Clarendon, so the whiskey supply in the Pease country's dry as Methuselah's chewing tobacco."

Tom snorted in disgust. "Clarendon. Dry as a bone. That bunch of chicken-eatin' Methodists over there don't know how a cowboy lives. No wonder they call it Saint's Roost." He sighed. "God, this mother's son will be glad to get back to Tascosa where there's decent whiskey. Meantime, I guess coffee and a chunk of beef would help. I'm so hungry I wouldn't even care if it was LIT beef."

Jim helped himself to a final cup as Tom ate, then led the rangy cowboy out of hearing range of the wagon crew. The two friends settled down on a flat rock surrounded by scrub brush and prickly pear, and rolled smokes from Jim's tobacco sack as the sun touched the western horizon. With the approach of evening the southwest wind eased. Fine dust grains stirred by wind and cattle settled from the red-orange sunset and the deepening purplish-blue sky.

"What's up, Tom?"

Tom Emory took a deep drag from his cigarette and let the smoke trickle from his nostrils. "We've maybe got some problems ahead, Jim. First, though—what do you think really happened to Dink Edwards?"

Jim frowned. "I don't know. But I'm not buying Bill Moore's story that Dink escaped on the way to Mobeetie. Don't see how a man in irons could get loose from Moore and that big blacksmith."

Tom dragged at the cigarette, its faint glow showing the worry wrinkles in his forehead. "That's what I figure, Jim. Moore could have turned him loose. On the other hand, there's a lot of open range out there. Plenty of space for an unmarked grave." Tom picked up a pebble and tossed it toward a prickly pear leaf. "Anyway, three days after Dink's so-called escape, the blacksmith shows up in Tascosa with a couple of double eagles in his pocket. A week after that I'm riding drift over across the New Mexico line. There's Spade Diamond and Double H Connected cattle all over that country."

Jim ground his cigarette butt beneath a heel. "Never heard of the Double H Connected."

"That's another kick in the britches, Jim," Tom said. His tone was cold and flat. "Brand's registered in New Mexico. To Bill Moore. And he bought up the Spade Diamond brand a few days after the drift wagons pulled out."

Jim stared toward the western horizon for a few moments. There was only one conclusion to be drawn. Bill Moore was behind at least some of the sleepering and outright rustling going on in the Texas Panhandle. "Any way we can prove it, Tom?"

Tom grunted in disgust. "Hell, if I had any solid proof I'd hang the little bowlegged bastard to a cottonwood limb myself," he said. "If we keep an eye out, maybe we can catch him at it."

The two men fell silent for a moment. Jim felt the cold anger build in his gut. It made sense now why Moore insisted on taking Dink Edwards to Mobeetie instead of the Tascosa jail.

"That's not the worst news, Jim," Tom said. "Word's out that the big ranchers are fixing to clamp down on their hands. For starters, no more mavericking. The cattleman's association's decided that anything not already branded belongs to their outfits. The short of it is there won't be any way a cowboy can build a herd of his own. Not on thirty a month and found."

Jim's frown deepened. "A lot of the boys won't stand for that. It's the only reason they put up with the broken bones and can-to-can't workdays in the first place."

"Gives a man a bellyache to get pushed around." Tom's voice had a bitter edge. "What's more, the association's getting set to tell the little men they can't rep on roundups any longer."

The cold anger warmed in Jim's gut. "They can't do that, Tom. These small ranchers like Alton Moseley can't afford to put their own chuck wagons and crews on the range. Dammit, Moseley's a

good man, as fair and honest as I've ever met. He'd be forced out
of business sure as God made crabapples."

"That's what the big men want. When you cut it down to the
bone, they're setting things up to drive the little men out. The
cowboys and the small operators aren't going to stand for it. I'm
afraid we're looking at a range war, Jim. Not now maybe, but a few
miles down the road. It's coming. I can smell it. And that, my
friend, brings us to the reason I rode all the way out here. How
would you like to be Oldham County's next sheriff?"

Jim sat bolt upright. "What the hell are you talking about, Tom?"

"I've been thinking, Jim. Now, I've got nothing against Cape
Willingham. He's a good man. But he's an association man. The big
ranchers put him in office and they want to keep him there." Tom
reached out, broke a thorn from a prickly pear and slipped it into
the corner of his mouth. "I've been talking to a few of the cowboys,
kind of on the sly. We want one of our own wearing that badge,
somebody who knows cow piss from weak beer if trouble starts.
You're the best man for the job. It's not too early to start talking it
up with the boys."

Jim sat silent for a moment, stunned at the idea. Then he shook
his head. "I don't know, Tom. I don't see what I could do to
help—"

"Just be there," Tom broke in. "The cowboys trust you and the
big ranchers respect you. Everybody in the country knows they'd
get a fair shake from Jim East. You're one man who could maybe
keep the lid on if the pot boils over. All we're asking is that you
think it over. Let me know when roundup's done."

Tom stood and brushed the dirt from his backside. Then he
chuckled. "If it means anything, the pay's about a hundred a
month more than you can make punching cows."

Jim rose and offered a hand. "I'll think it over, Tom. I won't
promise you more than that."

"That's enough." Tom returned the handshake. "Now, if you can
spare a spot of ground for the night that doesn't have a rattler or a
scorpion in it, I'd sure like an invite to stay over for breakfast. Hell
of a long ride out to Yellow House."

"You've got the invite, Tom, but I won't make you any promises
about the rattlers and scorpions. If you have to kill a couple, don't
worry about it. We've got plenty to spare."

Jim East lay awake in his bedroll for an hour after turning in. Usually it took only a couple of minutes before he fell asleep, but now he lay on his back and stared at the wash of stars overhead.

In the near distance he heard the lowing of cattle as the herd settled down. An owl hooted twice from the cottonwood grove along the nearby creek, then fell silent, awaiting a reply. A coyote howled in the distance, mournful, as if it had just lost its only friend. From the bedrolls around him came the raspy sound of cowboys snoring, and the occasional rustle of a canvas groundsheet as one of them shifted his position. Near the herd the nighthawks sang, off-key voices flat against the still air. One of them sang a hymn, the other a bawdy cowboy ballad.

Tom Emory had handed Jim a tough biscuit to chew on. The thought of being a peace officer had never entered his head until now. Sheriff of Tascosa did have sort of a ring to it, he thought. Jim had never considered himself a politician, but he knew he had a knack for getting along with people. The appeal of the idea wasn't in the power that went with the badge. It was in the chance to maybe do something worthwhile in a life that so far had been drifted away behind trail herds and in cow camps and line shacks. He didn't have much to offer Hattie at the moment. They could do a lot more on a sheriff's salary than on a cowboy's pay.

He sighed heavily and stirred in his blankets. His bruised butt seemed to find every pebble on the Pease River. The job here was nearly finished. In a few days they would start the long drive back to the Panhandle. One thing was certain, Jim promised silently as his lids finally grew heavy. He wouldn't say yes or no to the idea until he'd had a chance to talk it over with Hattie.

Tascosa
June 1881

Jim East rested his elbows on the faded checked cheesecloth, coffee steaming in the mug before him, and cocked an eye at Hattie seated across the small table.

"Well, girl? What do you think?"

Hattie made a steeple of her fingers and peered across the tips at Jim. "I think you'd make a fine sheriff, dear," she said.

"It could be a dangerous job."

"More dangerous than what you're doing now? Jim, you don't know how much I worry about you. There are so many things that could happen out there on the ranch." She dropped her hands and leaned back in the chair. "I'm being selfish about this," she said. "If you were sheriff, I'd have you home almost every night instead of once a month. Or less."

Jim sighed. "Don't think I haven't considered that. And with the extra money I'd be bringing in, we could buy that house, get you some new clothes, a cookstove instead of a fireplace—"

Hattie leaned across the table and touched a finger to his lips. "Never mind the money and the house and the stove. I want you here with me, Jim." She dropped her fingers to his forearm. "Besides, I know you would be a good sheriff. Not that Cape Willingham isn't. He does his best. I'm prejudiced, but you could do better. This is *our* town, Jim. It needs you."

Jim rose, strode around the table and kissed her on the nape of the neck. "That's what I needed to hear, Hattie. I wouldn't go into something like this without your support. But for now, let's keep it between us. I want to talk to Tom again, and to Cape Willingham. I wouldn't try to put a man out of a job without looking him in the eye first."

Jim felt Hattie's body tense as the sound of distant gunfire echoed through the streets of Tascosa. He patted her shoulder in reassurance. "Nothing serious, I'd bet. That was from over in Hogtown. Probably just some of the boys letting off a little steam before they point the sale herd toward Kansas and railhead."

Hattie looked up, a quick flash of disappointment and pain in her deep brown eyes. "Oh, Jim—does this mean you'll be gone *another* three months?"

Jim smiled. "Not this time, girl. I'll be closer to home. The LX wants me to run a floating wagon up in the Coldwater Creek country. Lon Chambers drew the black bean on the Kansas drive this time around. I'll get to come home at least twice a month until fall roundup starts."

Jim was relieved at not drawing the trail drive duty. Before Hattie he had looked forward to trailing the herds north despite the danger of flooded rivers, the occasional stampede, even being ambushed by gangs of thieves along the way. Now the only thing that mattered was being able to come home once in a while. *Must be getting old,* Jim thought. *Next thing you know I'll be in a rocking chair out front of the house watching the young ones ride by.* The report of another gunshot rattled through the streets.

"Sounds like this might be serious, Hattie," Jim said. "Maybe I'd better go see if Cape can use some help."

"It's not your job yet, Jim," Hattie protested.

Jim patted her shoulder again, then strode toward the door and his gunbelt hanging on a peg nearby. "Not my job, girl, but like you said, it's our town." He strapped on the gunbelt and pulled his hat into place. "Almost forgot my manners, Hattie," he said as he reached for the door latch. "That was one mighty fine supper. I'll be back in a bit."

"You watch yourself out there, Jim East," Hattie scolded. "I'd like to have you back here for breakfast, and still in one piece."

Jim flashed a smile of reassurance. "I'll watch out, Hattie. I'm not near as reckless as I used to be in my younger days."

Jim studied the town anew as he strode toward Hogtown. Tascosa had grown a lot this spring. New buildings sprouted along the streets and the town's population swelled by the day. Not all the growth was welcome.

Texas Ranger Captain G. W. Arrington had finally gotten his fill of the rowdies, gamblers and assorted riffraff in Mobeetie and chased them out. Those who didn't chase got carried out. The problem was that the majority of those evicted from Mobeetie had drifted into Tascosa. Most of them settled in Hogtown, where they followed their chosen occupations of drinking and whoring and fighting. Sometimes they spilled into Tascosa proper, where such goings-on were not looked upon kindly.

Jim tested the Colt's fit in the holster as he crossed into Hogtown. Technically the place was Lower Tascosa. It had earned the name "Hogtown" after one of Upper Tascosa's ladies remarked in disgust that everyone who went there behaved like swine and got hog-drunk. The name stuck.

Jim stopped in the middle of the dusty street as Sheriff Cape Willingham and Constable Henry Brown stepped through the doorway of the Emporium, a three-room adobe saloon, each dragging a man in range clothes. Jim knew the two captives by sight. One was an LS cowhand named John Lang. The other was J. B. Gough, a saloon hanger-on, gambler and sometime gunman known as the Catfish Kid for reasons Jim could never fathom. The side of Gough's head was bloody.

"Problem, Sheriff?" Jim asked.

Willingham shrugged. From hat crown to boot heel, Cape Willingham wasn't a big man. From side to side he was big enough— thick chest, heavy sloping shoulders, and hairy forearms almost as bulky as a corral post. "Nothing serious. These boys got a little too much panther piss in 'em and decided to shoot up the place. Henry had to massage Catfish's head a bit with his sixgun to get his attention."

Jim glanced at the constable. He didn't much care for Henry Brown. The man was tall and lean, with prominent ears and a quick temper; he was a former buffalo hunter who had ridden with Billy the Kid in the Lincoln County War. Jim suspected Brown might have had a hand in the Kid's rustling business around Tascosa, but the man had stayed behind when Billy's bunch made their run for New Mexico. Brown, Jim thought, looked a bit smug over tonight's affair. He liked hitting people. Jim promised himself that if he won the sheriff's race he'd ask Henry Brown to find another line of work.

Jim touched the brim of his hat to Cape Willingham. "I'll be on my way then, Cape," he said. "Just thought you might have run into something you might need help with."

"Thanks, Jim. Appreciate the offer. Come along while we lock these two up until the whiskey wears off 'em. Got something at the office you might be interested in."

The small adobe jail stood at the south end of McMasters Street, not far from Jim's home. Willingham opened the door of the single cell. Brown roughly shoved the men inside and locked the door. Jim watched Willingham open the bottom drawer of a small, scarred desk and drop the prisoners' weapons inside. He picked up a newspaper clipping and handed it to Jim.

"The Kid broke out of the Lincoln jail before they could hang him," Willingham said. "Killed two deputies, Bob Olinger and J. W. Bell."

Jim scanned the clipping. It recounted, in somewhat florid prose, the deaths of the two guards—Olinger blown almost in half by shotgun blasts from a window of the Lincoln lockup, Bell shot with a pistol on the stairs inside the jail—and the Kid's escape. It added that Sheriff Pat Garrett was again on the fugitive's trail. Jim handed the clip back to Willingham and shook his head. "Maybe I should have let Barney Mason kill the Kid after all," he said. "Billy told me he wouldn't hang."

Willingham dropped the clipping casually onto the cluttered desk. "Likely he won't. I expect Garrett'll get a slug or two in the Kid this time around."

Jim hesitated for a moment, then decided this wasn't the time to bring up his notion of running for sheriff against Willingham. Especially not with Henry Brown hanging around. He nodded a good-night to Cape, turned and stepped through the door into the last hour of daylight. He had never before noticed how close the jail was to his home. He made a mental note to check the loads in Hattie's shotgun before he rode out.

SEVEN

Tascosa
July 1881

Jim East sat in an overstuffed horsehair chair, his right leg propped across a pillow atop a low bench. The knee was swollen to twice its normal size, and it sent a knifepoint of pain up his leg each time his heart beat. His shoulder was less painful. It was badly bruised, but for the most part undamaged. His head still hurt and every time he took a breath the cracked rib ripped a double-bit axe blade across his chest.

Jim didn't remember all that much about the fall but the details he did recall were vivid enough to bring on cold sweats. He especially remembered the sheer terror of those few seconds that were the worst nightmare of the working cowboy.

He had the blue roan in a dead run with all the flat-out speed the horse could muster, trying to turn the lead steer of a dozen LX cattle before they reached the dense thicket on Coldwater Creek. The roan's forefoot hit a badger hole. The fall was too quick and too hard for Jim to kick free of the stirrups. He remembered seeing the ground slam into his face and feeling the fleeting, crushing weight of the horse as it rolled over him. Most of all he recalled the gut-ripping fear when the horse regained its feet with Jim's right boot hung up in the stirrup. He vaguely remembered a hoof grazing his head, rocks and brush tearing at his body as the panicked horse bolted.

Then Lem Woodruff's horse appeared from somewhere and charged alongside the roan. Lem leaned in the saddle, grabbed the headstall of the roan's bridle and yanked the horse to a stop, pushing its head around to keep the hooves clear of Jim's body. Jim remembered looking up at the roan's side, his foot still twisted in the stirrup, before the red haze came and the lights winked out.

The lights flickered on once, briefly, and Jim lay confused until he realized he was stretched out in the back of a flatbed wagon. Then the pain roared back and the world went dark again.

The memories triggered a chill in Jim's bones. He had seen men dragged to death. It was a brutal and messy way to die. He had been lucky. If Lem Woodruff had been another twenty yards away or riding a slower horse, there wouldn't be much left of one James H. East today.

The knee wasn't broken, just badly sprained. His whole body was an impressive collection of bruises and scrapes that ached and stung. It seemed to Jim that he wore more bandages than skin at the moment. But he was still alive. He could stand a little pain, considering how it could have worked out.

Jim's only complaint at the moment was that the small adobe house was too crowded for comfort. And the crowd was drinking up a month's supply of his coffee. *That stuff is expensive,* Jim grumbled to himself. Figured cup against shot glass it cost more than good whiskey.

Sheriff Cape Willingham lounged against one wall. Constable Henry Brown sat at the table, polishing off the last piece of Hattie's dried-apple deep dish pie. LX foreman Bill Moore fidgeted in a hard chair across from Brown. Lem Woodruff, the lean young cowboy whose dark eyes twinkled with mischief and an almost constant grin that flashed stark white against sun-browned skin, sat on the fireplace hearth. He cradled a coffee cup in both hands and grinned at Jim.

Hattie darted from one visitor to the other, refilling mugs. Jim noticed the frown crease her brow as she served Henry Brown. Hattie disliked Brown as much as he did, but it was part of her nature to feed everybody who came calling at the East adobe. It seemed to Jim that every animal from stray pups to out-of-work cowboys stopped at the East place. None went away hungry.

"How you feeling, Jim?" Willingham asked. There was genuine concern in his tone.

"Like I've been dragged behind a horse," Jim said. The cuts inside his mouth tasted like copper and his swollen lips had trouble forming the words. "But I reckon I'll make it. I've got a good nurse."

Willingham smiled at Hattie. "Yes, I suppose you do."

Moore finished his coffee and reached for his hat. "Jim, Bates and Beales have agreed to keep you on the payroll until you've healed enough to ride again. They'll pay you top hand rates."

"Tell them I said thanks." He watched the foreman leave. He welcomed the news Moore had brought. Not many of the big ranch owners would keep paying a bunged-up cowboy when he couldn't work. But Jim wasn't especially unhappy to see Moore walk out the door. He couldn't shake the feeling that Bill Moore would rather have seen him dragged to death.

Lem Woodruff stretched and yawned. "Guess I better get back to cowboying. Sitting around listening to Jim East try to grow skin isn't near as much fun as chousing stock." He turned to Hattie. "Thanks for the coffee and hospitality, Missus East. Take care of that broken-down saddle tramp over there. I sure would miss having him around. Keeps life on the drift wagon exciting."

Woodruff started for the door.

"Lem, did I say thanks?" Jim asked.

Lem shrugged. "*De nada.* Do me a favor sometime and we'll call it even." Woodruff lifted a hand in salute and strode from the cool adobe into the blazing sun.

The sheriff pushed away from the wall and handed his cup to Hattie with a nod of thanks. "By the way, Jim," he said as he reached into his shirt pocket and produced a sheath of bills, "I finally got a definite identification on that rustler you killed. It was Bud Cochran. Real hard case. Killed three men in Nebraska besides the store clerk in Kansas. There was a two hundred dollar bounty on him. It's yours."

Jim shrugged and immediately winced. The bruised shoulder let him know that wasn't a good idea. "Give it to Hattie. She'll put it in the house kitty."

Hattie took the money with a nod of thanks. "Part of this is going into a fund to try to get a doctor to come to Tascosa," she said. "Lord knows we need one, with the kids getting sick and breaking bones and cowboys who keep getting into one mess after another."

Willingham turned to his deputy. "Better start your rounds,

Henry," he said. "Time to check out the goings-on in Hogtown. Saturday night, you know. I'll be along shortly."

Henry Brown grunted, pushed back his chair and left without a word, not even thanking Hattie for the pie and coffee. The sheriff waited until the door closed behind the deputy, then turned back to Jim. "Thought you might be interested to know Billy the Kid's dead, Jim. Just got word in from New Mexico this morning. Pat Garrett caught up with him last week—night of the fourteenth—at Pete Maxwell's place in Fort Sumner. Shot him twice. Billy died almost as soon as the slugs hit him. Also, Dave Rudabaugh broke out of jail. Rumor is he headed for Mexico."

Jim sighed. "Billy was right, then. He told me when the shackle rivet popped that he would die and Rudabaugh would go free. Billy also told me he would never hang."

"Just as well it worked out that way for the Kid and everybody concerned," Willingham said with a frown of disgust. "Saved New Mexico the expense of a hanging. Jim, I'll never understand people. They've already started to make some kind of hero out of Billy. Like he was something more than a small-time bandit turned killer. Makes no sense to me. I guess you knew Billy about as well as anybody besides Garrett."

"I knew him well enough," Jim said. "Billy was a likeable sort, but I don't think I'll waste much time mourning over him."

"Anyhow, he's buried alongside Charlie Bowdre and Tom O'Folliard at Fort Sumner. Good riddance, as I see it." Willingham reached for his hat. "Jim, if you need anything, just let me know," he said. "Thanks for the coffee, Hattie. I'd better get back on duty."

When Willingham had gone Jim shifted his backside in the over-stuffed chair and groaned aloud. Any movement at all seemed to rekindle the fire in the knee and put a fresh edge on the axe in his chest.

Hattie came to him and traced a finger along a patch of un-bandaged stubble on his jaw. "Are you comfortable, Jim? Is there anything I can do?"

Jim patted her hand. "I'm all right. I just need a little time to get the pieces back together."

Hattie squeezed his hand in reply, then set about washing the dishes.

A soothing silence fell on the adobe house. Jim was glad to finally be away from the center of attention. It made him uncomfortable.

After several minutes Hattie looked over her shoulder, her forearms buried in dishwater. "That does it, Jim East," she said.

He raised an eyebrow. "Uh-oh. Am I in trouble again?"

"Except for darn near getting yourself killed again, no. I was just thinking. If you're going to insist on chasing outlaws, getting shot at and crippled up anyway, you might as well get paid more for it. I had some doubts before but I didn't voice them. Now there's no question in my mind. You'll make a good sheriff, Jim."

Jim grunted. "Well, at least I'll have some time to study on it. Looks like it'll be a spell before I get horseback again."

Tascosa
September 1881

Jim East limped along Main Street, savoring the cool of the morning. It was his favorite time of year, this brief bridge between the fading days of summer and the onset of autumn. A few cottonwood leaves already showed the first tinges of yellow that would turn them into splashes of burnished gold before the first strong north wind stripped them to the bones of winter.

The knee still pained a bit when he turned it a certain way, but it was almost back to full strength. Jim had gone through a bout of moving around on crutches, then to a stout cane, and finally was able to walk without any help from man-made legs. The bruised shoulder was only a memory now. The cracked rib had healed except for an occasional twinge and most of the skin he had left on the Coldwater had grown back. *Nothing like nearly getting dead to make a man appreciate life,* Jim thought.

His daily walks served a double purpose. They strengthened the knee and kept him in touch with the town's supply of local gossip. He was pleased with the way the leg was healing. He wasn't quite so happy with the turn Hogtown had taken.

Tascosa proper had never been exactly tame, but it hadn't been all that wild. Not like Dodge City or Ogallala at trail's end in the old days. Upper Tascosa occasionally had its share of brawls in the three saloons now in operation, and sometimes a cowboy grew a little too much whiskey hair and tried to tree the town.

Hogtown was a boar from a different litter.

While Upper Tascosa grew, Hogtown boomed. There were at least three whorehouses in operation now, not counting the one-girl or two-girl stables that worked the smaller saloons or ran their own business from their homes.

Ranger Captain Arrington's cleanup of Mobeetie had contributed the most to the growth of Hogtown. Gamblers, swindlers, and drifters who had no visible means of support other than somebody else's livestock or pocketbook had doubled Hogtown's population in the last few months. The women who made their livings on their backs had followed. They went by names such as Frog Lip Sadie, Gizzard Annie, Rowdy Kate, Midnight Rose and Box Car Jane, among others. Throw a mixture like that in with a bunch of off-duty cowboys who had a month's wages burning holes in their pockets and most anything could happen these days in Hogtown.

Upper Tascosa's growth was watered from more respectable streams of commerce. New merchants moved in to share the gold spent by the big ranches. Freight wagons lumbered in almost daily from Dodge City to the north, Fort Worth to the southeast, and Mobeetie downriver. Others rumbled west toward New Mexico. Cattle buyers crowded the hotels and boarding houses, and there was an almost constant flow of salesmen of all lines of goods into and through Tascosa.

Mexican craftsmen and laborers sweated and prospered. Six days a week they built new adobe homes, businesses, corrals, even pig pens and chicken coops. On Sunday they stopped work to attend Catholic services in Casimiro Romero's sprawling double-adobe home on the hill north of Hogtown.

The civic leaders of Tascosa proper were still trying to lure a doctor to the community. There was still talk of building a church and a school. Jim had no reason to believe they wouldn't succeed. Tascosa's civic pride ran high and optimistic. Almost to a man the town leaders were convinced that soon the railroad would come. After all, they reasoned, there was no better crossing of the river than at Tascosa. The gentle slope of valleys to the north and south meant a shallower grade for the rails to follow, without the expense of cutting through sheer bluffs that stretched up and down the river.

Tascosa seemed destined to become a metropolis on the grassy plains. There was even talk of an opera house. But so far, Jim reminded himself, it was still a small adobe village dependent on the cattle trade. And it still had its share of poverty.

Jim paused outside the North Star Restaurant on Main Street as the door swung open and Cape Willingham emerged, a toothpick jutting from beneath his thick mustache. *Might as well get it done,* Jim thought. He returned the sheriff's nod of greeting. "Got time for a private talk, Cape?"

Willingham grinned. "Sure. Haven't had a single bit of trouble yet and it's already past seven o'clock in the morning." He waved to a bench beside the door. The narrow sidewalk was stained a brownish black with the residue left from the daily meetings of the local spit-and-whittle club. "Take the weight off the knee, Jim. Doing better?"

Jim sat and stretched the injured leg out before him. "Better every day. I'll be back in the saddle in a week or so. Maybe sooner if Hattie picks up a butcher knife and runs me out of the house."

Willingham chuckled. "Does get a might tiresome just sitting around listening to your whiskers grow. What's on your mind?"

Jim took a deep breath. "Cape, I've been asked to run against you next election. I thought I'd tell you in person before word started to get around on the street. That's not to say I think you haven't been a good sheriff. It's just that—well, some of the cowboys have asked. Nothing personal between you and me."

"Hell, Jim, I know that," Willingham said. He plucked the toothpick from his mouth, flipped it into the street and reached for his battered pipe. "Doesn't take any real genius to see trouble's coming between the cowboys and the big men. Everybody knows the association ranchers back me. Makes sense the punchers would want somebody in office who savvies their side. If I was chasing cows I'd want the same thing." He paused to light the pipe and puff it into serious action. "Don't reckon there's any need to ask you to keep the campaign clean?"

Jim shook his head. "I hadn't planned on letting it get nasty. Didn't figure you would either, Cape. No need to badmouth each other. That would mean I'd have to lie about you and the job you've done. If I've got to lie to get a job I don't want the damn thing. Thought we might just put out the word that we're both candidates and let the voters pick."

Cape Willingham sucked at the pipe and nodded. "Sounds fair." He grinned around the pipe stem. "What the hell. It's a long time to election day. Both of us could get killed before then."

EIGHT

Texas Caprock
August 1882

Jim East pulled the big buckskin to a stop on the high bluff over-looking the Valley of Tears.

The broad stretch of rugged, brush-studded country below had gotten its name in the days when Comanches ruled the Texas High Plains. It was here that captive families were separated among different bands to make escape attempts less likely, or were traded for goods offered by Comancheros.

Jim swung from the saddle to rest his knee and let the horse blow before the steep descent from the crest of the Caprock.

The knee still ached after several hours in the saddle. Jim had resigned himself to the notion it would give him trouble for a long time to come. His concern now wasn't the dull pain in the knee. It was the long, winding trail of dark shapes in the distance.

Jim was taking his turn at what the cowboys now called the "Winchester Quarantine." The Texas Fever had been especially bad this year and the Panhandle Cattleman's Association decided to crack down on the movement of trail herds through their own grass. Except for a four-mile-wide corridor from the southern Plains through Tascosa and on to Kansas, all cattle trails through the Texas Panhandle were now closed.

Jim understood the cattlemen's concern. Texas Fever could wipe out a whole herd in one season. No one knew what it was, but they knew it followed the trail herds north from central and southern Texas. They had no real choice but to stop the herds from crossing their lands—or, at best, confining the drives to the one narrow strip. The only way to do that was by association decree backed up by rifle and handgun.

Jim doubted that the owners cared much about his worries at the moment. *Nothing to it,* he thought. *One man, one Winchester, to stop a trail drive of more than a thousand cattle herded by a dozen men armed to the teeth. Just another working day in the life of a Panhandle cowboy.* He sighed, flexed the knee once more, and swung back into the saddle. He reined the buckskin toward the narrow trail that snaked down the side of the Caprock to the floor of the valley some six hundred feet below. The horse stopped and snorted, head down and ears pointed toward the steep trail.

"I know, Buck," Jim said as he patted the horse's neck. "I'm not real crazy about the idea myself." He touched spurs to the buckskin's ribs.

An hour later he pulled the lathered gelding to a stop to let the animal catch his wind. He could feel the horse's heart thump against the inside of his knees. While he waited for the horse's breathing to settle, Jim pulled his rifle from its boot, checked the loads, and stared toward the herd in the near distance. He slipped the rifle back into its sheath. Most men got testy if you rode up on them with a gun in your hand. Jim knew from experience that trail bosses were testy enough to begin with. He kneed the buckskin into motion.

He rode at an easy trot toward the herd, making no attempt to conceal his approach. He lifted his fingertips to his hatbrim as he neared the lead rider, a lean and weathered old-timer who rode easy in the saddle. The man's saddle and chaps were as trail-worn and scarred as the rider himself, Jim noted. Cold blue eyes rode above a skewed nose that appeared to have been broken more than once.

"Howdy," Jim said.

"Howdy." The tone was as chilly as the pale blue eyes.

"You the boss of this outfit?"

"I'm him. Name's Wade Turner. I got all the hands I need, you're looking for work."

"Wish it was that simple, Mister Turner." Jim's voice was calm, but he felt the yips in his gut. One of the point riders rode up, hand on the butt of a Colt at his belt. "Afraid I've got some bad news. I'm Jim East of the LX. Rep for the Panhandle Cattleman's Association."

Wade Turner twisted his head and spat. The spurt of tobacco

juice knocked a tarantula from the side of a rock. "Don't like bad news, East. Speak your piece."

Jim glanced at the point rider. The man had eased his pistol from the holster and held the weapon at his side, thumb on the hammer. "The association's put a quarantine on trail drives through the Panhandle, Mister Turner. There's one strip set aside. If you agree to keep your herd in that strip, we'll lend you any extra hands you need as long as you're on association range. Otherwise, you have to turn your herd back to Doan's store and trail north through Indian Territory, or go south of the Panhandle to New Mexico and then turn north. Or hold your herd here until first frost."

Turner glared in silence at Jim. A mixture of anger and disbelief burned in the pale blue eyes. "Now, that's kind of a high-and-mighty attitude, ain't it?"

"I suppose it seems like it. But we've had a Texas Fever problem up here, Mister Turner. The Panhandle ranchers don't want to lose any more stock."

Jim had begun to wonder if the trail boss could stare down an owl before Turner finally blinked. "Suppose I tell you and the association to go to hell?"

Jim shrugged, trying to ignore the man with the pistol. "I do my best to stop you."

Turner's jaw muscles twitched. The lines deepened in a face the color of worn saddle leather. "You got some help to do that little chore?"

"No. Just me."

"Look around, East. I've got a dozen hands here, all packin' iron. Don't see how one man can stop me."

"I didn't say I'd stop you, Mister Turner," Jim said. "I said I'd do my best to stop you."

"You could get pretty damn dead, too."

"Could be." Jim sat with his forearms crossed casually over the saddle horn. He kept his hands well away from his weapons.

Turner's gaze remained locked onto Jim's eyes. "Ain't you gonna say something stupid about how I'd be the first man dead?"

Jim inclined his head toward the point rider. "No, Mister Turner, you wouldn't be. That man over there with the pistol would blow me out of the saddle before I could blink. But if you kill me and move this herd onto Panhandle grass you'll have a hundred cowboys from a dozen brands on your tail inside of a day. You might give that some thought."

"You threatenin' me, East?"

"No. Just telling you where the badger holes are."

Turner slowly shook his head. Then the old-timer's scowl softened and finally faded into a grin. "Damn me, Jim East, if you ain't got bigger balls than a Mexican stud. I admire a man with sand, by God." The trail boss turned to the point rider. "Put the hardware up, Gus," he said.

The rider holstered the weapon. Jim breathed a silent sigh of relief.

"You'll show us where this strip is, East?"

"Be glad to. Runs from the head of Palo Duro Canyon up through the Tule country and north into Tascosa. You catch the Dodge City Trail there. There's good grass and water along the way."

Turner nodded. "I reckon I can go along with that." The pale blue eyes suddenly narrowed. "You the Jim East helped catch Billy the Kid?"

"I was there. Can't say I was all that much help."

The trail boss chuckled. "Gus, good thing you didn't throw down on this man. I hear he's poison with a Winchester and faster'n a greased snake with a pistol."

Jim had to grin. "Somebody's been tamping sand in your flour sack, Mister Turner. I'm just a dollar-a-day cowboy."

"Yeah. And the Rocky Mountains is pimples on a whore's butt." Turner stuck out a hand. Jim took it; the grip was warm and firm. "Ride along with me, East," Turner said. "Don't expect to live through this drive, though. Our cook's sourdough'll probably kill you."

The two men rode without speaking for half a mile. The lowing of cattle and calls of cowboys stirred Jim's memories of earlier trail drives, when he was the man out front of a herd on the move. It was a feeling that couldn't be described and couldn't be forgotten.

Wade Turner was the first to break the silence.

"Still live in Tascosa, East?"

"I think so. Haven't been home in three months. My wife may have traded me for a better horse by now."

Turner clucked his tongue. "Damn shame a man has to stay away from home that long at a time. I'm already missing that old bat I'm married to, and I ain't been gone two full months yet." The trail boss sighed. "What're we gonna do, East?"

"About what?"

Turner waved back over his shoulder. "Our lives. This ain't gonna last. Trail drives, open range, the days a man could make somethin' of hisself and be proud." He spat out the used-up chew, pulled a plug from a shirt pocket, bit off a chunk and settled the tobacco into his jaw. "You know, there's some big old bones stuck in the rocks up in Montana. Big lizards lived a long time ago. Dyno-sewers, the smart boys calls 'em." He worked the chew for a moment, then spat. He was a good spitter, Jim noted. Almost none of the tobacco juice dribbled down the gray-stubbled chin.

"That's us, East. Dyno-sewers. Last of our breed. Pretty soon they won't be none of us left, just bones layin' somewhere." Turner sighed. "What the damn politicians, railroads and bankers don't steal and the damn British and rich Yankees don't buy up's gonna be covered with that newfangled barb wire 'til a man can't ride a mile in a straight line. God, I'm gonna miss it."

LX Ranch
October 1882

Jim East kicked the last of the sullen steers from the Coldwater Creek thickets toward the main LX herd two hundred yards away and wondered if this was his last roundup.

There were fewer Longhorns this year than last and more of the red cattle with white faces called Herefords that Bates and Beales had shipped in to upgrade the herds. Jim knew it was good business. The shorthorns fleshed out better, were worth more on the market, and nobody could say they weren't easier to handle.

But he was already starting to miss the Longhorns. There was something about them that was like the land itself. Tough and stringy and mean most of the time, but they came through droughts and blizzards and took care of themselves. Maybe, Jim thought, the Longhorns were some of Wade Turner's "dyno-sew-ers."

There were already a few bones showing up in the Panhandle. Major George W. Littlefield was gone now, the LIT sold to a bunch of Britons calling themselves the Prairie Land & Cattle Company. Luis Bausman had stayed on at the LIT for about ten minutes after he heard the news.

Tom Emory had told Jim of Luis's emphatic departure from the LIT. "Ain't workin' for no damn Brits," Bausman had growled as he packed his few belongings. "We whipped them bastards in three, four wars and still can't cut loose from 'em. But by God, this mother's child can." Several other LIT hands headed out before Luis's dust had settled. Bausman moved into Tascosa and made his living gambling and doing odd jobs or ranch day work now and then. Some of the others stayed, switched to different outfits, or just packed up and left the Panhandle.

The LS, with W. M. D. Lee at the controls, had nearly doubled in size. Lee had bought up Ellsworth Torrey's LS Connected. He also acquired the claims to several smaller spreads and nester shacks and now claimed an area as big as the state of Connecticut. What the LS didn't own outright Lee took simply by declaring the land LS range even though it was technically in the public domain and belonged to no one.

The LX had followed Lee's lead and now grazed a swath of Panhandle grass that stretched sixty-five miles north to south and thirty-five miles east to west. Now there were rumors that the British were getting ready to make a move to buy the outfit. Jim frowned at the thought. He didn't agree all the time with Luis Bausman's ideas, but in this case Bausman was right. Foreign syndicates buying up Panhandle grass rubbed Jim's fur the wrong way. It would be damned hard to have the same loyalty to the brand when the work was for people who never got their own hands dirty.

The Panhandle Cattleman's Association hadn't made life any easier for the cowpunchers. The orders had come down that a cowboy could no longer run a few head of his own cattle or horses on land claimed by the big ranchers. Mavericking, once accepted as fair open range practice, had been outlawed. The association claimed that any unbranded stock grazing a member's land belonged to the ranch owner. That, Jim knew, just about killed a cowboy's chances of ever building his own place; he was a peon on horseback, a name on a payroll, and would be for the rest of his natural working life if he stayed on a ranch. If he didn't, he wouldn't be missed. Young men drifted into the Panhandle every day, looking for work. If a cowboy quit, three men were waiting to take his place.

If the association had made life miserable for the cowboy, they'd made it impossible for the men who owned small spreads. The so-called "little men" were now banned from participating in the spring and fall roundups run by the big ranches. Many of them had already been forced out of business. One of the first to go had been Alton Moseley of the Bar M, a good, honest man whose life's work was now only a memory. His land wound up in the hands of one of the big spreads. Others followed and Jim wondered how many of their cows now wore the LS, LX, Diamond F or other big ranch brands without the original owner's having been paid for them. The little man's cows gathered in the big ranch roundups were mostly unbranded. The big outfits claimed them, slapped their brands on them and kept them. Jim had trouble seeing the difference between that and outright rustling. It just didn't strike him as fair.

The association had put a standing bounty of two hundred fifty dollars on any man caught rustling from the big ranches. That didn't work in reverse, though. Any thefts from the smaller outfits were just their hard luck, in the association's eyes.

Cowboys had always bitched about the hard work, long hours, low pay and dangers of their job. The difference now, Jim noted, was that the tone of the bitching had changed. The cowpunchers were serious about it these days, not just making noise.

Now there was talk of building a drift fence north of the Canadian to keep Kansas and Colorado stock from reaching the shelter of the river breaks to survive the brutal northers that swept down the plains. It didn't take much of a cowboy to know what that would mean. Cattle would reach the fence and then, unable to move south, would stand and freeze to death while others stacked up behind them and died. Barbed wire was coming to the Panhandle.

Jim edged the steers into the herd and reined his tiring horse toward the remuda. It was time to change mounts before the sorting and branding started. The young wrangler had Jim's rope horse caught and waiting by the time Jim got to the horse herd. He stripped the saddle and bridle from the gray he had been riding and watched him shake himself, lie down and roll in the dust. Jim saddled the deep-chested sorrel rope horse.

At least, he thought as he pulled the cinch tight, Wade Turner wouldn't have to see the end of a way of life. Word had reached Tascosa that the old man was dead, crushed when a horse fell on him in Kansas ten miles from railhead.

Jim stepped into the saddle and reined the sorrel toward the herd. The gelding's muscles quivered in anticipation. The horse liked his job and was eager to get on with the work.

Jim shook out his first loop and realized that it might well be his last time, at least for a while. The association might have made life hell for cowboys and small ranchers, but it had also swung a lot of votes in his direction and the election was little more than a month away. The cowboys would vote in a block for one of their own. The association helped Jim's cause by openly backing Cape Willingham for another term.

Jim hadn't campaigned much. Bill Moore and the LX hadn't given him the time. Jim figured that was part of the association strategy, and it fit all right with Jim's plans to let the big men do most of the talking. Among Oldham County's cowboys, its few remaining small ranch owners and its working poor, resentment ran high toward the rich. Every time the big men opened their mouths they pushed a few more votes Jim's way. There were a lot more poor folks than rich people in the county.

Jim had found the time for an occasional quick visit to the smaller ranches and the isolated line camps on the bigger spreads. He had made a couple of brief trips into Hogtown and a few stops in Upper Tascosa. He hadn't set up drinks at the Equity or any other Tascosa saloons. He just dropped by and talked with the cowboys and townsmen, made no promises, and went on about his business. Although he had a feeling the vote would be close, his confidence grew by the day. He had handled himself well in the Pecos War. People knew he could handle touchy situations. But so could Willingham. Cape had proved his courage and competence several times over. There were two graves in Boot Hill that had been filled by Cape's shotgun and pistol, and one or two others in the rocky hills overlooking the Canadian.

The election, Jim now knew for certain, wasn't between two men. It was between two factions whose distrust and hatred for each other grew by the day.

Jim eased the sorrel into the herd, swung the loop overhead once and then dropped it in front of the back feet of a halfbreed yearling. He pulled the slack from the rope as the yearling stepped into the loop, dallied and turned the sorrel. The yearling bawled and fell to its side, and the sorrel leaned into the rope, dragging the calf behind. This heifer would be the first to feel the iron on this day's work.

Tascosa
November 1882

Jim East felt Hattie's grip tighten on his upper arm as C. B. Vivian, Oldham County's one-armed clerk, scribbled the final vote tally on a cracked slateboard tacked to the outside wall of his combination office and home.

Jim let a grin spread over his face as the first wave of cheers broke from the cluster of cowboys crowded on the sidewalk. He had won by just over twenty votes.

Hattie reached up, caught Jim by the ear and pulled his head down far enough to give him a quick peck on the cheek. Her face was flushed with pride and admiration. "Congratulations, Sheriff East," she whispered.

Before Jim could reply the crowd surged forward, eager to shake his hand. Cape Willingham was one of the first.

"Jim," Willingham said, "it was a fair contest and a clean campaign. Congratulations."

Jim returned Willingham's sincere handshake. "Cape, I'd be a lot more proud if it had been somebody except you put out of a job. What will you do now?"

Willingham chuckled. "Try to stay alive until you take the oath of office January first," he said. "To the victor, as nobody has said, go the hazards. I'm not all that disappointed. I'm tired of wrestling drunks and getting shot at, to tell you the truth."

"Gentlemen," Vivian shouted, "the saloons may now reopen! The election is over!"

The announcement triggered a fresh surge of jubilation from the crowd. "Be pleased to buy you a drink, Jim," Willingham yelled above the din.

Jim started to shake his head but Hattie tugged at his sleeve. "Go ahead, Jim," she said. "You deserve a little celebration." She smiled again, mischief dancing in her brown eyes. "Just don't overdo it or Sheriff Willingham might toss you in our little jail. I'll be waiting for you at home."

Jim smiled back at her. "Thanks, Hattie. I promise I won't be long." Jim watched her push her way through the mob, then lost sight of her in the crush of outstretched hands. A cowboy in the back of the crowd pulled his pistol and fired a shot of celebration into the air. The blast triggered a volley of gunshots. The fire of muzzle flashes scored the darkening sky.

Willingham made no attempt to stop the celebration. He knew when to let men blow off steam, as long as it didn't last past regular folks' bedtime. "Meet you at the Equity in a few minutes," Cape all but yelled in Jim's ear.

It took Jim almost a half hour to work his way from Vivian's place to the Equity Saloon. His right hand felt swollen and sore from all the handshakes. He found Cape Willingham leaning against the bar. Constable Henry Brown was there too, frowning into a glass. He glared at Jim for a moment, then turned back to his drink.

Willingham raised his glass in salute, then pushed a bottle and an extra glass to Jim. Jim dribbled a single shot of whiskey into the glass and lifted it, returning the sheriff's toast. He sipped at the amber liquid and winced. It was pretty raw stuff.

"Seriously, Cape," Jim said, "what will you do after the end of the year?"

Willingham shrugged. "Got a few dollars squirreled back. Reckon I'll buy me a bunch of the meanest horses I can find and drift 'em into New Mexico. Always wanted a horse ranch." He lowered his voice so that Jim had to strain to hear. "Watch yourself,

Jim," Willingham said. "A man can get killed in this town. I got a
feeling it's going to get worse before it gets better."

Jim nodded. "I expect you're right, Cape. I'll watch it."

A hand on his shoulder interrupted the conversation. He turned
to a trio of grinning faces still dusty from the day's work—Lem
Woodruff, Tom Emory, and young Cal Polk. "By God, Jim," Lem
said, "we did it! I'll buy the next round for the new sheriff of
Oldham County!"

Jim shook his head and smiled. "Thanks, boys, for all the work
you did for me. And for the offer of the drink, but I best get on
home now. Hattie will be waiting on me. We've got a lot of plans to
make—"

A yelp of outrage and the clatter of a falling table at the far end of
the saloon interrupted the conversation. Jim craned his neck and
got a glimpse of the action through a break in the crowd. Two men
grappled on the floor, cursing and slugging at each other. Jim
knew them by sight, two saloon bums who had drifted into Tascosa
when Arrington chased them out of Mobeetie.

At Jim's side Cape Willingham groaned aloud. "Damn fools can't
hold their liquor." He thumped his glass onto the bar and turned
toward the fight, Brown alongside him.

"Need a hand, Cape?" Jim asked.

"Nah. I'm still sheriff for now. I'll handle it."

Jim watched as Willingham pushed his way through the crowd.
He grabbed one of the men by the belt, lifted him bodily from the
floor and tossed him against the wall. The man's head hit the wall
hard enough to crumble a few flakes from the adobe. At the same
time, Brown whipped out his pistol and cracked it against the second man's skull. The man flopped unconscious and bleeding to the
floor. Brown raised the pistol again, prepared to slam it into the
man's head a second time. Cape Willingham's fist closed around
the barrel of the Colt.

"That's enough, Henry," Willingham said. "No need to beat a
half-drunk man to death."

Brown frowned and grumbled, but he holstered his pistol. Moments later the sheriff and constable half carried, half dragged the
moaning and dazed combatants toward the door. "Night in my
little hotel will take the starch out of their peckers," Willingham
said to Jim as the men passed by.

Jim saw the hard set of Henry Brown's jaw and the gleam of violence in his eyes. Brown's free hand rested on the butt of his holstered Colt. *No doubt about what I'll do first as sheriff,* Jim thought. *Brown's got to go.*

Jim turned back to the bar. He placed a five-dollar gold piece on the counter and told the barkeep to fill the glasses of his three cowboy friends until the money ran out. "After that, Lem," he said, "you boys are on your own. I'll see you later."

He pushed his way through the crowd, shook a few more hands and stepped onto the street outside. The chill had sharpened with the coming of sunset. Jim's breath left puffs of steam to drift on the north breeze as he made his way to the small adobe house at Main and McMasters. An oil lamp glowed beyond the flour-sack curtains at the lone front window, a golden rectangle against the deep blue of the early night. *Well, girl,* he thought, *we can get you that house soon. And some real lace curtains for it. We'll start looking just as soon as I tie up a few loose ends.*

LX Ranch
December 1882

Jim East found Bill Moore where he could usually be located when the wind was raw and the rain cold—seated behind the long table near a roaring stove, shuffling papers. The LX foreman glanced up as Jim stepped into the room and shook the raindrops from his hat. Moore nodded a greeting, but there was no welcome in his eyes.

"Thought you were out tracking strays, Jim. Find any?" Moore's tone was guarded.

Jim shook his head. "Found some. Maybe a dozen head. Rain washed the trail out a few miles this side of New Mexico. They weren't strays."

"Rustlers again?"

"Cattle don't drift northwest with the wind in their faces." Jim flexed his aching fingers. They had been stiff and achey in cold weather since the long, hard winter of the Pecos River War.

"Damn nesters," Moore growled. "Steal anything that's not

nailed down or too hot to pick up." He waved toward the stove. "Coffee?"

"No. I'll be drawing my time now, Bill."

Moore's eyebrows lifted. "Now? You still have two weeks before you get to be sheriff. That's half a month's wages."

"That's the way I want it."

Moore shrugged. "Hate to lose a good hand." He reached for the cash box, scribbled a notation on the pay ledger and counted out two week's wages. Jim tucked the money into a pocket.

"I'll get my stuff out of the bunkhouse and be on my way in a few minutes," he said.

Moore nodded. "Jim, you have any idea who's behind the sleepering and rustling up on the north side?"

"I have my suspicions," Jim said, watching the LX foreman's eyes. Moore averted his gaze, but not before Jim glimpsed the worry behind the eyes.

"Want to tell me about it?"

"Nothing to tell. Suspicions don't make proof. Last time I looked you couldn't jail a man—or hang him—on suspicion alone."

"I suppose as sheriff you'll keep looking into these things," Moore said. It was a question as much as a statement.

"Bet on it, Bill. On any ranch, no matter the size of the outfit. Whoever it is will make a mistake one of these days and I'll bring them in. Upright in the saddle or face down over it, depending. See you around."

Jim turned on his heel and strode through the door. He pulled his hat down tight against the wind. The rain had picked up. Within the day the whole of the Texas Panhandle would be soaked. If the temperature fell much more, they'd be looking at ice.

An ice storm was harder on livestock and men than a flat-out blizzard. And now that damned drift fence stretched across the northern Panhandle from the New Mexico line all the way to Adobe Walls. Dead cattle would be stacked against it like chunks of ice for miles if this weather got worse.

A sudden realization pushed Bill Moore and the drift fence from Jim's mind and brought a smile to his chapped lips. He didn't have to ride drift this winter. And for the first time in four years, he was going to be home with Hattie for Christmas. He quickened his step, anxious to gather his gear and head for home.

NINE

Tascosa
January 1883

Sheriff Jim East sat behind the cluttered desk in the cramped two-room adobe that doubled as single-cell jail and office, and surveyed his inheritance from Cape Willingham.

On the surface it wasn't much. One homemade badge. A battered pine desk scarred by spur rowels. A sawed-off double barrel ten-gauge shotgun. A potbellied stove with a diminished stack of firewood. A disorganized collection of papers that were supposed to be case records, official complaints and wanted notices, so jumbled that it would take weeks to restore them into something that resembled official files. *Cape may have been a good sheriff,* Jim grumbled inwardly, *but he sure wasn't much for paperwork.*

The inheritance included a half-dozen cases of cattle rustling still under investigation, two complaints of theft of other property, and several reports of lesser crimes still to be checked out.

Cape Willingham's legacy also included two men. One was a young cowboy awaiting trial for murder. He sat now on a cell bunk, singing an Irish tune in a clear and pleasant tenor voice. The second man stood before Jim's desk, a scowl on his sun-browned face.

"You wanted to see me, East?" Henry Brown's tone was as contemptuous as the expression in his eyes.

"I did, Brown," Jim said. "You won't be needed here any more."

Brown's jaw muscles twitched in a flare of anger. "You firing me?"

"Let's say I'm offering you the opportunity to resign, Constable."

"How come?"

Jim sighed. "Because, Brown, you're dog-ass mean. I don't hold with pistol-whipping drunks and unarmed men. I don't hold with shooting a man who could be talked into giving up. I don't hold with slapping a woman around, even if she is a Hogtown whore. You've done all that. You're not doing it in this town any longer, at least not under the protection of that constable's badge."

Brown leaned forward and shifted his weight onto the balls of his feet. His fingers twitched near the butt of the Colt at his belt. Rage flamed in his squinted eyes.

"Touch that gun, Brown, and I'll be on you like a rooster on a cricket," Jim said.

Brown stared at Jim for several heartbeats. The cowboy in the cell had stopped singing. Jim knew the conversation would be clearly audible to the man in the jail cell. The silence grew as heavy as the tension.

A flicker of caution tempered the anger in the constable's eyes. "You think you're stud hoss enough to do that, East?"

Jim shrugged. "One way to find out."

For a moment Jim thought Henry Brown was actually going to make a move for his gun. Then the constable spat a curse. "You can go to hell, East. I ain't workin' for no lace-pants cowboy playin' sheriff." Brown lifted his hand from the gun butt, reached into a pocket and tossed a scratched and tarnished badge onto Jim's desk. "I quit."

"That's the best decision you've made in months, Brown," Jim said. "What you do from here on is your business unless you break the law in Oldham County. Then it's my business. I don't think either of us wants that."

Brown glared at Jim for a moment, but the bluster was gone. "The hell with it," Brown muttered. "I was gettin' damn tired of this town anyway. There's places in Kansas need a good lawman."

Jim watched as the former constable spun on a heel, yanked the door open and slammed it behind him. He sighed in relief, lifted the cocked Colt from his lap, lowered the hammer and dropped the weapon back into its holster.

"Sheriff?"

Jim rose and strode the few feet to the doorway of the cell in the adjoining room. Ed Norwood leaned against the bars, a grin on his face.

"What is it, Ed?"

"Just wanted to thank you on behalf of the citizens of Tascosa,"

Norwood said. "That Brown was bad medicine. Hell, I killed a man, sure enough, but at least I had a reason. Brown just did it 'cause he liked it."

"I know that, Ed," Jim said. "I'm going to leave the office for a spell. You need anything?"

"If you can spare a cup of coffee. And maybe a deck of cards? Gets kind of boring in here with nobody to talk to." The young face suddenly brightened. "Say, Sheriff, maybe you could arrest two, three others? Then at least we could have a poker game or something back here."

"I'll see what I can do." Jim found a tattered deck of cards in a desk drawer, filled a tin cup and returned to the cell. "Last of the coffee, Ed. It might be a little strong," he said.

Norwood's grin widened. "Maybe I'll pour some of it on these bars and see if they melt."

Jim paused in the small office, glanced at the double shotgun and his Winchester on the pegs along one wall, then decided to leave both. *No sense in making my first tour carrying more guns than the Tenth Cavalry,* he thought. He strode through the door into the raw north wind. Bits of paper and last fall's tumbleweeds swirled along the street. The town was all but deserted at this hour.

Tascosa still suffered the pangs of last night's New Years celebration hangover. Jim suspected things would liven up a bit as the day wore on and people who still had money left would start looking for the hair of the wolf that bit them the night before.

As he walked he made a mental note to follow up on the investigation of the killing that had put Ed Norwood behind bars. It had been a revenge killing; Norwood's brother was shot in the back of the head and robbed some time back, in the bed of a girl named Ginny who worked Captain Jinks' Saloon in Hogtown. Willingham's notes indicated that bartender Johnnie Maley might have been behind the robbery. There was no solid proof of Maley's involvement in the killing, but it was worth a closer look, Jim thought. Ed Norwood had sent Maley to Boot Hill with a forty-five shortly after his brother's death.

Maybe, Jim thought, Cape had overlooked some solid evidence. Norwood was a happy-go-lucky kid, well liked by everyone who knew him. He didn't seem the sort of man who would kill another in cold blood unless he was sure he had good reason.

All was quiet along Main and McMasters, the stores and saloons not yet open for business. Hogtown also slept as it nursed its hangover.

The bitter north wind slapped at Jim's coat and pushed against his hat as he made his way back to the office. *At least I'm not out in this chasing a bunch of cows,* he thought. *If there's a colder place anywhere than on horseback in the middle of a Texas Panhandle winter I don't know where it is and I don't want to find out.*

Back in his office Jim stoked the stove with cottonwood limbs from the bottom of the woodbox. The limbs sat for a moment on the glowing coals before small tongues of flame licked up from the dry wood. It would burn hot and keep the chill at bay, but it would also burn fast. Jim found a nicked axe in a corner and strode to the woodpile in back of the jail.

The main thing he had found so far, he thought as he swung the dull axe, was that early-morning foot patrols in Tascosa didn't accomplish much. The town was dead as last year's Christmas goose until the sun was a couple of hours over the eastern horizon.

Tascosa was still growing as fast as a yearling colt. The population had nudged past three hundred. The town had five saloons. Jess Jenkins had a share of one bar in Upper Tascosa, but it was his Emporium in Hogtown that drew most of the cowboy traffic. Jenkins was the unofficial boss of Hogtown and one of the most influential men in all of Tascosa. Jenkins was emerging as a leader in the cowboy and small rancher faction against the big men in the rift that grew deeper by the day. Jim made a mental note to call on Jenkins soon. The man could be either a problem or an asset if trouble came.

New adobe buildings sprouted quickly when weather permitted. The girls who worked the saloons now lived in a cluster of small houses in the flats behind the bars and the two major mercantile stores. When the weather was decent, freight wagons rolled in an almost steady stream from north and east into the town. The stage from Dodge usually carried at least one new resident into town on each trip. Not all of them were outstanding citizens. Add to that the cowboys coming into town on weekends to "wet whistles, deal pasteboards and dip wicks"—whiskey, cards and women to those who didn't speak the slang of the range—and Jim East knew he was in for a busy time.

He finished chopping a supply of firewood and restocked the kindling box in the jail. *Next order of business,* he promised himself, *is to get a deputy, somebody dependable and with a good head on his shoulders.* Jim glanced up at a timid knock on the door.

"Come in," he called.

An aging Mexican stepped into the room, a battered sombrero in his hand. He wore open-toed sandals and a coat with more holes than cloth despite the icy bite of the wind. "*Señor* Sheriff, I hate to bother you on your first day, but there is a problem . . ." His voice trailed away.

Jim waved him toward the stove. "Warm yourself, friend," he said. "The reason I'm here is to help with problems. Tell me about it."

The Mexican bowed his head as if in shame. "My name is José Cantos. The problem is a small thing to anyone but myself and my family," he said. "Last night, one of my hogs was shot and killed. I had but four sows and the one boar. The boar is now dead, and without him I can make no more pigs. With no more pigs I cannot feed my family."

Jim ran a hand across his jaw. "This is not a small thing, *Señor* Cantos. Not when a man's means of supporting his family is threatened. Did you see the man who shot your pig?"

The Mexican nodded warily. "Yes. It was the man called Gough. The one known as the Catfish Kid. He and some friends were making bets on how well he could shoot."

"Do you know where he is now?"

"He is with the woman in red from *Señor* Jenkins's saloon, the Emporium. She is called Frog Lip Sadie."

Jim tugged his hat down on his head and nodded to the Mexican. "Come with me, friend. I can't get your hog back, but maybe I can help you buy a new one."

Ten minutes later Jim East pounded on the wooden door of a two-room adobe shack in Hogtown. He heard the muttered protest inside and banged again on the sagging portal. The door swung open. J. B. Gough, the Catfish Kid, stood in the doorway clad only in his longhandles. Over his shoulder Jim saw Frog Lip Sadie pull the blankets up to her chin.

"What the hell do you want, East?"

"This man Cantos says you killed one of his pigs last night. That right, Catfish?"

Gough scratched an armpit. "What the hell difference does it make? Just a damn pig and a damn Mexican."

Jim leveled a steady glare at the Catfish Kid. "The difference is that pig meant a lot to this man. You destroyed personal property."

"So?"

"So you pay this man for the pig or I lock you up, Catfish. It's that simple."

Gough's bloodshot eyes went wide. "Ah, hell, East. We were just funnin' some. You can't hold that against a man."

Jim held out his left hand, palm up. "I sure can, Catfish. Pay up or get dressed. I figure that hog was worth about ten dollars."

"Ten dollars! My God, man! Are you out of your mind?"

Jim glanced at the frightened Mexican standing nearby. "That all right with you, *Señor* Cantos?"

The Mexican bobbed his head up and down.

"What'll it be, Catfish? Pay for the hog or be the guest of the county for a few weeks?"

Gough's face turned red, then almost purple, beneath the beard stubble. "East, are you serious?"

"Try me if you think I'm not."

Gough sighed in disgust. "Oh, the hell with it." He strode to his pants draped across a chair, fished a ten-dollar gold coin from the pocket and tossed it to Jim.

Jim handed the gold piece to Cantos, then stared hard at Gough and gestured toward the hog farmer. "Remember this man's face, Catfish." Jim put a hard edge on his voice. "Pray for his continued health, because if anything happens to him, his family, or his pigs, I'm coming straight after you. You'll pay a damn sight more if I have to do that."

"You threatening me, East?"

"No. I'm making you a promise." He glanced past Gough's shoulder and tipped his hat to the wide-eyed whore. "Morning, ma'am," Jim said. "Hope you have a fine day." He turned away from the sputtering Gough. "Come along, *Señor* Cantos. You can buy another pig now and have a few dollars left over to pay for your troubles."

Tascosa
February 1883

Jim East half dragged and half carried the drunken teamster through the blinding snow, kicked open the door of the office and shoved the big man toward the jail cell.

"Brought you some company, boys," he said to the three men inside. Two of the three were suffering the agonies of the damned from their sins of the night before. *God must have made hangovers when he decided whiskey was a mistake,* Jim thought.

Ed Norwood looked up and grinned.

"Sheriff, I don't plan to ask you to bring me any more company," he said. "Got to where it's downright crowded in here all the time."

Jim turned the key, opened the cell door and pushed the teamster inside. "Quit complaining, Ed," he said. "Play poker with *these* guys for a change. You already got seventy cents of my money." He locked the cell and strode back into his office.

Wrestling drunks, breaking up fights and collecting payment for dead pigs, Jim mused, wasn't exactly a glamorous and exciting job. He nursed a shiner that would have taken first prize at anybody's county fair, courtesy of a cowboy whose speed with a fist Jim had underestimated. It wasn't a mistake he would make again. The toothmarks on his arm had almost healed, and he just hoped the whore who had bitten him during that saloon brawl in the Emporium didn't have hydrophobia. He had thought about hauling her in for assaulting an officer of the law, then realized that he had only one jail cell and it was full of men. She probably would make more money in the lockup than her fine would cost. So he let it drop.

Jim East was learning fast about this job of being sheriff. For one, winter was a bad time for men who carried a badge. People didn't have much to do except drink, fight, gamble and carouse. The fall roundups were over. The last trail drive had gone through months ago, and cowboys who had jobs during the summer were now out of work and generally broke—or heading that direction in a long lope. A few hands who had ridden for the smaller ranches were now without jobs. They had been cut loose by the LS, the LX and other big spreads that had forced out the little men and taken over their grazing lands.

It was bad enough without the blizzard that had howled down from the north two weeks ago and showed no signs of letting up. Wind-whipped snow piled up in drifts that touched the sod and pole roofs of Tascosa's one-story adobe buildings and closed all the roads to freight traffic. Supplies were running low. A few of the less scrupulous merchants had doubled or tripled prices on the smattering of staples available. That grated on Jim, but there wasn't a thing he could do about it. They weren't breaking any laws.

The sickness had come before the blizzard. The lung fever didn't discriminate between the wealthy and the poor, the respectable and the shady. The town was still without a doctor. Hattie and the other women of Tascosa who had so far escaped the illness scurried about tending to prostitute and merchant's wife, drifter and cattle buyer alike, until they were worn down like horses ridden two miles too far. But they didn't slow down, except to attend the occasional funeral when they lost a patient.

Jim listened to the screech of the wind outside the office. The drift would be bad this year, with heavy stock losses, and the damn fence across the Panhandle would make it worse. Four strands of Glidden wire—a trap of thorns for cattle trying to escape the bitter blast from the north.

The door swung open, interrupting Jim's thoughts. Deputy L. C. Pierce ducked into the room, slammed the door against the blast of frigid air, and started slapping snow and ice from his hat and coat.

At least Jim had found the right man to be his deputy. L. C. Pierce was in his thirties, his shoulder-length hair and thick mustache already showing touches of gray. He wasn't a big man—about five-nine or so—and carried only a hundred fifty pounds on a slender build. But there was an air of calm confidence and authority about Pierce that made even total strangers respect him at first glance. Those who didn't soon learned. The soft-spoken deputy was as tough a man as Jim had ever met, slow to anger but quick to act when necessary. He carried a Smith & Wesson New American forty-four in a holster high on his right hip. As far as Jim knew Pierce had never drawn the gun, but there was no doubt in anyone's mind that the former store clerk knew how to use his weapon.

It was said he could talk a mad possum out of a tree and have the critter tame as a house cat by the time it hit the ground.

"Evening, Jim," Pierce said as he strode to the stove and held his palms toward the glowing iron. "Nasty out there. Sometimes I wonder if this storm will ever break."

"Everything stops sooner or later, L.C.," Jim said. He nodded toward the cell. "Got a couple more drunks back there. I don't expect any trouble from them, but watch that big teamster. He's an argumentative sort." Jim flexed his sore right hand with its skinned knuckles. "Got a jaw like an anvil, too."

Pierce nodded, shrugged out of his coat and reached for a ceramic mug on a peg beside the stove. "I'll watch 'em, Jim. Want to feed them breakfast?"

"Just Ed Norwood. No sense in the county feeding the others. I don't think they're going to be all that hungry, anyway."

Pierce filled his cup and stared at Jim for a moment. "You look like you've been rode hard and put up wet," he said. "Go get some rest."

"I could use it. See you in the morning." He pulled on his hat and coat, stepped through the door and slogged through the wind-blown snow toward home.

Hattie stood by the new cookstove, her back to Jim, as he pushed the door open. The scent of ham steaks, redeye gravy and fresh bread set his stomach to rumbling. "Girl," he said, "you sure got it smelling good in here—" He stopped abruptly as Hattie turned toward him. Her cheeks were wet with tears, the brown eyes deep pools of hurt and pain. "Hattie? What happened?"

Hattie's lower lip trembled. "We lost the little Smith girl. She died about three hours ago."

Jim crossed the room and pulled Hattie into his arms. He held her, rocking back and forth on his heels as if soothing a child. "I'm sorry, Hattie. I know you did all you could."

She was silent for a moment. Her shoulders twitched in quiet sobs, her face buried against his snow-damp coat. "Jim, sometimes I don't understand," she said. "I know the preachers say God works in mysterious ways, but how could He take such a sweet and pretty young child? She was only four years old . . ." Her voice trailed away.

"I don't have an answer for you, Hattie," Jim said. "I don't guess anyone does."

The grumble in his belly subsided. The death of a child was not an unusual event in Tascosa, but it still took a man's appetite away. Especially now. Jim remembered Tessie Smith's perky upturned nose with its freckles and the way it wrinkled when she laughed. She had been one of those rare children full of laughter and love. Jim felt the sting at the corners of his own eyes. *It isn't fair,* he thought. *God shouldn't take the best ones all the time.*

Hattie finally pulled away. "Supper's going to get cold, Jim." She dabbed at her eyes with a plain cotton handkerchief and tried to force a smile.

Jim ate mechanically, his normal enthusiasm for Hattie's considerable kitchen talents dulled by the vision of a small freckled nose. He wondered how much hurt a family could endure and still survive. *It could have been our daughter,* he thought, *but the Lord seems disinclined to give us a child. Is it better to have them for four years and lose them, or never to have them at all?* He tried to push the thought aside. It wouldn't leave. Hattie wanted children even more than he did, and she had endured one disappointment after another. Maybe that was why she took the death of a child so hard, he thought.

Hattie made no effort to eat. When Jim finished his supper she covered the leftover food with a tin pie pan and placed it on the warming plate of the cookstove. As she washed the dishes Jim stood at her side, drying and putting them away.

"Hattie," he said, "I don't know what to say."

She leaned a shoulder against him. "You don't have to say anything, Jim. Just be here. That's enough."

Jim had stowed the last of the dishes and settled into his overstuffed chair when a knock sounded on the door. *Damn, not some trouble in town—not tonight,* he thought as he got up and swung the door open.

Cal Polk stood in the doorway, hat already in hand. Ice and snow packed the folds in his clothing.

"Cal, what the hell—come in, son. You look half frozen. Trouble somewhere?"

"Sorry to be a bother, Jim," Cal said. His words were choppy, his teeth chattering from the cold. "I didn't know where else to go. Hotels are all full."

Jim led Cal to the stove. Hattie thrust a mug of coffee into the young cowboy's stiff hands. Jim waited until the warmth of the fire and the coffee chased away the worst of Cal's chill, then he motioned to a chair.

"What is it, Cal?"

"I quit the LX, Jim," Cal said. "I just couldn't take it—"

"Take what?"

"That damn drift fence." Jim saw the pain in Cal's eyes. "Jim, there's hundreds of cattle stacked up on that thing froze to death. More piling up behind them. I cut the damn fence and herded as many as I could through the hole. Then I rode back to the LX and drew my time." Cal dropped his gaze to the coffee cup in his hand. "I just couldn't stand it, Jim. All those cows, dying like that."

Jim nodded in understanding. "Any cowboy worth the salt on his saddle blanket would have done the same thing, Cal. It's the nature of the animal. What will you do now?"

"I don't know. I can't go back to the LX. Or any other association outfit. I guess I'll try to find a place to stay until the storm quits—"

"You have a place, Cal," Hattie interrupted. "You're welcome to stay here."

"Missus East, that wouldn't be right. I mean, you and Jim—I just couldn't impose like that. I left my horse down at McCormick's stable. I can sleep in the hayloft."

"Nonsense," Hattie said, her tone firm. "We'll rig a cot. You're welcome here any time, Cal, for as long as you want. Are you hungry? When did you eat last?"

Jim saw the flush of embarrassment crawl up Cal Polk's neck. "Missus East, I couldn't—I don't want to cause you any trouble."

"Cal Polk, you hush up about trouble. If you get to be trouble, I'll boot you out the door." Hattie busied herself at the stove, filling a plate with the leftovers.

At least, Jim thought, Cal's arrival would take Hattie's mind off the death of Tessie Smith for a spell.

Cal sipped at his coffee. A frown creased his normally smooth brow. "Something else bothering you, Cal?" Jim asked.

"Yes. There's an awful lot of unhappy cowboys out there, Jim. There's even been talk of a cowboy strike."

"Strike?"

Cal nodded. "A bunch of the boys have been talking. They think the only way they can get fair treatment is to walk out, refuse to work unless they get more money and the chance to run a few head of their own cows." The young man's smooth face twisted in a grimace. "When President Lincoln freed the slaves, Jim, he forgot all about cowboys."

"This strike—is it coming soon?"

"Probably in the spring, just before the first big roundup."

Jim rose and started pacing. "It won't solve anything, Cal. The ranchers are likely to fire the whole lot without so much as a faretheewell. There are people drifting into the Panhandle every day looking for ranch work. Most of them don't know which end of a cow eats, but they're warm bodies and they need work. I tell you, Cal, I don't like the sound of this."

TEN

Tascosa
April 1883

Jim East leaned against a porch post of the Wright and Farnsworth general store on Main Street and watched the steady procession of cowboys file past.

Three of the riders—Tom Emory, Tom's brother Charley, and Lem Woodruff—reined away from the latest group, pulled their mounts to a stop before Jim, and nodded a greeting. Tom's expression was drawn and serious. Woodruff still wore his perpetual grin. Charley just stared toward Hogtown.

"Light and set a spell, boys," Jim said.

Tom Emory stepped from the saddle and tossed the reins to his brother. Charley and Lem remained mounted, Lem sitting loose in the saddle with his forearms crossed over the horn.

"The strike's on, Jim," Tom said. "Nearly all the cowboys in the Panhandle have laid down their ropes. The big outfits won't have a choice now but to go along with us. Spring roundup's due to start any day now."

Jim arched an eyebrow. "How'd the owners react?"

"Fired a bunch of us on the spot," Tom said with a shrug. "Maybe half the hands on the LS, LX and LIT are out of work. But we've all got a little money saved up, knowing it was coming. We'll wait 'em out."

Jim sighed. "I'm not sure you can pull it off, Tom. There's too many men around here looking for work. Plus, the big outfits have the money to sweat you out."

Tom snorted in disgust. "Nesters. Kids who don't know the first damn thing about cattle. They can't handle a roundup, let alone drive a herd to railhead. The owners will have to come around."

"Don't count on it, Tom. You're dealing with a bunch of pretty hardheaded men there."

Lem Woodruff chuckled aloud. "They're not the only ones can be hardheaded. Tom Harris put this thing together and I never met a more stubborn man."

There was more than a little truth to that, Jim thought. Harris was as tough as he was stubborn, and he could carry a grudge a long time when he thought he had been wronged. He also was Jess Jenkins's brother-in-law.

Lem straightened in the saddle. "You two can stand around and yammer all day if you want. Me, I've got some business in Hogtown. Lady named Sally." He raised a hand in salute and kneed his horse toward Lower Tascosa.

Tom watched his friend ride away, then turned to Jim. "You're one of us, Jim. I expected a little more support from you."

"You know where my sympathies are, Tom," Jim said, "but sympathy doesn't wear a badge. I don't have the authority to step into a squabble between owners and cowboys unless somebody breaks the law. I'll talk to the ranch bosses and the strikers both." He leveled a steady gaze at Tom Emory. "We've ridden many a mile together, Tom, but I'll warn you just like I will everyone else. I'll do what I can to keep the peace. I'll jail anybody who starts trouble."

Tom returned Jim's gaze for a moment, then shrugged. "Aw, hell, I know that, Jim. I shouldn't have shot my mouth off. No insult intended."

"None taken."

Tom half smiled. He reached for the reins. "Guess I'd best get on to Hogtown before old Lem gets all the whiskey and women tied down. See you around."

Jim East watched as Tom nudged his big bay into a trot down Main, Charley riding alongside. Then he sighed and stepped off the porch. It wouldn't be long until the whiskey started hitting thirsty cowboys. He rolled a smoke, hitched up his pistol belt and started his patrol.

Tascosa
May 1883

Jim East tried to shrug the exhaustion from his aching shoulders and blinked against the grainy feeling in his eyes. Tom Emory had been wrong about the ranchers caving in to the cowboys' demands. The combination of idle cowhands with a little money in their pockets and the whiskey, women and card games of Tascosa left a sheriff with little time for rest.

He leaned back in his chair behind the desk, hoping to catch a short rest before starting his evening rounds. At least, he thought, there hadn't been any serious trouble yet. The ranchers had black-listed the fired strikers. None of the cowpunchers on the list could find work with association brands. But the cattleman's group had agreed not to take stronger action against the strikers.

The out-of-work cowboys in turn caused no problems with the men who had taken their places. There were some hard stares exchanged from time to time between blacklisted punchers and new riders, but no lead had been thrown.

Leadership of the opposing factions became more clear by the day.

Tom Harris and Jess Jenkins were the backbone of the loosely organized "little men," the small ranchers and the cowboys who had lost jobs in the strike.

The Panhandle Cattleman's Association hauled the wagon for the "big men." But the man who held the whip was W. M. D. Lee, the majority owner of the LS ranch. Word of the strike had reached Lee, who headquartered in Leavenworth, and in less than four days he rode in behind a lathered buggy horse to take charge. Lee was a man who wouldn't be pushed. Even the association members with power and money backed off when the little LS banty rooster got his feathers ruffled.

Jim knew those three men were the ones who held the aces in this poker game. Where they led, the others followed. Jim just hoped the herds stayed pointed in the right direction. The only blood spilled so far had been from noses broken in brawls over

cards and women. Jim idly wondered how much longer his luck
would hold.

"Jim?" Ed Norwood's call from the cell interrupted Jim's mus-
ings. "Can you spare another cup of coffee?"

Jim sighed. "Ed, son, you're eating this county into bankruptcy. I
guess we can stand another cup of coffee. If you'll forget that fifty
cent monte debt I owe you."

"Jim, that's blackmail!" Ed feigned indignant outrage, but Jim
heard the low chuckle. "That's downright unethical, what with you
being a man of the law and all. But I sure would like to have some
coffee."

Jim filled two cups and carried them to the cell. He handed one
to the clean-shaven young cowboy and sipped at the other as he
perched on a low stool outside the cell, studying Ed Norwood's
smooth face and his eyes that twinkled with humor just below the
surface. It wasn't hard to figure out why Norwood had a steady
stream of visitors, from cowboys to dance hall girls, almost every
day. Lem Woodruff and Luis Bausman dropped by like clockwork
to lose money to Norwood at cards. Jim knew Woodruff and Bausman were top hands with the pasteboards; they let Ed win just to
keep him in tobacco and a few other necessities of life. It was impossible to dislike the kid even if he had gunned down a man.

"Ed, I've got some good news for you," he said. "The girl, Ginny
—she finally broke down. Admitted to me that Johnnie Maley had
gone to her room after your brother passed out. She heard a shot,
muffled, like somebody had fired a gun through a pillow. And she
said Maley showed up the next day with a handful of Mexican
silver like your brother was carrying. She's agreed to say so in court
when your trial comes up."

A grin brightened Ed Norwood's face. "Does that mean I can go,
Jim?"

"Sorry, Ed. It might get you off the murder charge, maybe re-
duce it to manslaughter. I'll write the district attorney and see what
we can do. If you have a good lawyer and a jury with a sense of real
justice they might even turn you loose. In the meantime, I'll have
to keep you here."

"But Jim, that bastard Maley killed my brother!"

"We both know that now, Ed. We both also know that you killed
Maley. At worst you should be looking at maybe four, five years in

prison instead of a hangman's noose." He paused for a sip of coffee and winced. As usual it was strong enough to double as an anvil. "I think you should be satisfied with that."

Norwood half smiled. "I reckon. Maybe it was worth it after all." The cowboy riffled the battered deck of cards. "Want to try your hand again, Jim? I'll forget the four bits."

Jim grinned back and shook his head. "You're not going to sucker me in again, Ed. Drink your coffee and play solitaire—"

A rattle of gunfire in the distance brought Jim off the stool. The abrupt movement splashed hot coffee on his hand and triggered a sharp curse. He rushed to his desk, plopped the cup down and grabbed the sawed-off shotgun.

The office door swung open and Deputy L. C. Pierce poked his head in. "Trouble in Hogtown, Jim," he said as he lifted his revolver from its holster and spun the cylinder. "Sounds like it came from Jenkins's place."

Jim broke the action of the shotgun, checked the loads, and closed the breech with a solid chunk. "Let's go."

The two lawmen entered the Jenkins bar out of breath and out of sorts, weapons at the ready—and found nothing amiss.

Three card games were in progress with other gamblers waiting for an open chair. Cowpunchers stood two deep at the bar. There wasn't a single squabble going on.

"What was the shooting about?" Jim snapped.

Blank stares were the only response. Luis Bausman glanced up from one of the tables. "Didn't hear a thing, Jim." A slight grin touched the corners of Bausman's mouth. "Any of you boys know what's going on?"

An LS cowboy who had lost his job in the strike strode into the saloon from a back door in time to hear the question. "Just a few of the boys letting off a little steam, Sheriff East," he said. "Nobody shootin' at anybody else."

Jim let a steady gaze drift around the saloon crowd and settle on Jess Jenkins's florid face. The bar owner sat at a corner table, a deck of cards in his hand. "Any trouble here, Jess?" Jim asked.

Jenkins shrugged. "Like the man said. Just a few boys funning around out back. No trouble."

Jim lowered the shotgun. "All right, if you say so." He raised his voice. "I don't want to hear one more gun go off in Hogtown tonight, boys," he said. "The next man who decides to do some funning around can play with me." Jim glanced at Pierce. The deputy's eyes reflected Jim's own disgust and exhaustion. "Let's go, L.C. Before I lose my temper."

The two men strode back to the jail. Twenty yards from the building Jim barked a curse. The front door stood open. He sprinted inside. His boot clanked against a prybar; the cell was empty, the thin iron plate twisted away from the wrecked lock. Ed Norwood was gone.

"What the hell?"

Jim glanced at his deputy. "We've been suckered like a greenhorn," he said. "While we were off chasing a gunfight that never happened, somebody slipped in behind us and broke Norwood out."

"What do we do now, Jim?"

"Keep an eye on the town, L.C. I'm going after that fool kid."

Jim East pulled the slicker tighter about his neck and listened to the hammer of raindrops on his hat. The storm had turned the narrow trail along the Cimarron into a small river. The rushing water had carried away the last of Ed Norwood's tracks.

Jim sat for a moment and stared into the wind-driven deluge. Lightning danced overhead, the boom of thunder shaking the muddy ground beneath his horse's hooves. Then he touched a finger to his dripping hat brim.

"Well, Ed," he muttered, "you made it this far. Maybe you can make it on into Colorado or Wyoming. At least you won't be looking at five years in the pen for killing a man who damn well deserved it."

Sometimes, Jim thought, the best justice was none at all. This seemed to be one of those times. He reined his horse away from the region called the Cimarron Strip toward home. There was enough work at Tascosa to keep a man too busy to scratch.

Tascosa
June 1883

The stage from Dodge City creaked to a stop in front of the Exchange Hotel. Jim East stood by the driver's seat and watched the passengers climb from the carriage, a habit he had followed since he first pinned on the badge. A sheriff needed to know who was coming into town—and who was leaving.

Today's coach held four passengers. The first to dismount carried the brand of the professional gambler. Jim had learned to read the type. The second was a cattle buyer from Chicago, a portly man who had become a seasonal fixture in Tascosa. The buyer offered a hand to the woman who followed. Another dance hall girl, Jim noted. He could spot them as quick as he could professional gamblers.

The last man off the stage was David T. Beales, the Bostonian who owned the majority share of the LX Ranch. Beales was of medium height, beardless, and wore an air of quiet confidence along with a slightly dusty but expensive silk suit and beaver hat. Beales glanced about, caught Jim's gaze and extended a hand.

"Sheriff East," Beales said, "good to see you again." His accent was heavily Bostonian, but he still had the firm grip of a craftsman who had turned a small shoe business into a considerable fortune that included several thousand head of Texas cattle. His smile was genuine. "Rather unusual to be greeting you as sheriff, Mister East. The last time we met, you were—how do you Texans say it? Oh, yes—topping off an LX bronc, I believe."

Jim had to laugh. "The bronc won that battle, Mister Beales. But he turned into a good horse."

"Your letter said there was a matter of some importance we should discuss upon my next visit." It was obvious to Jim that the small talk was over. Beales was a direct man. "Should we get down to it?" He gestured toward the Exchange Hotel. "I have a room booked here. It should be sufficiently private." Beales led the way. If the crude adobe hotel seemed primitive to the Bostonian, he made no mention of the fact.

A half hour later Beales sat across from Jim at a small table, a frown bunching his heavy eyebrows. "Are you telling me, Sheriff East, that my foreman is stealing cattle from my ranch?"

"No, sir," Jim said. "I'm telling you only what I've seen and what I suspect. If I had solid proof that Bill Moore was rustling your stock, he'd be in irons right now."

"And what are the chances of getting that proof?"

"I'd say slim, Mister Beales. Moore is slick. He's been around ranches a long time. He knows how brand registries and mavericking work, and he knows how to buy stolen cattle without making a dumb mistake."

Beales fell silent for a moment. His sturdy fingers curled into a fist on the table. "Sheriff East, I appreciate your candor in this matter. I will discuss this in considerable detail with Mister Moore." The expression in the Bostonian's eyes was hard and cold. "I cannot abide theft by an employee. It is the worst kind of slap in the face one man can deal another."

Jim pushed back his chair. "I agree, Mister Beales. That's why I wrote you in the first place. Now, if you'll excuse me, I have rounds to make. Tascosa gets a bit rowdy sometimes."

"One moment, Sheriff," Beales said. He reached into a coat pocket and produced a sheaf of bills. "I would like to reward you for your information."

Jim shook his head. "I won't take your money. You treated me fair when I worked for the LX. Let's just say I'm paying back a debt for that."

A wisp of a smile touched the Bostonian's lips. "You have an interesting code of honor, Mister East. I don't believe I've met more than a half dozen men in my life who wouldn't accept a gratuity for services rendered. Back in Boston all I see is upturned palms." Beales tucked the money back into his pocket, stood and offered a hand. "Thank you again, Sheriff East. I assure you the source of the information you've given me here will remain confidential, and that I *will* have a serious talk with Mister Moore."

Jim nodded and reached for his hat.

"Sheriff," Beales said, "I've had reports that conditions are quite touchy in the Panhandle. Now that the so-called cowboy strike has ended, do you think tensions will ease?"

Jim stared straight into the Bostonian's eyes. "No, Mister Beales.

It's going to get worse, not better. We could be heading straight into a range war between the little men and the big outfits like yours. I'm going to do my best to make sure that doesn't happen."

Jim strode from the hotel into the bright spring sun. Tascosa was reasonably quiet. The cowboy strike had ended with barely a whimper, petered out like a small spring-fed stream disappearing into dry sand. It had ended as the strike funds saved by the cowboys disappeared into the saloons and gaming tables and whorehouses. From start to finish the strike had lasted barely a month.

Now many of the cowpunchers Jim had ridden with were gone. They had followed young Cal Polk south, or headed north to Colorado and points beyond, looking for work where the cowboy blacklist meant nothing.

Quite a few of the old hands had stayed on. Lem Woodruff, Luis Bausman, and Charley and Tom Emory now made their livings almost exclusively at the gambling tables. It was a good thing Tom Emory was better at poker than he was at forecasting the future, Jim thought.

The big ranches had not only survived the strike, they had prospered and expanded. The spring trail herds had moved north as scheduled—maybe not as expertly handled as in the past, but they moved. Several more small ranchers had been squeezed out, their lands bought up by the LS, LX, LIT, Turkey Track and other spreads.

Now a new ranching syndicate loomed just over the ridge of hills northwest of Tascosa. The state of Texas had deeded thousands of previously unclaimed acres of land in the northern and western Panhandle to a group of Chicago investors in exchange for construction of a new state capitol building. The ranch would run the XIT brand. Jim couldn't predict what impact that would have on the town or its people, but another big syndicate outfit on range that was already getting crowded wouldn't help the situation a lot.

It may be quiet around here now, Jim thought, *but one thing's for sure —if some fool on either side makes a dumb move, Boot Hill may not be big enough.*

ELEVEN

Tascosa
March 1884

Jim East settled into the hard wooden chair behind his desk, fresh from his first bath and home-cooked meal in more than a week.

By his guess he had ridden better than three hundred miles in the last nine days. The stiffness in his knees, the leaden feel of his shoulders, and his sore butt reminded him of every mile.

For his efforts he now had two small-time rustlers in the Tascosa lockup awaiting the next term of district court to open in a couple of weeks. *Two out of God only knows how many,* he grumbled inwardly. These two hadn't resisted. A man tended not to put up too much of a fuss when you caught him red-handed with a hot running iron on an LIT cow and stuck a Winchester muzzle under his nose.

The Texas Panhandle rode the edge of violence, but it still hadn't exploded. It smoldered and fizzled just beneath the surface of the deepening split between the big ranch and little man factions. Jim knew the fuse was burning hotter and faster by the day. He could feel the heat.

The cowboys left behind after the strike fizzled took their revenge on the big ranches not with lead but with iron—running irons. The amount of mavericking and rustling that plagued the big outfits now made the work of Billy the Kid and his Pecos River gang look like a gaggle of boys stealing candy from the local store.

The Panhandle cowboys were expert horsemen. They knew cattle and markets and brands and every creek and thicket along the Canadian and the Cimarron as well as they knew the path to the outhouse. They also loved the rich, rolling grasslands and knew it was some of the best cow country in the world. They were as determined to have their share of it as the big men were to have it all. That made the Tascosa cowboy the best stock thief in the business.

There were other factors at work too. The big ranches had kept expanding, claiming still more free range as their own personal property. When a nester family or small rancher tried to settle on a piece of land they could expect trouble by sundown of the same day. But some of the tougher and more savvy cowboys could handle trouble in pretty big doses. There were more nester outfits and one-section cow ranches in the Panhandle now than there ever had been.

Tom Harris, leader of the cowboy strike, established a base of operations across the state line at Liberty, New Mexico, and registered the Bar WA brand. The Bar WA was now universally known among the Panhandle cowboys as the "Get Even Cattle Company."

Bill Moore, fired from the LX less than a week after Jim's talk with Beales, didn't exactly suffer the pangs of starvation. His Double H Connected brand, also just across the state line, was growing fast. So fast, in fact, that the standing joke was that Moore must be one hell of a cowman, because every mama cow he owned had two sets of triplets each year.

A complex network of so-called "outlaw" brands cropped up as the stock thefts increased. Most notorious of all was the Tabletop, a spidery brand with "legs" extending outward from a rectangular "table." It could be burned over almost any brand in the Panhandle. Other suspected rustler marks included the Hondo, which changed ownership as often as a wind-broke horse; the Pipe, owned by Joe Dyke, formerly of the LIT; and Bill Gatlin's K Triangle.

Most obvious of the lot was the T-48 brand registered to Tom Harris. All it took to change an LS brand to a T-48 was two quick strokes of the iron. There were others of lesser importance, six-cow ranch brands designed primarily to cover the trail of stolen stock.

The politics and geography of the area simplified the process of rustling. Eastern New Mexico was far from any site of government. New Mexico authorities were less than concerned about the activities around Liberty and other points north. While Tascosa was now a county seat, it had no active courts except for twice-yearly sessions when the district judge brought his bench from Mobeetie a hundred and thirty miles downriver. Indictments had to be obtained in

Mobeetie because Tascosa had no grand jury, and indictments handed down in Mobeetie on offenses in Oldham County had little chance of standing up in court. The question of jurisdiction muddied the waters of judicial procedure.

Conditions favored the rustlers, and they weren't shy. Cattle rustled in New Mexico went into the Texas herds. Stock rustled in Texas soon found a new home in New Mexico. It had gotten to the point, Jim mused, that a Texas cow would look up, see a man on horseback, and just start on the trail to New Mexico, and vice versa. Some of the cattle had changed hands so many times there wasn't space left on their hides for a fresh brand, even if a man had clear title to the critter.

Compounding the problem was the increasing ownership of Texas lands by British or Eastern money interests. Bates and Beales had sold the LX to a British outfit called the American Pastoral Company Limited. The LIT belonged to Britain's Prairie Land & Cattle Company. Now the XIT was starting up operations on the Chicago syndicate's grants in the northern and western Panhandle. The XIT planned to put barbed wire around its holdings—hundreds of miles of what the cowboys called the devil's string. Jim snorted in disgust at the thought.

The wire brought to his mind the comments of Wade Turner, the old trail boss. "You're right, Wade," Jim muttered under his breath. "Dyno-sewers. That's what we'll be soon, you and me and the other cowboys of this world."

Absentee ranch ownership brought a new problem to the Panhandle. When the old-time cowmen left, any sense of loyalty to the brand went with them. As one grizzled old cowboy had remarked to Jim, "Hell, Sheriff, it ain't no crime to brand no syndicate calf."

Rustlers had hit every one of the big ranches, the LS especially hard. Members of the Panhandle Cattleman's Association were pitching a bigger fit than a bronc under saddle for the first time. It would be funny, Jim thought, this idea of the big ranches caught in a coyote trap they had set and baited themselves—except that one Tascosa lawman was caught in the middle of the whole mess.

"Hey, Sheriff," a gruff voice called from the cell in back, "how about gettin' some grub in here?"

"Hold your water, Bailey," Jim yelled back. "You'll get fed when the North Star cook sends it over."

"Damn poor way to treat a man, starvin' him half to death. Sorriest jail I ever been in, and I been in 'em from Montana to San 'Tone."

"Maybe it'll be better at Huntsville, Bailey," Jim replied. "I expect you'll have plenty of time to get used to it down there."

A mumbled curse from the cell was the only reply.

Jim pulled out his pocket watch, flipped open the lid and checked the time. He had four hours left before L.C. came on duty and he could go home to Hattie. He thought for a moment about asking L.C. to take over the rest of his shift, but discarded the thought. The deputy was just as exhausted as the sheriff. Pierce kept a handle on Tascosa while Jim was off chasing rustlers, and that was a job that wore a man down. Still, Jim would be happy to see L.C.

The only good thing about being gone so long and so often, Jim thought, was the homecoming. Hattie made a fuss over him, and Jim groused about all the attention, and he loved every minute of it. Hattie could always find a way to make him laugh. These days he needed a good chuckle every chance he got.

He tucked the watch back into his pocket and glanced up as the office door swung open. A familiar figure ducked under the low frame.

"Hello, Jim," Pat Garrett said, a slight smile on his lips. The smile wasn't reflected in the eyes.

"Come in, Pat." Jim rose and extended a hand. "What brings you back to Tascosa? If you're hunting somebody, I've got a couple in back you're welcome to."

Garrett shook his head. "Afraid it's a little bigger than that this time. The star looks good on you."

"Thing gets mighty heavy at times." Jim waved toward a chair. "Have a seat. I'll put on some fresh coffee."

"Don't bother. This is a business call."

Jim cocked an eyebrow in question.

Garrett sat and leaned forward, his elbows resting on his bony knees. "I've come to ask your help again. The Cattleman's Association has hired me to put a stop to the rustling hereabouts. They want me to put together a company of rangers. I've got some men lined up. I could use another good hand."

"I didn't think the Texas Rangers were adding more men," Jim said. "I asked for a couple not long ago. They turned me down."

Garrett shrugged. "We won't be an official company. The governor tossed that idea into the outhouse quick. My group will be called the Home Rangers. Financed and backed by the association, mostly by the LS."

Jim settled into his chair and stroked his chin. "Sounds like a vigilante group to me."

"On the surface, maybe it does sound that way. But I've stressed to the association that the Home Rangers will work only within the framework of the law. There won't be any lynchings as long as I'm in charge."

"Who else is in on it?"

"Barney Mason, Lon Chambers, Charley Reasor, Ed King, Frank Valley, John Lang, and a couple of others you may not know. Men new to Tascosa."

Jim winced inwardly. Except for Lon Chambers, there wasn't a man in the group he would trust even if they carried two pounds of badges. He shook his head. "I don't like the sound of it, Pat," he said. "Deal me out."

"Want to tell me why?" There was a hint of a challenge in Garrett's tone.

"Ed King for starters," Jim said, his voice calm and steady. "That man is a killing waiting for a place to happen. Gets downright mean when he's drunk. Which seems to be most of the time. He's going to shoot somebody for no reason except an overload of Old Skullbuster one of these days." Jim let a wry smile touch his lips. "Besides, King's been my guest here a couple of times. I had to bust him in the ear to break up a fight in the Dunn and Jenkins Saloon just last week. I don't think he likes me too much."

Jim leaned forward, his gaze locked on Garrett's eyes. "Pat, I won't run with that pack, and not just because of King. Several of those men don't care who they hurt. I won't have any part of them."

Garrett's eyes narrowed. "You don't think I can handle them?"

"That's not what I said," Jim replied. "I just said I won't have any part of it. I'm a sheriff, not a night rider with a gun and a rope. This badge means something to me."

"Suppose we brought in warrants based on indictments from district court? Would you help serve them?"

Jim sighed. "You know I wouldn't have a choice. As sheriff of the county I'd have to help serve any warrants that were legal and binding. I'll work with you when the law says I have to, but like I said—deal me out as far as the rest of it's concerned."

Garrett shrugged and stood. "I guess that's it then, Jim. I was hoping you'd see it my way."

"I see it your way. What I see is dead wrong." Jim let a hard edge creep into his tone. "And remember this, Pat. If you or any of your Home Rangers break the law in my jurisdiction, I'll come after you like I would any common thief."

Garrett tugged his hat into place. "I don't doubt that for a minute, Jim. I just hope it never gets to that point. I'll see you around." The lanky New Mexican ducked through the doorway and strode into the midafternoon light.

Jim sat for a moment and stared toward the door. He tried to shake away the dread that sat like a lump in his gut. Then he pushed himself out of the chair, strapped on his gun belt and reached for his hat. He had a town to patrol.

Tascosa
May 1884

Jim East folded the tattered copy of the Dodge City newspaper with care, placed it on a corner of his battered desk, and glanced up as Deputy L. C. Pierce strode into the office. Pierce's thumb and forefinger were clamped securely on the left ear of a tousle-haired lad about ten years old.

"Caught Widow Thoreson's chicken thief, Jim," the deputy said. He released his grip on the boy's ear. The youngster's eyes were wide with fear and pain as he rubbed the abused flap of skin. Tears pooled in the lids of the boy's eyes. "What do we do with this desperado?"

Jim leaned back in his chair and glared into the boy's frightened eyes. "Well, Clint," he said grimly, "you've got yourself in a mess of trouble this time. You know what happens to stock thieves around here."

Clinton Scarborough tried to stare back defiantly, but the tremble of his lower lip and the trickle of a tear down a dirty cheek wrecked his attempt at arrogance. Clint was from one of the poor families in town. His shoes were worn through at the toe and his britches and homemade shirt had more patches than original material.

"Well, Clint? Why did you take to rustling the widow's chickens?"

"I"—the boy hiccuped a sob—"we didn't have no money. Daddy don't make much workin' at the stable. I stole them chickens 'cause the cook down at the North Star cafe buys 'em from me." Clint dropped his gaze to the floor and shuffled his oversize feet. "I didn't mean the widder no harm. Heck, it was just some dumb ol' chickens."

Jim winked at L. C. Pierce over the boy's bowed head. He kept his voice firm with an effort. "Son, it wasn't just some dumb old chickens. Widow Thoreson's as poor as you folks are. Those chickens are her only cash income. If you steal all her chickens, Widow Thoreson's going to starve to death. Rustling chickens is stock theft, just like stealing a man's cows, as far as the law is concerned." He paused for a moment to let the concept sink in, then rose and reached for the manacles hanging on a peg near the desk.

"Sheriff," L.C. said, "do we hang this rustler now, or wait until after the trial?"

Jim studied Clint's face. It had gone the color of chalk. Sheer terror showed in the boy's eyes when Clint looked up. "Sheriff, please—"

Jim clanked the manacles a couple of times, then tossed them onto the desk. "Maybe there is a way we can keep a jury from hanging you, Clint," he said. "We'll go talk to the Widow Thoreson. Maybe if you offer to help her out around the place—clean the coops, gather eggs, fix up things when she needs it—she might drop the charges." He stroked his chin as if in deep thought. "She's a good woman, the widow. Has a charitable streak in her. Of course, I'll have to make sure that's all right with your dad. He's a poor man, but proud—"

"Sheriff, my pa'll skin me alive if he hears about this! You got to help me out!"

Jim scowled at the boy for a long moment. "Tell you what, Clint. You go talk to the widow on your own. If you can make a deal with her, we'll keep this just between you, L.C., me and the widow. You come back here and tell me how it works out." He pointed a stern finger at the boy. "You skip out on me, I'll be mighty disappointed. I'd have to come after you."

The youth swallowed hard. "I won't, Sheriff. I promise."

"All right. Go talk to the widow."

The boy turned and scurried out the door.

Jim settled back into his chair. "Well, that's another case solved by the fearless law enforcement officers of Tascosa," he said to L.C. "Clint's not a bad kid. He's just at the age where he doesn't stop and think things through. Come to think of it, we've got a lot of grown men around like that."

L.C. helped himself to some coffee and toed a chair around to face Jim's desk. Jim pushed the copy of the Dodge City paper to the deputy. "You might be interested in this, L.C.," he said. "Henry Brown's dead."

"Well, I'll be damned," Pierce muttered. "What happened?"

"After I fired him, Brown drifted into Kansas. Got himself appointed city marshal at Caldwell, married and seemed ready to settle down." Jim shrugged. "A few days back Brown and three others tried to rob the bank at Medicine Lodge. They got caught. Brown collected a double load of buckshot trying to outrun a lynch mob. The others took a long drop on a short rope."

Pierce scanned the article and tossed the paper back onto the desk. "Can't say I'm real surprised. I never did like the looks of that man." The deputy grunted in disgust. "Does give lawmen a bad name, trying to rob a bank and all. The least he could have done was to do the job right. People will start thinking lawmen don't even know how to pull off a bank holdup."

The deputy dismissed Henry Brown's demise with a shrug. "You heard the news about the courthouse, I reckon?"

Jim nodded. "It's the talk of the town. Folks are mighty grateful to the LS outfit for putting up the money to build us one."

"You don't sound all that pleased, Jim."

Jim picked up a stub of pencil and tapped it against the edge of the desk. "I don't think the LS has all of a sudden developed a streak of civic pride, L.C.," he said. "Study on it for a minute.

Garrett says his LS Rangers won't try to arrest anybody without an Oldham County indictment. To get an indictment you need a grand jury. To get a grand jury you need a courthouse."

Pierce scratched a thumb across a stubbled jaw. "You've got a point there, Jim. I was just thinking how we would get us a new office and a decent jail. What you said puts a whole new kink in that rope." The deputy fell silent, staring into his coffee cup.

Jim knew what was running through Pierce's mind. So far Garrett's crew hadn't spilled any blood, just made a nuisance of themselves. The Rangers prowled the line camps, roundups and floating crews, kept an eye out for rustled stock, and enforced association decrees. One of the first rules the association issued was to ban cowboys from carrying pistols. That set off a howl of outrage, but nobody openly bucked Garrett and the Rangers. Instead, there had been a run on harness shops until now almost every cowboy wore his gun under his armpit in a shoulder rig. There were just as many revolvers around as before. The only difference was that the cowboys were developing a new set of calluses from carrying them in a different place.

Pierce sipped at the cooling coffee in his mug. "When Garrett gets the legal papers he wants, there's going to be hell to pay on the Canadian," the deputy said.

Jim sighed. "You don't have to tell me, L.C." He rose and reached for his gun belt. "You get some rest. Catching hard cases like that chicken thief can wear a man down. I wish they were all going to be that simple."

Trujillo Creek
August 1884

Jim East pulled his sorrel to a stop on the ridge above a shallow canyon on the tributary of the Canadian. In the sandy flat of the canyon floor some thirty head of cattle milled and bawled. Three riders held the small herd as a forth piled wood onto a branding fire.

Jim glanced at the deputy astride a big roan beside him. "L.C.,"

Jim said, "there are times I wish I'd never had the notion to be a lawman. This is one of them."

L. C. Pierce turned his head and spat. "Me too. Looks like that's the bunch we're looking for down there. Don't see anything but Tabletop brands on the herd."

Jim slipped the tiedown thong from the hammer of the Colt at his belt. The Tabletop changed hands more often than a good whore on cowboy paydays. Now it belonged to the blocky man at the branding fire. "Watch the other three close, L.C.," he said. "I'll take care of Lochenburg. This is a tough bunch. If anybody even looks like he's about to go for a gun, shoot him." Jim touched spurs to the sorrel.

The man on the ground looked up as the two peace officers rode into the flat. Deke Lochenburg was a short, broad-shouldered, powerfully built former LS rider with a weathered face that seldom showed a grin. He wore a pistol on the shell belt around his hips. Lochenburg stared without speaking as Jim rode up and dismounted.

"What you doing here, East?" Lochenburg's voice was like the grating of a shovel over sandstone.

"Brought some bad news, Deke," Jim said. "I have to take these cattle."

Lochenburg stared at Jim for several heartbeats. "The hell you say. Who give you a bill of sale on 'em?"

"Oldham County Commissioners Court," Jim said. "The Tabletop brand's been outlawed."

"I don't know what you're talkin' about, Sheriff."

"The court's taking over several brands. The Pipe, K Triangle and the Tabletop, among others. All cattle wearing those brands belong to the county now."

"What?" Lochenburg's confused expression gave way to a look of growing anger. "Hell, East, they can't do that! It ain't legal!"

Jim shrugged. "Legal or not, Deke, they did it. I've got a paper in my pocket that says you have to turn any Tabletop stock over to me. Garrett's men are picking up outlaw brand stock at other cow camps up and down the river."

Lochenburg's face flushed. "By God, East, nobody takes my stock! I'll see you in hell first!" Lochenburg's right hand slapped at the butt of his pistol. Jim reached out with his left hand, clamped

Lochenburg's wrist against his side, and slammed a doubled fist between the burly man's eyes. Jim felt the cartilage of Lochenburg's nose crumple under the blow. Lochenburg staggered. Jim hammered him again. His knuckles thumped against Lochenburg's windpipe. The man's eyes glazed and his knees buckled. Jim yanked the Colt from Lochenburg's holster and let him fall.

"Hold it!" L. C. Pierce's voice was sharp against the thin morning air. Jim glanced up. One of the three riders froze, his hand on the stock of a Winchester in a saddle boot. "Make one more move, cowboy, and I'll kill you," Pierce said. His voice was cold.

Jim turned his attention back to Lochenburg. The stocky man was on his knees, one hand wrapped around his throat. Blood poured from the broken nose. Lochenburg wheezed as he tried to pull air through his bruised windpipe.

"Goddamn you—to hell—" Lochenburg's words came in pained, short gasps. "I'll kill—you for—this, East."

"Any time you get the urge, Deke, I'll be around." Jim reached down, grabbed Lochenburg by the collar and dragged him to his feet. He frisked the man, found no hideout gun, and turned to glare at the others. "Drop the hardware, boys. Slow and easy. You're going to help us trail these cattle back to Tascosa. After that, you're all free to go. I have no warrants for your arrest, just a paper for the cattle. They're not worth getting killed over."

The riders scowled and cursed, but one by one they let their gunbelts and rifles fall. L. C. Pierce gathered the weapons as Jim levered the still wheezing Lochenburg into the saddle of Deke's horse.

"Next time—you come at me—you better have a gun in your hand, East." Lochenburg's voice sounded like the croak of a tromped frog.

"I'll remember that, Deke. I truly will," Jim said. "Now, let's head these cattle to Tascosa."

Tascosa

Jim East lounged in the saddle on the flat south of Tascosa and watched as the last of the "outlaw brand" cattle disappeared around a bend of the Canadian, bound for sale in Springer, New Mexico, as decreed by Oldham County.

Jim spat. The cowboys had elected their sheriff, but the Lee and Scott LS brand owned the county commissioners court. The governing body of Oldham County was, in effect, an extension of the LS. The court's actions in declaring the suspect brands outlawed and confiscating the stock were illegal as hell, Jim grumbled to himself, but there wasn't anything he could do about it. And despite his own feelings he had to admit there was no question that at least some of those three hundred cows now headed to market at Springer had been stolen.

Almost a third of the herd wore the Tabletop brand. *Only the good Lord knows what brands are on the inside of those hides,* Jim thought.

As promised, he had turned Deke Lochenburg and his friends loose. He had no legal reason to hold them. The brands had been outlawed, not the owners. But Jim knew that more trouble was ahead with the stocky rustler. Lochenburg wasn't the sort of man who made idle threats.

"Well, Sheriff," said one of the county commissioners standing beside him, "there goes the county's first profit from the sale of stolen beef. That herd will certainly add a nice sum to the county coffers."

Jim shot a quick glance at the county official. "Don't count the coins yet. I know those men driving the stock. I doubt you'll ever see them again. Or the county's money." He abruptly reined his horse about and headed back for Tascosa at an easy trot.

Outlawing the so-called rustler brands was more than just illegal, Jim thought as he rode; it also was going to drive an even bigger wedge between the association and the little men. Garrett's group, now commonly known as the "LS Rangers," had opened a few more wounds.

Garrett had kept his word as far as Jim knew. The rangers hadn't killed anybody. But a lot of Garrett's former friends had gone over to the other side. When Garrett came to town now, the New Mexico lawman had to buy his own drinks.

Jim rode past the building taking shape at the corner of McMasters and Court streets. Workmen, mostly Mexican laborers, swarmed over the pile of rock that soon would be Oldham County's courthouse.

Jim admitted he had to give the Cattleman's Association some credit. They had bought a rundown one-room building for Tascosa's first school, which now had better than thirty students during the winter. And even if the LS's motive in supplying funds for the courthouse was self-serving, at least the county would have a decent lockup and sheriff's office. He idly wondered how much the trade-off would cost in trouble and blood before it was over.

The wind had kicked up again, hot and dry and out of the southwest. It whipped sand from the riverbed and peppered the buildings of Tascosa. *Hot days, cheap whiskey and bad tempers,* he thought. *A dangerous combination.*

Jim still had several stops to make on his rounds before he headed to the new home he and Hattie had purchased.

The thought of Hattie brought a slight smile to Jim's face. They had owned the house for only a week, but already she had turned it into home. It was as if they had lived there for years. Tonight she had promised him a deep-dish dried-apple pie dusted with cinnamon. She would smell like baking apples and the rose water she used in her daily bath. Hattie knew how to take a man's mind off his worries.

Jim's last stop was Jess Jenkins's Emporium in Hogtown. The place was crowded, but not uncomfortably so. Luis Bausman looked up from the poker game at a corner table and waved a greeting to Jim. Lem Woodruff stood at the bar laughing and joking and still reasonably sober, his arm around the auburn-haired dance hall girl named Sally. The sight bothered Jim a bit. Lem seemed to be getting serious about Sally. That in itself was no problem. Many of the dance hall girls and prostitutes in Tascosa married former clients and settled down to become devoted wives and mothers.

What worried Jim was that he had seen Sally appear to make a play for Ed King on evenings when Lem was not around. It wasn't unusual for woman trouble to set off a fight or even a shootout in Tascosa. Sally was playing a dangerous game, flirting with one man from the so-called "little man" or "nester" faction and another from the ranks of the big landowners.

Jim made a mental note to keep an eye on Sally. If it looked like she was deliberately trying to stir up trouble he'd see that she caught the next stage out of town.

TWELVE

Tascosa
October 1884

Sheriff Jim East closed and locked the new jail door and yanked on the doubled-strap iron slats that served as bars. The door barely wiggled. At least, he thought, the county hadn't skimped on its lockup; it would take several sticks of dynamite to even loosen the doors of this jail.

He heard the scrape of boots and chairs on the wooden floor overhead. The association hadn't wasted any time convening its first grand jury. The mortar was still damp between the stones of the two-story courthouse, and the grand jury upstairs was already loaded with association backers.

"Might as well get ready," he muttered to himself. "There'll be a paper stampede coming down those stairs pretty quick."

He had barely settled into the chair behind his old desk—the county had decided the expense of a new one wasn't warranted—when Pat Garrett clumped down the stairs, a sheaf of papers in hand, followed by County Judge McMasters. Garrett was smiling. McMasters looked grim. But then, Jim thought, McMasters most always looked like he'd just swallowed a handful of red ants. Garrett handed the sheaf of indictments to Jim.

"Well, Sheriff," Garrett said, "we've got the legal papers. You game to go help us haul in some rustlers?"

Jim leveled a cold stare at Garrett. "I told you I'd help as long as it was legal." He dropped his gaze and studied the indictments one by one. Most of the names were familiar. All were associated with the small rancher and cowboy faction.

Jim sorted the indictments into two piles, then tapped a finger on the top paper of the shorter stack. "I'll take care of these myself, Pat," he said.

Garrett's eyebrows arched. "I thought we were supposed to be a team again."

"Not on these two. Your LS men ride up on Tom Harris, there'll be a killing for sure. Same with Deke Lochenburg. They'll shoot first and then ask how come you're there." He shoved the other indictment papers to the corner of the desk. "There's enough others to keep you and your boys busy for a while without me, Pat." He stood and reached for his hat.

"Where are you going, Sheriff?" Judge McMasters was a bit red in the face. He expected the duly elected officials of the county to jump when he hollered "frog." Jim East didn't feel a single twitch in his leg muscles.

"I'm going after Harris first, then Deke. I'd kind of like to bring them both in alive, Judge." Jim saw the flicker of disgust in the judge's eyes. The association, it appeared, would prefer to see them brought in face down over a horse. Jim tucked the two warrants into a shirt pocket, slipped into his coat and lifted his rifle from the rack by the door. He paused at the doorway.

"By the way, Judge," Jim said casually, "how much did the county make off that herd of rustler brand cattle?"

McMasters sputtered, his face flushed. "You know damn well those cowboys never came back with the money."

Jim nodded. *Shouldn't be baiting the county judge like that,* he thought, *but a man takes his fun where he finds it.* He stepped through the door into the cool October air. The golden leaves of the cottonwood trees by the courthouse rustled in a gentle breeze. The air had a fresh smell to it, crisp and clean, flavored with a hint of woodsmoke. *Going to be one of those days that's a keeper,* he thought, *if some fool doesn't spoil it with gunsmoke.*

The sun was just past its midpoint when Jim reined his sorrel to a halt in the narrow canyon ten miles from Tascosa where Tom Harris spread his bedroll when he wasn't at his ranch in Liberty.

A wisp of smoke curled from the chimney of the small rock house nestled against the side of the canyon amid a jumble of sandstone boulders and stunted cedar trees. Tom was at home, it appeared.

Jim slipped his rifle from its scabbard, cocked the weapon and rested it in the elbow of his left arm. He kneed the sorrel forward. He made no attempt to sneak up on the house. That was the quickest way to draw a bullet. Tom Harris was not only stubborn, he was also a dangerous man with a quick temper and a fast gun. But he wasn't the type to shoot a horseman who rode straight into camp like he belonged there. Jim pulled the horse to a stop ten yards from the cabin door.

"Hello, the camp!" Jim called.

Tom Harris stepped through the doorway, a Winchester in his hand. "Hello yourself, Jim East," Tom said. "What brings you out this way? Social call?"

"Nope. I've got a warrant for your arrest, Tom. I've got to take you in."

"You bring some help for that little chore?"

Jim shook his head. "Just me. I looked the paper over myself. It's legal."

"What's the charge?"

"Rustling. Specifically, twelve head of LIT cows. Back in August."

Tom Harris snorted. "Hell, Jim, you know I never stole any LIT stock. Besides, I was over in Liberty the whole of August."

Jim shrugged. "Then you've got nothing to worry about, Tom. Fetch your possibles sack and saddle up."

Tom Harris's eyes narrowed. "What if I decide I don't want to be arrested?"

"Then we'll do it the hard way."

"Maybe I'm faster with this Winchester than you are with that one."

"Maybe. Maybe not. Think it's worth betting your life on, Tom?"

There was a moment's silence before Tom said, "I'm studying on it."

Jim shifted his weight in the saddle. The slight movement brought the muzzle of his own rifle into line with Tom Harris's gut. "Tom," he said, "you may be a lot of things, but I've never figured you for a killer. It's getting a little late in life to start picking up some more bad habits."

Harris stood for a few heartbeats, poised on the balls of his feet, thumb on the hammer of the Winchester. Jim felt the steady thump of his own heart against his ribs. In the silence he thought he could hear the tick of his pocket watch. Then Tom Harris grinned and lowered his rifle. "I'm no killer, true enough. I'm not a fool either. I've seen you work a Winchester. You reckon I can get a fair trial? Tascosa's association country."

Jim lowered his own weapon. "I can't deny that, Tom. And you'll be up against Temple Houston. He's a top hand district attorney, one of the best, but he's fair. With a good lawyer on your side you'll stand a chance."

"How do I know the association won't bust me out of jail and lynch me to the nearest tree?"

"Because I won't let them."

"That's good enough for me, Jim. I'll get my stuff."

Moments later the two men rode side by side toward Tascosa. Harris had handed over his pistol and rifle. Jim saw no reason to put the man in irons. Harris had given his word he wouldn't try to run. The word of a thief might not be something a man took to the bank, but Harris's promise was enough for Jim. Besides, they both knew Jim still held the Winchester.

"Jim? Are you sure that paper said LIT cattle? Didn't mention LS stock?"

Jim half smiled. "I'm sure of it, Tom. Just LIT."

Harris chuckled. "Then I reckon I'm in the clear this time."

Jim put the Winchester back on the rack and hefted the sawed-off ten-bore shotgun. Deke Lochenburg didn't have as much common sense as Tom Harris did. He had a worse temper, and a hate for Jim East that went back to that day on Trujillo Creek. Deke had told Jim that the next time he'd better have a gun in his hand. Jim figured the ten-gauge qualified as a gun. The biggest one he could find.

Tom Harris lounged on a cot in the new jail cell. He seemed pleased, in an odd sort of way, to be the first to "break in" the new lockup. He would have some company soon—if not Lochenburg, then someone else. Garrett and his men had already started a swing through the Canadian, looking for others named in the indictments.

Jim hadn't bothered to tell Garrett that Lochenburg was already in town. It was going to be chancy enough facing Deke without a half-dozen LS men getting in the way and maybe getting dead in the process. Jim broke the action of the ten-bore, checked the loads and strode into the fading light of dusk.

It didn't take long to locate Lochenburg. All Jim had to do was ask the whereabouts of Frog Lip Sadie. Tonight she was working the Emporium in Hogtown.

Jim eased through the saloon doorway and paused to survey the crowd. Frog Lip Sadie wasn't on the floor. That meant she was already at work. Jim strode to the table where Jess Jenkins had just dealt a hand of blackjack.

"I'm looking for Deke," Jim said.

Jenkins waved a card toward the doorway to the back rooms. "First door on the right," he said. "You going to kill him?"

"If he wants it that way."

Jenkins grunted. "Don't let Sadie get hurt. She's one of my best."

The crowd of cowboys stepped aside after a quick glance at the twin bores of the big shotgun. Conversations stopped and card games went still as Jim walked past.

He knocked on the door of Frog Lip Sadie's room. It wasn't polite to walk in on a woman, even a five-dollar whore, without warning. Also, some of them carried nasty little forty-one caliber derringers.

"Deke, you in there?" Jim called.

"East, is that you?" The voice rumbled back, the words slurred a bit from too much whiskey and a touch nasal from the busted nose. To walk straight in on Deke would be like chewing a handful of live scorpions. Jim moved away from the door and pressed himself against the rough adobe wall.

"I've got a warrant for your arrest, Deke. Come out slow with your hands empty."

"The hell you say, you sonofabitch!" Splinters flew from the flimsy door; three slugs slammed into the adobe wall atop the reports of a big-bore pistol. Bits of dried adobe speckled Jim's cheek.

"Sadie, get down! I'm coming in!" Jim called. He waited a second, then tapped the barrel of the shotgun against the doorknob. Two more slugs tore through the wood. They were belt high to Jim. He grunted aloud as if hit, then scraped the stock of the shotgun down the wall as he crouched beside the door.

Moments later the shattered door banged open and Deke

Lochenburg stepped into the short hallway, a Colt pistol in his fist. Jim raised the shotgun. "Drop it, Deke!" he yelled.

Lochenburg whirled toward Jim, the muzzle of the pistol swinging into line. Jim squeezed the front trigger of the smoothbore. The heavy buckshot charge picked Deke up like a big fist and slammed him to the floor. Jim knew the blocky man with the big pistol was dead before his head bounced twice. Still, he kept the other barrel trained on the body as he stepped to the door and glanced inside. Frog Lip Sadie cowered naked beside the bed, her face stark white beneath the smeared kohl and rouge.

"Sadie, are you all right?"

The woman swallowed, tried to speak but managed only a croak, then nodded.

"Get some clothes on," Jim said calmly. "This place will be full of people real quick." He ignored the woman and edged closer to Deke's body. The charge had taken Lochenburg squarely in the chest. Jim stared at the dead man for a moment. He had forgotten how much blood could come out of a man.

A nervous cowboy peered around the doorway leading to the main saloon. "Better get the county judge, friend," Jim said. "We're going to need an inquest here."

Tascosa
December 1884

Jim East sat at his desk, pieces of the stripped-down Winchester spread before him, and listened to the growing moan of the north wind outside.

So far it had been a mild winter in the Panhandle. Only one snowstorm worth noting had come, a six-inch blanket that covered the countryside. Three days after the snow stopped it was gone, melted by a bright winter sun and the Chinook winds that swept down the eastern slope of the Rockies into the northern Texas Plains.

Jim picked up the sear and trigger assembly of the rifle, cleaned the powder residue away with a dry rag, and wiped the mechanism lightly with an oiled cloth. The rifle showed a bit of scabbard wear

along the octagonal barrel and the stock was scarred from en-
counters with brush and an occasional rock. But the bore was still
bright, lands and grooves crisp and well defined.

Upstairs the scuffle of chairs and occasional voices raised in argu-
ment sounded from the second session of the Oldham County
Grand Jury. Jim smiled wryly at the loud words from above. The
association was not altogether pleased with the results from the first
round of trials.

Tom Harris was once again a free man, a jury of his peers having
found him not guilty of the charge of stealing LIT cows. District
Attorney Temple Houston had accepted the ruling with class and
grace. The dark-haired, dark-eyed son of the man most Texans
called the father of the state merely shrugged and smiled at the
verdict. "Hell, Sheriff," he had told Jim in private after the trial,
"the state—meaning in this case the Panhandle Cattleman's Association—didn't have a shred of solid proof to begin with. We tried
the man on his reputation and for leading the cowboy strike, not
for stealing cows. He's guilty as sin, but not of the charge he was
tried on."

Another former LS cowboy and a nester rancher had been cut
loose by juries. Young D. B. Swarthmore was beginning to make a
name for himself as a defense attorney. He was new to Tascosa, not
long out of law school, and still operated under the assumption that
men were innocent until proven guilty. He might get over that
eventually, Jim knew, but in the meantime he was winning nearly
as many cases for the little men as Temple Houston was for the big
boys. Houston didn't seem to mind. He seemed to like watching a
good young lawyer at work.

Houston was still a few cases ahead in the courtroom game. Four
small-time rustlers were now in Huntsville or on their way to enjoy
the state's hospitality for a number of years. Two more sat in the
new Oldham County jail waiting for the long trip to the state pen.

Of those convicted, Garrett's LS Rangers had brought in two on
their own. Jim and L. C. Pierce had helped Garrett run the others
to the ground. Garrett still seemed to be keeping his word that
there would be no Ranger lynchings. Only two men had been
killed resisting arrest and Jim freely admitted both of them deserved it. Jim knew the association was upset with these results. The
big men wanted the accused rustlers shot or lynched on the spot,

not brought to trial. A trial was a hell of a lot more expensive than a bullet or a rope.

If they had done nothing else, the Tascosa lawmen and the LS Rangers had helped swell the populations of New Mexico and Colorado of late. At least a half dozen of the men indicted had left the Tascosa country at a long lope once word got out that the situation had turned serious. Rustling along the Canadian had slowed. It hadn't stopped.

The role Garrett's LS Rangers played in the full-bore attack on cattle and horse thieves had backfired as far as public sentiment went. Resentment against Garrett and the big ranchers was stronger than ever now among the owners of the small spreads and the cowboys who sided with them. Jim knew for a fact that many of the men who currently rode for the big brands resented the high-handed approach their bosses had taken in hiring Garrett. The gulf between the cowboy-nester faction and the association faction widened by the day.

Jim had finished cleaning and assembling the Winchester by the time the familiar footsteps sounded on the stairs. He fed a couple of cartridges into the loading port, worked the action to chamber and then eject them, and grunted in satisfaction. The weapon's action was smooth and fluid. He was confident it would function even in weather well below zero. He was loading the rifle when Garrett and McMasters stepped into his office. Garrett carried a handful of papers. The stack was smaller than last time.

"Got some business for us, Sheriff," Garrett said as he handed over the indictment papers. McMasters merely glanced at Jim and grunted a surly greeting before he stalked from the office. Jim ignored the judge's snub. He thumbed through the indictments and set one aside.

"No problem with that one, Pat," he said. He studied the others for several moments, then glanced up. "These could be touchy. Tough bunch."

Garrett nodded. "Wade Woods, Bill Gatlin and Charley Thompson. I expect we'll have to burn some powder on those boys." Garrett strode to a window and stood for a moment, watching the sand and debris swirl down the street in the freshening wind. "Know where they are, Jim?"

"I'll find out."

Garrett turned to face Jim. "Those three will most likely have others with them. Gunmen, not just cowboys. What we need is a good blizzard. Like on the Pecos campaign against the Kid's bunch."

Jim could almost feel the pain in his fingers just thinking about it. "You're right. God, I sure wish you weren't. I hate being horseback in one of these blue whistlers. Never quite got over the frostbite from that little trip to Sumner and back. But that's the best way to take them with the least chance of a shootout. If a man's all cozy and warm he doesn't figure any lawman would be crazy enough to ride in that weather— Wait a minute, Pat."

Jim strode to the window. A cowboy on a paint horse was riding past, his hat jammed down over his ears against the wind. Jim stepped outside. Garrett followed. "Hey, Ben!" Jim called.

The horseman glanced at Jim, then reined his paint toward the courthouse door. "Am I in some kinda trouble I don't know about, Sheriff?"

Jim grinned. "No. But in case you don't remember, you did have yourself a good time last night. You headed back to the Bar CC?"

The young man nodded. "No place else to go and it's another whole month 'til payday."

"Tell Jesus Quintana I've got a warrant for his arrest, Ben. Tell him to get his butt in here before I have to go get him. Jesus doesn't want that."

Ben nodded. "I'll tell him, Sheriff. See you next month." He reined the paint about.

"That's all there is to that one?" Garrett seemed a bit mystified. "Will Quintana come in just like that? Just because you told him to?"

"He'll come, Pat. Quintana's got a big case of the 'fraids when it comes to *Señor* Sheriff East and his big smoothbore shotgun." Jim sniffed the wind. "No snow close yet, but it won't be long. In a week or so we'll have our blizzard." He turned and strode back inside. Garrett tagged along.

"Pat, do me one favor."

"What might that be?"

"While your boys are in town, keep Ed King under a tight rein. There's bad blood building fast between King and Lem Woodruff.

I'd just as soon they didn't decide to have a go at each other. I like my town quiet."

Garrett shrugged. "I'll do what I can. King does get a little antsy when he gets a snoot full of cheap whiskey. But he has his uses."

Jim leveled a steady glare at Garrett. "Maybe he does," he said, "but I'd just as soon he didn't put those uses to work around Tascosa." Jim strode to the desk and picked out two indictments. "Let's go see if we can't pick up these boys while we're waiting for that blizzard."

Red River Springs
January 1885

Jim East scrunched deeper into his trail-worn buffalo hide coat, trying to escape the knife cut of the north wind.

The blizzard—Pat Garrett's "hunting weather"—had wailed into the Panhandle two days ago, a white wall of wind-driven snow and below-zero cold. Drifts as tall as a man on horseback grew on the downwind side of thickets, cliffs, and any other natural or man-made structures that turned aside the bitter onslaught from the north.

The snowfall had stopped at midnight but the wind still raged, whipping ground flurries from the drifts. Overhead the sky showed a weak gray light as the clouds thinned. *A bad turn of luck,* Jim thought; *now they'll be able to see us coming.* He shivered beneath the coat. His hands ached and stiffened despite his thick leather gloves lined with rabbit fur. He had lost touch with his feet miles ago. Winter boots of thick mule hide, a full size too big in order to accommodate three pair of socks, seemed to do little to turn aside the cold. His only solace was that the men who rode with him suffered as much as he did.

He glanced over his shoulder at the line of men. Their horses plodded along the trail broken by Jim's powerful buckskin gelding. Pat Garrett rode behind Jim, his tall frame bent against the blast of wind; he was followed by Deputy L. C. Pierce and LS Rangers Ed King, Frank Valley, Charley Reasor, Barney Mason and Fred Chilton. Kid Dobbs, the one LS man Jim trusted enough to swear in as a special Oldham County deputy for this job, brought up the rear. Dobbs knew the Red River Springs country as well as Jim did.

Jim had failed to convince Garrett to leave three of the men behind. Jim didn't trust King, Valley and Mason; the three men were gun-crazy, always looking for an excuse to drop a hammer on someone. Chilton and Dobbs were more like Jim. They saw no need for shooting when it could be avoided. Jim could only hope Garrett could keep the other three in line. King already had his rifle out and a round chambered, and they still had two miles to go before they reached the rock house at Red River Springs.

The posse was showing signs of trail wear. They had ridden out the night and covered better than forty miles in the pitch dark of a winter storm. The horses were hurting worse than the men. Jim doubted if the animals had more than one good burst of speed left in them.

The posse's objective was a rock house built into the side of a hill by Kid Dobbs's father-in-law many years ago. The house had been abandoned for the last five years except to provide temporary shelter for cowboys, hunters and drifters. Now it was occupied once again—by the men named in the indictments Jim carried in an inside pocket. Jim's sources of information had been correct. Dobbs had confirmed the wanted men's presence at the rock house the day before the blizzard hit. He had also brought back some unwanted news. There were a dozen horses in the rock corral beside the house. Fugitives Woods, Thompson and Gatlin had company. That tilted the odds if it came to a fight.

Dobbs urged his tiring horse alongside Jim's mount. "When we top that rise up ahead they'll be able to see us, Sheriff," he said. "Can't sneak up on 'em from this side. To get behind 'em we'd have to ride another twenty miles."

"And cross the river twice," Jim added, thinking aloud. "The horses are nearly worn down now."

"Then, by God, we go straight in," Garrett said. "If we put the steel to these horses we'll be on them before they can get organized."

Jim bit back a sharp retort. Garrett knew damn well who was wearing the badge in this posse. But Jim had to concede that Garrett had a point. There wasn't any other way to tackle the bear's den up ahead.

"All right, Pat," Jim said. "But I don't want any shooting unless we're fired on. Is that clear?" Jim heard the challenge in his words.

Garrett's eyes narrowed as he glared at Jim. The lanky New Mexican turned his head and spat. "Yeah. I seem to recall how you just can't stand the sight of blood, Sheriff." Sarcasm lay heavy on his words.

Jim quit fighting the anger that rumbled in his gut. "Dammit, Garrett!" he snapped, "if I didn't have a job to do I'd yank you off that horse and beat the living hell out of you right here and now!"

Garrett returned Jim's stare for a moment, then shrugged. "Be interesting to see if you could handle that little chore. But like you say, we've work to do."

Jim tore his gaze away from Garrett and turned to the others. He was seething inside. "Put the damn rifle up, King. I don't want any weapons drawn until we're within a hundred yards of that house. No shooting even then unless we're fired on. Now, let's go." He touched the spurs to the buckskin.

The posse swept toward the house at the best speed the tired horses could manage in the snow. Jim saw no flashes of gunfire from the windows as they charged to within a hundred yards. *So far so good,* Jim thought. He pulled his Winchester from the saddle boot.

The Tascosa posse's charge thundered past the house without a shot being fired. Behind the house Jim saw one man dump an armload of wood and sprint for the door. Kid Dobbs's mount almost ran the man down. Moments later Jim had his men deployed behind and on either side of the house, where there were no doors or windows to fire from. Jim crouched beside Garrett behind a clump of junipers at the back of the house.

"East and Garrett are out there!" he heard the man who had dropped the firewood call from inside.

The words had barely reached Jim when he heard the door creak open. Tom Harris stepped into view around the side of the building. He was unarmed.

"You after me again, Jim?" Harris yelled.

"Not you, Tom," Jim called back, "I have no warrant on you. We're after Wade Woods, Charley Thompson and Bill Gatlin. The rest of you stay out of it and everybody will live a lot longer."

Harris backed away. "Woods isn't with us. I'll talk to the other boys."

Jim glanced at Garrett. The tall lawman had his jaw set and his rifle at full cock, muzzle pointed toward the house. "Give them a chance to talk it over, Garrett," Jim said.

A few minutes later, nine men walked from the house, hands empty and held at shoulder height. Gatlin and Thompson stayed inside. Garrett barked orders for Chilton and Mason to herd the nine into the rock corral and keep an eye on them. Then Garrett turned to Jim. "Let's go dig the other two out, Sheriff."

"Wait a minute, Garrett," Jim said. "I know Charley Thompson. Maybe I can talk him out of there."

Garrett shrugged. "It's your funeral."

Jim stepped into the open and slogged through the snow to the side of the house. He turned the corner and pressed his body against the rough wall beside an open window. The muzzle of a rifle rested on the window sill.

"Charley, it's Jim East," he said.

There was no answer from inside.

"I don't want to see you hurt, Charley." Jim's voice was steady and calm. "There's no sense in getting yourself killed."

"Jim, I ain't done nothing, ain't broke no law." Thompson's voice quavered. "Whatever that paper says I done, it ain't right."

"I know that, Charley. The only thing you've ever done wrong in your life, right up to this minute, is join that cowboy's strike. Give yourself up and I'll help you get a good lawyer."

"I got no money for no lawyer." Jim heard the note of desperation in the young cowboy's voice.

"We'll find a way, Charley. Have I ever lied to you before?"

"No. I reckon you ain't."

"Then you know I won't be lying if I tell you this—if I have to come in there after you I'll have to kill you. It sure would tear me up to have to tell your mother I shot you. It would break her heart, your getting killed for no good reason."

A momentary silence fell in the conversation. Jim waited patiently.

"Jim?" Thompson's tone was plaintive. "How's Mom? I ain't seen her in over a month."

"She's fine, Charley. Helping out the sick folks, working to help get money together to build a church. She misses you, son. Asks about you all the time." Jim paused to let the words sink in. Charley Thompson maybe had some drawbacks, but he was devoted to his mother. "She's getting on in years, Charley," Jim said. "What's going to happen to her if you're not around to help her out in her old age?"

The silence returned. Jim let it drag on. Charley Thompson took a little longer than some folks to think things through.

Finally the door creaked open. Thompson stepped outside, hands raised. Tears streamed down his cheeks. "Don't shoot, Jim," he said. "I'll go along peaceful."

"Good, Charley. I'm mighty relieved to hear that." Jim edged his way to Thompson's side, careful to keep out of direct view of the window in case Bill Gatlin had a twitch in the trigger finger. He draped an arm around Charley in fatherly fashion and led him toward the waiting posse. He felt the tension tighten the cowboy's shoulders as Garrett and the others came into view.

"Don't worry, Charley. They won't hurt you. I won't let them." He led Thompson to where Barney Mason waited. "Mason, I'm putting Charley here in your care. You make damn sure nothing happens to him unless you want something worse to happen to you."

Mason's face flushed; the man's jaw muscles tightened, but he nodded silently.

"What you going to do now, Sheriff?" Kid Dobbs asked.

"Go back to the house and see if I can talk some sense into Bill Gatlin. That might take a while. Bill can be mighty stubborn at times."

Jim East stood beside the window for better than two hours, cajoling, pleading, even threatening. Bill Gatlin wasn't in the mood to parley. Finally Jim gave up. He strode back to Garrett.

"I can't get through to him, Garrett," he said. "Maybe you could talk him out of there."

Garrett grunted. "I've heard enough talk for one day." He turned to two of his riders. "Reasor, you and King climb up on the roof and start ripping off some of those rafter poles. Watch yourselves. He might start shooting." Garrett raised his voice and called toward the house. "We're coming in, Gatlin! You fire at one of my men or pull a gun on us and you're a dead man!"

Jim waited, rifle at the ready, as the two LS Rangers clambered onto the sod roof held in place by weathered and weakened rafters. It took only a couple of strong tugs to break the rafters loose. Then Reasor and King yanked off the third pole. The hole in the roof was growing fast.

"Garrett!" The voice from inside held a note of desperation. "Hold off! Let me talk to East! Give me five minutes! Then either East or me will walk out alive!"

Jim came to his feet. Garrett reached out and grabbed his arm. "Where the hell do you think you're going?"

Jim yanked his arm free. "You heard the man. He wants to talk, I'll talk."

"He also said just one of you would come out alive. He'll kill you, Jim. Bill Gatlin's no Charley Thompson. He'd as soon shoot you in the gut as look at you. Better wait and let us smoke him out."

Jim sighed. "It's *my* gut at stake, Garrett. I'll take the chance. If I don't make it, you've got him on a murder charge—and you've got me out of your hair for good." He raised his voice. "I'm coming in, Bill!"

Jim felt sweat dampen his palms despite the cold as he walked toward the house. Gatlin was dangerous enough to begin with. He would be worse now that he was cornered. Jim knew from the yellowed flyers in his old desk that Gatlin had killed two men up in the Dakota country. Jim lifted his rifle to waist level and toed the door open.

Bill Gatlin stood with his back to the far wall, a Colt revolver in each hand. The pistols were trained on Jim's chest. The muzzle of Jim's Winchester pointed straight at Bill Gatlin's belly.

The two men stood, both poised to kill, and stared into each other's eyes for several seconds. Jim felt the throb of blood through the arteries in his neck as the tension built. The bores of the pistols in Gatlin's hands seemed to grow bigger in the strained silence.

"Well, Bill," Jim finally said, "what's it going to be? You put the guns down and we don't have to kill each other." Jim felt his heart hammer against his ribs. Then a curious calm settled over him. His muscles relaxed and his heartbeat slowed. *If it ends here,* he thought, *at least I have friends to watch over Hattie.* "I don't want to kill you, Bill," Jim said. "I sure as hell don't want you to kill me."

Gatlin's eyes narrowed. "I'd rather die here, clean and quick."

The outlaw jerked his head toward the back of the house. "Those LS Rangers out there'd hang me to the nearest tree."

Jim tightened his finger on the trigger until he felt the delicate balance of sear against hammer spring. "Think it through, Bill," he said, his voice soft. "You shoot me and they'll lynch you for sure. But if you're determined to get yourself dead, a rope would be a damn sight quicker than a Winchester slug in the belly. I've seen gutshot men die, Bill. It takes a long time and it hurts like hell."

Indecision flickered in Gatlin's eyes. "If you hand me those Colts," Jim said, "I promise you'll get to Tascosa alive. You're in a box, Bill, and I'm in it with you. There's no need for this."

The muzzles of the pistols wavered. "You swear you won't let them lynch me, Jim?"

"You have my word on it."

Gatlin's shoulders slumped. He lowered the pistols, eased the hammers and handed the weapons to Jim. "I guess I trust you to give me a fair shake."

Jim sighed in relief as he tucked the Colts into his waistband. "You can trust me." He turned his back on the wanted man. It was chancy, but Jim didn't think Gatlin had a hideout gun—or would shoot a man in the back. "I'll go out first, just so nobody out there makes a mistake."

THIRTEEN

Tascosa
April 1885

Jim East filed the last of the wanted notices that had come in on the noon mail coach from Dodge City, leaned back in his chair and stretched the stiffness from his shoulders. Paper work was a necessary part of the job, but Jim never had developed a taste for it.

He listened for a moment to the good-natured banter coming from the cell. Bill Gatlin, Charley Thompson, Jesus Quintana and two other prisoners played a harmless game of poker, idling away the time until the spring session of district court opened in Tascosa. The game was harmless because the rules were simple. It was penny ante, table stakes, and when one man had won all the money they divided it equally and started over again.

It was getting downright crowded in there, but some space would be opening up soon. Attorney D. B. Swarthmore had agreed to defend Charley Thompson free of charge and was taking Jesus Quintana's case for the princely fee of four dollars. Jim had loaned Jesus two of those dollars. Gatlin had decided to plead guilty and do his time. The others had different lawyers and, Jim figured, a fifty-fifty chance of getting cut loose. The Panhandle Cattleman's Association was probably going to take another licking in district court.

Jim stood as Pat Garrett strode into the office. The New Mexico lawman's frown exaggerated the weather lines in his angular face. Jim nodded a greeting.

"Just came by to say adios, Jim," Garrett said. "The Rangers are disbanded. I'm headed back to New Mexico."

Jim's brows arched in surprise. "Rangers disbanded? Mind if I ask why?"

Garrett snorted. "Hell, Jim. You had it right all the time. The association didn't want me to bring in live prisoners. It took me a while to figure that out, but it finally soaked in. I just got back from an association meeting over in Mobeetie. I told them if they wanted a hired gun there were plenty of them out there, but I wasn't doing any killing for them."

Garrett offered a hand. Jim took it. "Barney and I'll be pulling out for home this afternoon," Garrett said. "Jim, we've had our differences. But, by God, you're one of the best lawmen I've ever worked with. No hard feelings over those little squabbles?"

"None here, Pat. Good luck."

Garrett turned to walk away.

"Pat," Jim asked, "what about the rest of the boys in the Home Ranger company? Are they going to form up again with a new leader?"

Garrett shook his head. "The association's tired of spending the money and not getting any dead men in return. I suppose the rest of the boys will go back to work punching cows on their old outfits." He touched fingertips to his hat brim in a final salute. "See you around, Sheriff East."

Jim watched the tall lawman mount up and rein his horse toward the trail to New Mexico, Barney Mason at his side. Jim had to admit he wasn't especially sad to see the two men go; he just wished they had taken the rest of the LS Ranger outfit with them. About the only thing the Rangers had really accomplished was to make matters worse between the big landowners and the little men. And with the likes of King, Valley and Lang still hanging around, things could go from touchy to hurt in a hurry.

Jim made one last check on his prisoners, found everyone as fat and happy as could be expected of men behind bars, and strode from the courthouse into the unseasonably warm spring sun.

Winter had blown itself out in the January blizzard. February had brought slow, soaking rains instead of the usual ice storms, and March thunderheads had left an abundant supply of moisture in the Panhandle. The grass was already tall and green. It would be a good year for cattlemen, Jim mused as he strode along Main Street. But that didn't mean it would be a good year for sheriffs.

Tascosa
September 1885

"Jim East, I don't know what I'm going to do with you," Hattie scolded as she dabbed a wet rag across the scrapes and cuts on the knuckles of Jim's right hand. "Why don't you just get yourself a thick stick and whop these rowdy cowboys on the noggin instead of breaking up fights with your fists?"

Jim grunted and flexed his sore hand. The movement started the blood oozing again. "That would save some wear and tear, Hattie," he said, "but there's always the chance I could accidentally kill a man if I hit him with a club."

Hattie frowned at him, then suddenly leaned forward and kissed him on the forehead. "I guess that's one of the reasons I still love you after all these years, Jim. Under that grizzly bear hide of yours is the gentlest man I've ever met."

Jim felt the color rise in his face. "No need to insult me, girl. Just fix up the hand. I've got to get back on duty." He smiled for Hattie's benefit. "It's Saturday after payday, you know. Tascosa gets to feeling its oats when the eagle screams. It won't last long. Cowboys get separated from their money in a hurry here."

Hattie's lips turned down in a frown. "All that money wasted on gambling, whiskey and women," she said with a snort, "and all the while we're fighting to get a decent schoolhouse and a church."

Jim chuckled. "Then all you civic-minded ladies of the town have to do is open your own saloon and whorehouse. You could build a school on every pile of horse apples and a church on every corner." He patted her affectionately on the rump. "Why, girl, you'd bring top dollar yourself in the dance hall market."

"Jim East! Of all the nerve!" The scowl stayed on Hattie's face, but mischief danced in the depths of her eyes. "Get out of my house, you crude scoundrel! Go beat up some poor drunken cowboy!"

Jim pushed himself out of the chair and studied his battered knuckles. A bit of blood still seeped from the scraped skin, but the hand worked. He kissed Hattie, reached for his hat and started for the door.

"Wait a minute, Jim. I'll walk with you a way." Hattie plucked a shawl from the back of a chair and wrapped it over her shoulders. "Frog Lip Sadie's baby is due any minute. I promised I'd be there to help. I just wish that new doctor we finally talked into coming from Mobeetie was here now instead of next week."

Jim held the door open for Hattie. The night air was cool and fresh. It carried a hint of autumn. He glanced at his wife as they strode arm in arm down Main Street. *Jim East,* he thought, *you've got to be the luckiest man alive to catch a woman like Hattie.* At the same time he realized Hattie had seemed to age a bit since he pinned on the badge. She had a few more worry lines about the eyes, more gray in the dark brown hair. *Being a sheriff's wife must be a hell of a lot harder than being a sheriff,* Jim thought. At the corner of Main and Water Street Hattie pulled him to a stop, rose on her tiptoes and kissed him lightly on the cheek.

"Jim, be careful out there." Concern tinted Hattie's tone. "I'd like to get you back tonight in one piece."

Jim watched her walk toward Frog Lip Sadie's two-room adobe and shook his head in wonder. Tascosa still amazed him at times. A respectable woman could walk the streets at night without fear of being molested. The same God-fearing Christian woman had no qualms about helping deliver a whore's baby. The children of the prostitutes played as equals with the kids of the honest couples of the community. The whores contributed whatever they could afford to the school fund and the drive to build a church, and they showed up with food and sincere tears at funerals of the rich and poor alike.

Tascosa was wild but civilized, as serene as a mother's smile and as explosive as a charge of buckshot, honest as a good man's word and crooked as a shaved deck. In some ways, Jim thought, it was a puzzle inside a puzzle in a locked box without a key. Jim shook the thoughts away. *Cowboys and sheriffs aren't supposed to be philosophers,* he thought; *they aren't mentally equipped for the job.*

He found Deputy L. C. Pierce in the back room of the Exchange Hotel, keeping a watchful eye on a high-stakes poker game. The hotel owner was there, along with a cattle buyer, a land surveyor, a ranch manager, Lem Woodruff and Luis Bausman. The table was littered with gold and silver coins and U.S. greenbacks. Woodruff and Bausman had the biggest money piles. Those two, Jim knew, could hold their own with the top poker players in any town from Boston to California.

"Everything all right, L.C.?" Jim asked.

The deputy nodded. "All quiet in Upper Tascosa. Haven't been to Hogtown yet. How's the hand?"

"Touchy. Those XIT cowboys have the hardest heads I ever saw. But then a man's got to be hardheaded to be a cowboy. Or a peace officer. I'll check out Hogtown. You go get some rest. We may have a long night ahead of us."

Luis Bausman glanced up, winked a greeting at Jim, then turned back to the men in the card game. "Did I ever tell you boys about the time Charlie Bowdre's Mexican wife rearranged old Jim's ears with a branding iron?"

The cattle buyer grunted in disgust. "Not more than a hundred or so times, Luis. Deal the damn cards."

Jim grinned and shook his head at Bausman, then left the Exchange to continue his patrol. L. C. Pierce had been mostly right. Upper Tascosa wasn't quiet—there was plenty of carousing going on—but Jim didn't smell any trouble brewing. He made his way toward Hogtown, checking the doors of businesses that had closed for the night. The doors were locked, the goods inside the stores secure.

A half hour later he stood inside Jess Jenkins's saloon in Hogtown. The place was as noisy and smoky as usual. Cowboys stood three deep at the bar and there wasn't a spot to be had at a table. Jim frowned as he spotted Ed King and John Lang leaning against the bar. A nearly empty bottle stood before them. King had his hand around the waist of the girl called Sally. Lang was well on the way to being loaded on cheap whiskey, but he was generally a happy drunk. It was King a man had to worry about.

At the moment the two were busy regaling a handful of newcomers with yarns of their exploits as LS Rangers. Jim overheard a few of King's comments. Most of what he heard went past exaggeration to the point of outright lies. The former Rangers had earned the tag Tascosa had hung on them. They were called "barroom gladiators," since most of their fighting had been done with a bottle in one hand and a woman in the other.

King finished spinning his story, then turned away from the bar. His gaze caught Jim's steady stare. King lifted a glass toward Jim. "Care for a drink, Sheriff?"

Jim shook his head.

Anger flared in King's eyes. "What's the matter, East? You too good to drink with an old saddle-mate?"

Jim stepped up to King and glared into the LS rider's face. King had already had one too many, it appeared. "No, Ed, I'm not. But I don't drink on duty." He nodded toward the bottle in King's left hand. "You might consider going easy on that stuff. The jail's already full."

King's gaze wavered, the eyes momentarily glassy. "What you mean by that, Sheriff?"

"Just that I don't want any trouble in town tonight."

King rocked back on his heels, a mocking smile on his thin lips. "Damn if you ain't a suspicious man, Jim East. I wasn't plannin' on no trouble." He squeezed Sally's waist. "Me and the girl here got other things to do." The grin faded from King's face. "Where's that damned pretty boy friend of yours, that Woodruff?"

"Watch your tongue, King," Jim warned.

"Well, you give him a message from me," King said, the words slurred. "You tell Pretty Lem that old Ed King's done shot him out of the saddle with little Sally here. She's my girl now."

Jim leveled a hard glare at King. "You want to send a message, King, hire somebody to carry it. I'm not anybody's messenger boy." He fought back the impulse to whip his Colt from the holster and rap it against King's head. "You cause any trouble tonight, King— even so much as spit on the sidewalk—I'll come after you."

Indecision flickered in Ed King's eyes, pushing aside the challenge and drunken anger. Jim knew he had won this round even before King shrugged. "Aw, hell, Jim. You won't hear nothing about no trouble from me." He turned away and signaled the bartender for another bottle.

Jim waited a few more minutes, his gaze sweeping the crowd through the blue haze of tobacco smoke; then he strode for the door. He still had to finish his rounds.

Tascosa
March 1886

Jim East sat astride his buckskin gelding and watched as the drag riders of the trail herd from South Texas disappeared from view on the Dodge City Trail ten miles north of Tascosa.

Normally the sight of a railhead-bound herd brought back a wash of memories and set the cowboy blood that still flowed in his veins to pumping. Now it brought only a feeling of emptiness in his chest.

Jim sensed that he was watching one of the last trail herds to move through Tascosa. He thought of Wade Turner again; the old man's words seemed to come to mind more often these days. The trail herd that had just passed was one more of Wade Turner's "dyno-sewers." Maybe the last of its breed, one dying twitch of the tail of a big lizard. A lizard called the open range.

The damned wire was ruining the country, Jim thought bitterly. The XIT had almost completed fencing in its range. Jim knew the four strands of pointed barbs were not so much to keep XIT cattle in as to keep other men's cattle out. Now the thorned wire was creeping onto the LIT, the LX and the LS spreads.

"You were right, Wade," Jim muttered to the spirit of the old cattleman. "Pretty soon a man won't be able to ride a mile in a straight line."

For an instant Jim thought he heard the old trail driver sigh in pain. Then he realized it was only the wind whispering through the prairie grass.

The buckskin stomped its front foot and tossed its head, jangling the curb chain and bit. It was the big gelding's way of telling Jim they were too close to home after too long a ride to stop now. Jim touched the reins to the animal's neck. The horse snorted and stepped out toward Tascosa, anxious for its feed, stall and rest.

Jim knew how the horse felt. He was tired to the bone himself. Six days out, six days back, and all for nothing. The cattle rustled from the LS were now somewhere in Kansas. Another crime unsolved by the minions of Tascosa law, Jim scolded himself. The days had run together over the past few months, all different yet the same. Garrett's LS Rangers hadn't come close to stopping the cattle and horse thefts. The stealing had slowed for a time, but now it was worse than it had been before Garrett showed up. The small ranchers and the cowboys had hit back hard at the association for calling in Garrett and the Rangers, and the split between the two factions ran deeper than ever.

The association hadn't helped matters when it squeezed out two of the more popular and most honest small ranch owners in the business. The Slash B had been forced to sell out to the LX, unable to obtain credit in Panhandle stores dependent on association money. And a suspicious fire had burned two sections of the Rafter K's grass—almost the entire usable winter graze of the four-section outfit. The house, barn and corrals also had gone up in flames.

Even the weather had gone contrary in the Panhandle, Jim thought. A mild winter and dry early spring had dropped the water levels in the river and springs to half of what it normally would have been. And the heel flies were worse this year than at any time Jim could remember.

Heel fly time was one of the worst seasons on a working cowboy's calendar. The flies came in swarms and gave cattle unshirted hell. The tormented animals sought the only relief they knew, wading into the knee-deep mud of seeps and bogs along the creeks and river. It was the time when cowpunchers from every outfit got stuck riding bog, a back-breaking, dangerous job. Cowboys strained muscles and ropes and horses to pull cattle from the quicksands and sucking mud bogs, only to find the same cows back in the same muck again in less than a day. It brought to mind the comment of one old-timer: "The only thing dumber than a damn cow is a cowboy."

Jim had to admit heel fly time was one part of cowboying he didn't miss in the least. It made cowboys surly as well as muddy. That complicated a sheriff's life no end. There were more brawls, more shootings or near-shootings, and more drunks at heel fly time than at any other stretch that didn't include a major holiday.

Now the worst combination of all had come together at a place called Jerry Springs eleven miles upriver from Tascosa on LS range. Ed King, Frank Valley, Fred Chilton and John Lang were riding bog there. That put them too close to Tascosa to suit Jim

East. Of all the former LS Rangers, those four were probably the most hated. They were the core of the barroom gladiators, men unwilling to let go of what they saw as the glory days of their otherwise boring years in the saddle. They liked being hired guns a lot more than they liked tailing up a bogged cow. Blood wasn't as thick as Canadian River mud.

The buckskin stopped at the gate of the county livery stable and looked back at Jim as if to say, "Well, fool, we're home; get off and open the gate." Jim realized with a start that he didn't even remember riding the last mile. He had been too wrapped up in his worries. He unsaddled the buckskin and fed the animal before starting his walk home.

Jim paused at the corner of Spring Street and Main, his face drawn into a frown as he watched the four Jerry Springs bog riders move at a steady trot toward the hill on the east side of Tascosa. King, Valley, Chilton and Lang weren't the only ones in town today. Men and women on horseback, some in buggies or wagons and some afoot, filtered in a steady stream toward the big adobe home of Casimiro Romero north of Hogtown. Romero was famed far and wide for the lavish parties called *bailes* that he hosted from time to time.

Jim thought for a moment about following and confronting the four former LS Rangers, then pushed the idea aside. He had already had a talk or two with King and his bunch. There was nothing new to add. It could even make matters worse. If Ed King got mad before he started drinking, he would be in a full-bore rage after a few hits from the jug.

Casimiro Romero had strict rules for those attending his *bailes*. No guns, no cursing, no drinking to excess. The aging Mexican patriarch backed up his rules with a powerful personality and a Winchester when needed. It was unlikely the LS riders would cause trouble at Romero's.

Jim felt a pang of guilt for not having promised to take Hattie to the *baile*, with its lively dances, tables heavy with food and drink, and good company. He could never seem to find the time to take her to social gatherings these days. He knew Hattie would understand that he was dog-tired, hungry, saddle-stiff and needed a bath, a shave and a good night's sleep a lot more than he needed a party. He sighed and strode toward the footbridge over Tascosa Creek and the home that awaited him as twilight began to settle over the community on the bend of the Canadian.

The sound of gunshots brought Jim East awake with a start. The sharp crack of rifles and flat thump of pistol shots rattled down Main Street.

Jim was out of bed and grabbing for his pants before Hattie sat up in bed, alarmed. "What's happening, Jim?"

"I don't know, but it sounds like the Little Big Horn out there." The thunder of what seemed to be a dozen shots punctuated his words. Jim shrugged into his clothes, yanked on his boots, grabbed his gunbelt and was out the door before Hattie had time to call a warning.

Jim's boots pounded on the footbridge as he sprinted toward Main. The gunfire that had sounded in quick, ragged volleys died away for a moment, then a single final shot cracked the chill air.

Jim reached the corner of Main and Spring three strides ahead of Deputy L. C. Pierce. Jim skidded to a halt, cocked pistol in hand, in front of the Jenkins and Dunn Saloon. Ed King lay face up in a pool of blood, a bullet hole below his left eye. A second wound ringed by powder burns seeped crimson from his throat.

Jesse Sheets, the North Star Restaurant owner, lay in the doorway of his business, still in his nightclothes. He had a small, lethal hole in the center of his forehead. Fred Chilton's body slumped over a pile of plaster boards at the corner of the saloon. Blood soaked the front of his shirt and stained the porous boards beneath him.

"Jesus Christ," Pierce said, his voice hushed.

"Watch out, L.C.," Jim warned through clenched teeth. "This may not be over yet." He plucked a lantern from a bracket on a porch post and stepped into the darkened saloon. "Check around outside," he told the deputy.

Jim found Frank Valley dead near a bullet-riddled door in a back storage room. A single slug had hit him just below the left cheekbone and taken away a half-dollar size chunk of skull when it went out the back of his head. In the guttering lantern-light Jim saw pools of blood along a back wall of the small room. Someone else had been in here, someone hit hard, he thought.

Jim lowered the hammer of his Colt and holstered the handgun.

He left the lantern and stepped outside just as L. C. Pierce yelled "Halt!" toward a crouched figure running from the back of the saloon. Pierce yelled again, then leveled his rifle and fired. The running man went down. Pierce levered another round into his Winchester and sprinted toward the figure.

Lanterns bobbed along Main Street as Tascosa residents roused by the gunfire headed toward the saloon. A small crowd had already gathered. At the center of the crowd John Lang stood, his face ash-white in the feeble light of kerosene lamps. Jim pushed his way through the crowd to Lang. The man's clothing reeked of powder smoke. Jim reached out and plucked Lang's pistol from its holster. The barrel was still warm.

"What happened here, Lang?"

The LS rider blinked twice and shook his head. He seemed to be in a daze. Jim took him by the shoulder and shook him none too gently. "Listen, dammit, I've got four men dead here—"

"Better make it five, Jim," Pierce said as he strode into the cluster of men. "That was the Catfish Kid on the run. He's dying."

Jim mouthed a silent curse. He turned to the growing crowd. "Nobody touches anything," he called. "I want these bodies left alone." He picked out one pale face in the front of the crowd. "You there. Get the justice of the peace and the doctor." He waited until the man left at a trot, then turned to his deputy. "L.C., keep an eye on this crowd. If anybody gets out of line, take care of it. Lang and I are going to have a little private talk."

The deputy nodded, his face grim.

Jim borrowed a lantern from a bystander, ushered John Lang into the deserted saloon and pulled two chairs away from a table. "All right, John," he said, "tell me about it. Just the quick story—how it all started and who shot who."

Lang cleared his throat nervously. "It was after—the dance at Romero's. Ed and me, we was riding down Main Street when Ed's girl Sally walked up. Ed got down and handed me the reins. I was leading his horse off when I heard a voice from the front of the saloon."

Lang reached into his pocket for his tobacco sack. His hands and fingers trembled so hard he couldn't roll the smoke. Jim took the tobacco, twisted up a quirly, lit it and handed the cigarette to Lang.

"What was said and who said it?" Jim prompted.

Lang dragged at the smoke. "Didn't hear what. It was Lem
Woodruff's voice. Next thing I know I hear a shot. Ed spins around
and falls down. Sally takes off. Woodruff runs out of the shadows,
puts his rifle on Ed's throat and pulls the trigger. I rode back to the
Equity and hollered to Frank and Fred that they'd shot Ed. We
grabbed our guns and come back on the run."

Lang shook his head wearily. "They were waiting for us. Woodruff, Luis Bausman, Charley and Tom Emory, maybe a couple others I didn't see. Woodruff got hit in the gut the first time we traded
shots. He ran into the saloon here. I think Charley Emory got hit,
too. I was busy trying to stay alive, find me some cover, but I saw
Frank chase Woodruff into the saloon. Heard Frank shoot his pistol
four, five times, then heard one rifle shot. Frank didn't come out."

Lang took a final puff of the cigarette and dropped the butt on
the floor. "Fred and me ducked behind those plaster boards. The
café man stepped out the door. Fred shot him before I knew what
was happening. Then they opened up on us for sure. Slugs were
tearing those plaster boards to pieces. Fred got hit twice in the
chest. He handed me his pistol and I ran. They shot at me all the
way down Main."

Lang held up his coat sleeve and poked a quivering finger
through a hole torn in the cloth. "Nearly got me, too. That's about
all I can tell you. After the shooting stopped I came back to see if—
see who all was dead."

Jim studied Lang's face as the cowboy spoke. He seemed to be
telling the truth.

"Sheriff, those nester boys bushwacked us cold from out of the
dark. I know some of them were friends of yours. What you going
to do about it?"

Jim eased his chair back and stood. "First, Lang, I'm going to
lock you up, as much for your own good as anything. I wasn't the
only friend Lem Woodruff and the Emory brothers had. Then I'm
going after them."

Jim escorted the shaken Lang outside. The surprise and shock of
the gunfight had begun to fade from the crowd. The tone of muted
conversations had changed from curiosity to growing anger. Jim
knew he had to take control quickly, before another gunbattle
started. There were members of both factions in the group. He
picked out two men, one an LIT cowboy who was a solid associa-

tion backer, another a townsman who stood firm on the side of the small ranchers.

"Strouthers, I'm deputizing you and Dougan there. I want you to keep a close watch on these bodies. Don't let anybody near them." He raised his voice so that all could easily hear. "I don't want any more trouble to come out of this. If anybody gets out of line, they'll answer to me."

Strouthers and Dougan nodded. They didn't look too happy about it but Jim knew they would do their best to keep the crowd under control.

Jim waved his deputy alongside. "Let's go, L.C. We've got some suspects to find. We're looking for Lem Woodruff, Tom and Charley Emory and Luis Bausman. You know their hangouts as well as I do. I'll go after Luis and Tom Emory. See if you can locate Lem and Charley Emory. They're both hurt and probably didn't go too far. Don't shoot anybody unless you have to."

L. C. Pierce nodded and strode away. Jim set off toward Luis Bausman's nondescript adobe a few blocks away.

Jim pulled his Colt and opened Luis's door. Bausman lay on the sagging cot, the covers pulled up to his chin. The flame of an oil lamp flickered on a table nearby.

"Hello, Jim. What you barge in like that for? What's all the shootin' about?"

Jim reached for Bausman's Winchester leaning against the inside wall near the door. The barrel was almost too hot to touch. He motioned with the muzzle of his handgun. "You're under arrest, Luis. Suspicion of murder. Come along quiet."

Bausman grinned sheepishly and tossed the covers back. He was fully clothed, his boots and pant legs dusty. "Hell, Jim, I should have known I couldn't fool you." He got to his feet. "Them damn LS barroom gladiators started it, Jim. All we did was finish it."

"You'll get a chance to tell your side in court, Luis."

Twenty minutes later Luis Bausman and Charley Emory sat in the Oldham County jail. Charley was in bad shape. A slug had ripped through the heavy muscle of his thigh. He was bleeding heavily and moaning in pain.

"Found Charley in the doorway of the blacksmith shop," L. C. Pierce said. "I sent for the doctor. Looks like the new man in town's going to have all the patients he can handle—alive and dead."

"Let's just hope it doesn't get worse," Jim said. "We've got two of the men we want. Two more to go."

Pierce spat a sharp oath. "Make it three. I went to see if the Catfish Kid was dead yet. He wasn't there. No blood trail. Dammit, Jim, I couldn't have missed at that range."

Jim shrugged. "He won't be that much trouble. We'll put the word out for Catfish to come in and give himself up to save us the trouble of shooting him to pieces. He'll come." Jim strode back to the office, picked up his rifle and racked a round into the chamber. "I'm going after Tom Emory, L.C. I've got a good idea where he might be."

Dawn was a faint smear on the eastern horizon when Jim East pulled his horse to a stop in front of the small rock house all but hidden in a stand of trees and wild plum thickets at the headwaters of Tascosa Creek. A rifle barrel protruded from a window at the front of the abandoned wolfer's shack.

"Come on out, Tom!" Jim yelled. "I've got to take you in! I'd rather you be in the saddle than across it!"

Moments later the rifle muzzle disappeared. Tom Emory stepped through the door, the Winchester held muzzle down at his side. He strode up to Jim's stirrup. Moisture glistened at the corners of his eyes. "Jim, I'll let a lynch mob hang me before I'll shoot it out with an old friend."

"There'll be no lynchings from my jail, Tom."

Tom handed over the Winchester. "How's Lem and Charley? Looked like they were hit mighty hard."

Jim sheathed his own rifle and nestled Tom's weapon in the crook of an elbow. "Charley's in jail. If he doesn't bleed to death he'll make it. We haven't found Lem yet. You bring a horse?"

Tom shook his head. "Walked out here. Run most of the way. How'd you know where to look?"

"I remembered this place from the times we went hunting up here, Tom. Not too many people know where it is. Hard to find unless you know where to look. I just played a hunch you'd come back here." Jim kicked a boot free of the stirrup. "Climb aboard. This horse'll ride double. No sense in making you walk back to town."

FOURTEEN

Tascosa
March 1886

The sun was barely an hour above the eastern horizon as Jim East stood near a blood-soaked patch of sand on Main Street and watched as the justice of the peace and the doctor bent over Ed King's body.

The physician thrust a probe into the hole in King's face, worked the instrument a couple of times and grunted in satisfaction as he pulled out a deformed small-caliber bullet. The doctor held the slug out for Jim's examination.

"I make it a thirty-two," the physician said. He shook his head in wonder. "Little soft lead slugs cause a hell of a lot more damage than a man would think. This fellow never knew what hit him."

Jim frowned at the news. Lem Woodruff carried a thirty-two-forty Winchester, an uncommon caliber in the Panhandle. The slug wasn't positive proof, but it was a pretty fair indication of who had fired the fatal shot.

The dead men still lay where they fell, uncovered and open to the view of the crowd that milled about in front of the Jenkins and Dunn Saloon. Small boys slipped away from distracted fathers and darted in for awed peeks at the bloodstained bodies.

At the edge of the crowd Jim saw three LS riders mount and ride toward their home range. In a matter of hours, Jim knew, every cowboy riding for an association brand would be in town. They wouldn't be alone. Members of the nester faction already were gathering in the street, faces grim and pistols strapped on hips. *We're about three steps away from a war,* Jim thought.

He glanced up as L. C. Pierce strode up. "No sign of Woodruff yet, Jim. Blood trail played out behind the stores across the street. As much blood as he's lost, I doubt Lem's alive anyway."

"We'll find him, L.C., sooner or later. What I can't figure is how Jesse Sheets fits into this. It looks like he'd just rolled out of bed. He wasn't carrying a gun."

"Innocent bystander," the deputy said. "He told me yesterday he thought the cook was helping himself to supplies and the cash box after hours. Jesse said he planned to spend the night in the café and see if he could catch him at it. Jesse probably just stepped out to see what was going on and walked into a slug. Damn shame. He was a decent man."

Jim sighed. "In their own ways, L.C., I suppose they all were." He reached for the makings and rolled a cigarette as the doctor and justice of the peace finished examining the bodies. A few minutes later the four dead men were laid out on the saloon's narrow porch, the bodies draped in blood-soaked sheets. Blowflies buzzed over the gory bundles.

"What now, Jim?"

Jim took a slow, thoughtful drag on the cigarette. "What we do now is try our damnedest to make sure we don't have a full-scale war on our hands." He glanced around the crowd. "This thing's opened a powder keg. Some fool may decide to strike a match." He motioned to the two men he had appointed as deputies earlier. The two strode forward.

"Dougan, I want you to ride out to the small ranches and the cowboy camps. Spread the word I'll tolerate no trouble because of this. Strouthers, you go to the LIT and LX outfits. Tell them the same thing. L.C., I'd like for you to call on Jess Jenkins. Tom Harris too, if he's in town. They've got the most influence on the Tascosa cowboys and the town faction lined up against the association. Tell them I expect their help in keeping a lid on this thing."

"What are you going to do, Jim?" L.C. asked.

Jim dropped his cigarette stub and ground it beneath a heel. "I'm riding out to the LS and have a little heart-to-heart talk with W. M. D. Lee," Jim said. "It was his boys who were killed here. He's the boss bull in the association herd. That makes him the key to heading off any stampede."

LS Headquarters

Jim East stood before W. M. D. Lee's desk and studied the narrow face of the slightly built majority owner of the LS outfit. The brand registries said the LS belonged to both Lee and Lucien Scott, but everyone knew Lee was the man who had the final say.

Lee shoved back his chair and stood. The expression in his eyes was sharp and angry; the banty rooster had its neck feathers ruffled and was looking for a fight. "Let me get this straight," Lee said. "You expect me to tell LS riders they can't hit back when three of their own have been gunned down?"

"That's about the size of it, Mister Lee," Jim said. "I'm asking the other big ranchers—and the nesters and little men too—to keep the peace. If this gets out of hand we'll have a range war that'll make Lincoln County look like a lover's spat. I'm asking both sides to let the courts, not Winchesters, settle this."

"I don't see where you've got the right to tell me what to do, East. Hell, you've been on the side of the nesters from the start."

Jim felt the warmth of anger glow in his gut. "Mister Lee, I rode out here to ask your cooperation. Now I'm going to put it in a little stronger language. Whether you like it or not I'm the sheriff of Oldham County. I won't stand still for any shooting war. If it happens I'll throw you in the lockup first and think of a charge later."

Lee stared for a long moment at Jim, the muscles in his face twitching. Finally he exhaled a long sigh. "By God, East, I think you're serious about that."

"There isn't a circuit preacher in Texas more serious than I am right now, Mister Lee."

"I can't make any guarantees."

"I can," Jim said. "I've already made you one."

Lee picked up a pencil nub and tapped it against the edge of his desk. "Sheriff," he said after a moment, "I'll grant you one thing. You've got nerve." He tossed the pencil down in disgust. "All right. I'll talk to them. It may not do any good, but I'll try."

Jim nodded and snugged his hat down. "That's what I was hoping to hear, Mister Lee. Will I see you at the funerals tomorrow?"

"Maybe. I'm not sure yet."

Jim touched his fingertips to his hat brim and strode from the office. Outside, he paused for a moment and let his gaze drift over the half dozen LS riders who lounged on the porch or sat horseback. The men were surly and scowling. Jim nodded a silent greeting to a couple of the men he knew, then mounted and reined his horse toward home.

Tascosa

Jim East was about to dismount in front of the courthouse when a tall, slender man on horseback trotted up to his side.

"Sheriff, Lem's at my place," the man said. "He's hurt bad, real bad. He may not make it. He asked to see you."

Jim settled back into the saddle. "Lead the way."

A half hour later Jim stepped inside a small two-room house in a hay meadow two miles from Tascosa. Lem Woodruff lay on his side beneath a thin blanket, knees drawn up toward his chest. Sweat dribbled from his forehead down his stubbled face. His eyes were glazed and feverish when he looked up.

"Jim, I—" Lem moaned as a fresh wave of pain ripped through his body. "I reckon I've stepped in it—for sure this time."

"I reckon you have, Lem," Jim said. "Let me take a look." He peeled back the blanket. He almost shook his head in dismay before he realized Lem was watching. There was no sense in letting Lem Woodruff know he was all but dead. One slug had taken Lem low in the belly. A second had slashed into the hip near his groin. It was the belly wound that worried Jim the most. Few men lived through a rifle slug in the guts.

"Bad, ain't it?" Lem gasped.

"Bad enough, Lem. We've got to get you into town to the doctor." Jim turned to the hay farmer. "You have a flatbed wagon?" At the man's nod, Jim issued instructions to hitch up the wagon, pad the bed with hay and toss a mattress atop the padding.

When the rig was ready Jim slipped his arms under Lem's armpits. "Easy now," he told the farmer. "Take his feet. Try not to jostle him."

Lem Woodruff fainted from the pain before the two men had him settled in the wagon for the trip to Tascosa. Jim mounted his sorrel and nodded to the farmer on the wagon seat. "Take it slow," he said. "We don't want to kill him on the way in."

Back in Tascosa the two men placed Lem Woodruff on the cot in Luis Bausman's house. Luis wouldn't be needing it for a while and there were no rooms to be had in any of Tascosa's hotels or boardinghouses. Jim sent the hay farmer for the doctor and stayed at Lem's side.

Lem's eyes fluttered open a moment later. "Jim?" His voice was weak, distant.

"I'm here, Lem."

"We—we rode a lot of miles together," Lem said. Jim had to lean close to make out the words. "If I—don't make it, I want you—to have my saddle—and guns." He moaned through clenched teeth. "Sell my horse and—buy a marker."

"Hush that nonsense," Jim said. He reached for a bucket of water on a table by the bed, held a dipper to Lem's lips and let the wounded man have two small sips. He pulled a handkerchief from his pocket, dribbled water over it and wiped the damp rag over Lem Woodruff's forehead and cheeks. "You're going to make it, Lem," Jim said. "Cowboys like us are too stubborn and too tough to die."

Jim turned the nursing chores over to the doctor a few minutes later, then mounted and reined his horse toward home.

Hattie met him at the door, frown lines etched deeper in her face, her brown eyes red-rimmed from tears. She came into his arms and buried her face in his shoulder.

"Oh, Jim, it's been awful. Those men, all dead . . ."

Jim stroked her hair. "It's going to be all right, girl." He wished he felt as confident as he sounded.

"I've been over to Missus Sheets's house," Hattie said. "That poor family. All they had to their names was Jesse and the few dollars he made from the restaurant. I don't know what's going to happen to them now." Hattie released Jim and led him into the house. She dabbed at the corners of her eyes with her apron. "Missus Sheets is just shattered by grief," she said. "She told me she didn't want her husband buried beside those—those gunfighters, she called them. I told L.C. He said he'd make sure it was taken care of, that Jesse would be put in a corner of Boot Hill far away from them. Did I do the right thing?"

Jim squeezed her shoulder in reassurance. "Yes, Hattie. You did the right thing."

She turned away to dish up his meal. Jim told her about Lem Woodruff's surrender and that Lem was badly hurt. "I'll get right on over there and see if I can help as soon as you've eaten," she said. "He'll need a nurse—"

A knock on the door interrupted the conversation. Jim swung the portal open. A sheepish J. B. Gough stood in the doorway, hat in hand. "Hello, Catfish," Jim said. "You come to turn yourself in?"

The Catfish Kid nodded. "Heard it would be a damn sight less trouble than havin' you come after me." He twisted the brim of his hat in nervous fingers. "Jim, I didn't kill nobody."

Jim glanced over his shoulder at Hattie. "Keep my supper warm, girl," he said. "I'll be back in a while." He motioned toward the courthouse. "After you, Catfish."

The two men strode side by side down the dusty street. Jim became aware of the murderous looks thrown their way by cowboys and townspeople. The Catfish Kid had never been one of Tascosa's more popular figures. It wasn't difficult to understand the hard feelings toward a man who seemed to have no means of support beyond the card table. Jim loosened the Colt in his holster. He made sure the observers in general and the LS cowboys in particular saw the gesture.

"Catfish, you're supposed to be dead," Jim said. "L.C. thought he got a slug in you after the fight."

The Catfish Kid smiled wryly. "Quite a piece of luck I had there, Jim," he said. "I slipped in the mud where somebody had been making adobe bricks. Fell just as L.C. shot. The slug went over my head. I acted like I was hit, moanin' and rollin' my eyes and all, until L.C. went away. Then I got the hell out of there."

Jim ushered Catfish toward the cell in back. "You know, running away like that isn't going to make it look good for you. You packing a hideout gun on me?"

"I wouldn't try to slicker you, Jim. I'm clean. And as far as runnin', at the time it seemed a lot better than gettin' shot."

Jim swung the cell door open, let the Catfish Kid inside, and nodded a greeting to the other prisoners.

"Jim," Tom Emory said, "what's going on out there?"

Jim shrugged. "So far, not much. A lot of hard looks going back and forth across Main, but everybody's kept their tempers under control."

"Reckon it'll be that way tomorrow?"

"I sure as hell hope so," Jim said. He closed and locked the door. "I'll get somebody to rustle some grub for you boys. Charley, how's the leg?"

Charley Emory propped himself on an elbow on the bunk. "Hurts like old billy blazes. But it ain't bled any more."

"If it starts giving you trouble we'll fetch the doctor. I'll have L.C. come over in case you boys need anything."

Tom Emory grinned. "Most hospitable jail I've ever been in." The smile faded. "I'd sure hate to see it tore up by a bunch of guys with ropes."

"Relax, Tom. There won't be any lynch mob. If there's any more trouble it'll come after the funeral, I expect."

Jim East stood at the edge of Boot Hill, the ten-bore shotgun draped in the crook of an arm and the tiedown thong slipped off the hammer of his holstered handgun. A few feet away L. C. Pierce held a Winchester. He also had a Colt forty-four-forty in his holster and another tucked into his waistband.

Special deputies Strouthers, Dougan and Dobbs flanked the three freshly dug graves, rifles in hand. Jim wasn't sure he could count on Strouthers and Dougan if trouble started. But Dobbs was dependable. He would back Jim even if it meant throwing down on his friends.

Jim knew the mere presence of the three special officers should be enough to make anybody inclined toward trouble think twice. He also knew any confrontation wasn't likely to break out during the funerals. It wasn't the nature of the people of the Texas Panhandle to disrupt anything so solemn. Odds were that if there was trouble it would come later, when the bodies were buried and the saloons opened again.

It was one of those rare Panhandle days with no wind. The March sun seemed to have its seasons mixed up and thought it was August. Sweat trickled down Jim's back. Heat waves shimmered over the funeral entourage approaching the hill. A wagon carried the coffins of King, Valley and Chilton in dirge-step toward Boot Hill. A long line of LS, LIT and LX cowboys rode at one side of the wagon. On the other side a smaller but still impressive force of the "little men" faction walked or rode. Behind the wagon strode a contingent of Tascosa residents who had remained neutral in the struggle between the big outfits and the little men. That group was the smallest of the lot.

As usual Tascosa had shut down for the funerals. Women and older children were in the procession along with their men. Jim paid scant attention to the family groups. He concentrated on the two groups of armed men on either side of the wagon. The men wore pistols at their hips and carried rifles in saddle scabbards.

It was what he didn't see that bothered Jim East the most. W. M. D. Lee was not among the mourners.

The ceremonies began with the unloading of three pine coffins beside the open graves. The caskets were opened for a final viewing of the remains, which was good luck for Ed King—if a dead man could be said to have luck—because King's coffin faced the wrong direction. He would have been buried with his head to the west instead of the east if not for the viewing tradition.

The county judge removed his hat and opened his tattered Episcopal prayer book, the signal that final interment was about to begin. Jim removed his own hat. Seconds later all heads were bared to the blazing sun.

The judge recited the old-style Twenty-third Psalm:

"The Lord is my shepherd; therefore can I lack nothing. He shall feed me in a green pasture, and lead me forth beside the waters of comfort . . ."

The prayer was brief. The ceremony ended with the women of Tascosa leading two hymns. The closing notes of the final song had barely sounded when the second procession of the day wound up the narrow road to the hilltop cemetery. Jesse Sheets was about to be laid to his eternal rest.

As his widow had requested, Jesse's grave waited at a far corner of the cemetery, well removed from the other victims of the shootout. The crowd drifted in silence to his gravesite to pay respects to the innocent victim. For a second time that day both factions stood side by side as the burial ceremony was repeated for Jesse Sheets.

Then the men donned hats, re-formed ranks, and the crowd made its way down the hill. Jim mounted and rode the right flank, L. C. Pierce the left. The special deputies spaced themselves at either side of the wagons as the columns of armed men walked or rode back into town. Few of them spoke. Those who did talked in hushed tones. Occasionally one of the LS cowboys and a member of the opposing faction would exchange cold glares, but nothing worse developed. *The next few hours will decide whether it's war or peace,* Jim thought.

Jim East stood beneath the wind-gnarled branches of an ancient cottonwood beside the road to Mobeetie at the southeast edge of Hogtown, and studied the cowboys crowded into the small clearing.

He estimated there were more than fifty riders in the group, all but a handful from the LS. And they were in a surly mood.

"I tell you, boys, it's time we grabbed this ox by the tail and cleaned out that bunch of nesters," a loud voice called from the center of the group. "There's a bunch of 'em over at the Emporium right now, drinkin' and laughin' about how they bushwhacked three of our boys. And them that done the killin's in the jail. Wouldn't be no trouble to bust 'em out and lynch 'em."

An angry murmur rippled through the crowd. "Damn right," another man called. "We ought to hang every one of 'em and then tear this damn town down to the ground. Teach 'em all a lesson, by God!"

This thing's about to bust loose, Jim thought. *Maybe I can't stop it, but I can slow it down.* He glanced at the road leading from Tascosa to LS headquarters. *Dammit, where's Lee? I sent Strouthers after him three hours ago. He should be here by now.*

Jim stepped away from the bole of the cottonwood, the forestock of his shotgun cradled in his left elbow. The mutterings faded as the cowboys became aware of his presence. "Hold on a minute, boys!" Jim raised his voice so that all could hear. "Think this over before you do something we'll all regret!"

"You gonna stop us, Sheriff?" A lanky young cowboy stood at the edge of the crowd, his hand on the butt of his pistol.

Jim glared at the speaker. "Maybe I can't, but I've got to try."

"Fifty of us and one of you?"

Jim shrugged. "You've got the odds about right. You boys could take me. It might get expensive." He tapped a forefinger against the trigger guard of the smoothbore. It was a small gesture but one that spoke a lot of words. "Those of you who might get past me might want to think on this for a minute—the Texas Rangers don't take kindly to lynch mobs. Especially when a duly elected sheriff gets killed."

The young cowboy sniffed in disdain. "You hidin' behind that badge, Sheriff?"

"No," Jim said, his tone calm, "I'm standing behind a ten-bore sawed off. The badge goes with the scattergun." Jim kept his gaze steady on the young rider. The brash expression faded from the man's sun-browned face. His hand fell away from the pistol. *He might be young,* Jim thought, *but he's smart enough to know he'd be the first one to go down.* He dismissed the rider as no immediate threat and shifted his gaze, searching out the older and wiser faces.

"Boys," Jim said, "I've ridden with some of you in the past. You're not hired guns, you're cowboys. There's no sense in anybody else getting dead for a cowboy's pay. I'm not questioning your guts, just asking you to use your common sense. We've already had one innocent bystander killed. I don't want to see any others hurt, and a bullet doesn't care who or what it hits. Think about it for a minute—do you want to be the one who pulls the trigger and accidentally kills a woman, or a young kid who's done you no harm?"

Jim paused for a moment to let that idea take root. He knew cowboys. They weren't by nature violent men, and they had an ingrained respect for women, a genuine fondness for kids, and a soft spot for any helpless creature. They were hurt and angry and wanted to hit back at something, but they weren't cold and unreasonable men. It just took them a while to study things through sometimes.

"Enough of this yammering," one of the men called. "Let's go clean out that bunch of nesters!"

The solemn quiet broke into a low mutter. Jim could feel the anger build back in the crowd. The tension became almost a thing a man could touch. He cocked the shotgun hammers. *You've lost them, East,* he told himself, *this herd's about to stampede and one man isn't going to turn them.*

"Hold it!" The yell from the back of the crowd was like the roar of a mad grizzly. Jim glanced at the bear-voiced man, a rider nick-named Goose who had defied the cowboy strike and stayed with the LS. Goose shoved his way through the mob to Jim's side, an ancient and scarred Henry rifle in his hand. "You hotheaded young whippersnappers just wait a minute!" Goose jabbed a thumb over his shoulder. "The boss is comin' down the road yonder. Let's hear what he has to say."

Jim chanced a glance over his shoulder and silently sighed in relief. W. M. D. Lee's buggy moved toward the gathering at a stiff trot, Strouthers riding alongside. A sudden thought choked off Jim's sigh and sent a jolt through him—if Lee were of a mind to do so, he could whip this crowd into a killing frenzy that no man could stop. Lee and the big men had a lot to gain if the little ranchers and nesters were wiped out. The thought chilled Jim. He had put his own fate in another man's hands. One wrong word from Lee and Jim East would be so full of lead it would take nine people to carry the coffin.

Lee's buggy creaked to a halt. Dust eddied toward the crowd from the carriage wheels and filtered down in the long silence as the LS owner sat and stared at the gang of cowboys. Then Lee climbed from the buggy and strode to Jim's side.

"Boys," Lee said, "I've talked to everyone in Tascosa who knows anything about the fight. Nobody is madder about three of our men getting killed than I am. But there's a badger here we can't put back in its hole, and that's the possibility that our boys weren't lily-pure themselves in this whole thing."

Lee tapped the buggy whip against his boots and waited for the mutter of the crowd to settle. Jim finally felt the tension begin to drain from his muscles.

"Some of you probably heard it was an ambush," Lee said. "I can't buy that idea. I'm satisfied that it was nothing more than a drunken shootout that started over woman trouble. That's not a good enough reason to start a war. Sheriff East and his deputies have the killers in jail. They'll stand trial. Let's leave it at that."

Lee abruptly turned away, climbed into the buggy seat and picked up the reins. "Boys," he called, "the LS is paying you to punch cows, and right now you're wasting company money. Saddle up and let's get back to work. We've got a ranch to run."

It seemed to Jim that a collective sigh of relief swept over the crowd, as if they were glad the boss had made the decision for them. Now nobody could say they hadn't stood up for the brand or their saddlemates. Singly and in groups the men moved toward their horses picketed at the side of the Mobeetie road.

Jim stepped alongside the buggy. "Mister Lee, I want you to know I appreciate what you've done. We were headed for a blood-bath for sure."

Lee nodded, but anger still smoldered in his eyes. "I didn't do it for you, East. I did it for my riders, my brand and my associates. Dead cowboys can't work cows and the Cattleman's Association would be blamed for any war. It would be bad economics and bad politics."

Lee glared hard at Jim. "I'd like nothing more than to see that nester bunch run out of the Panhandle once and for all. I passed up a good chance to do that here today. The big ranchers built this country, and the three-cow outfits and nesters can't run us out, war or no war." His tone turned even colder. "Sheriff, I want you to understand one thing: I didn't do it because I'm afraid of you or that badge."

"That particular thought never entered my mind," Jim said.

Lee lifted the buggy whip, then lowered it. "East, we both know that gunfight wasn't really over a woman. It went a lot deeper than that and it started a long time ago. I doubt it will be over in our lifetimes. As long as there is land, there will be people fighting for it."

Lee flicked the whip against the buggy horse's rump, sawed the reins about and headed back to the road to the LS. Jim watched the ranch owner go. Small rooster tails of dust kicked from the buggy wheels. The cowboys rode two by two behind the rig.

Jim stood alone in the clearing for several minutes. Then he shouldered the shotgun. "No, Mister Lee," he half whispered toward the retreating column of riders, "it won't be over in our lifetimes. But for now, I'll settle for what we have."

Jim found L. C. Pierce riding shotgun on an unusually subdued crowd at the Emporium in Hogtown. "Looks quiet in here, L.C. Any troubles?"

The deputy shook his head. "Got a little touchy at one point, but Jess Jenkins and Tom Harris talked the boys down. Tom left town an hour or so back. He took some of the more gun-happy boys with him. I saw the LS punchers ride out behind Lee's buggy. Guess it's all over."

"It's over, L.C. There won't be a shooting war now."

Jim spotted Jess Jenkins seated alone at a table, a bottle of rye before him. Jim strode to the saloon owner's table, toed out a chair and sat.

"Thanks, Jess," Jim said. "You and Tom helped save a lot of killing here today."

Jenkins grunted. "Sure was tempted to turn 'em loose," the saloon owner grumbled, "but it's bad business to get your customers killed. Drink, Sheriff?"

Jim nodded. His nerves were still a bit raw. Maybe a shot would help. It wasn't likely to make things worse. Jenkins gestured to the bartender, who brought another shot glass to the table. Jenkins filled the glass from his own bottle.

Jim East raised the shot glass in a silent toast to Jess Jenkins, then tossed back the liquor and winced. The stuff burned the throat like lye unless a man drank enough to get calluses on his gullet. He waved away the offered refill.

Jim realized that his belly hurt and his eyes felt like half the Canadian River sand was trapped under his lids. He hadn't eaten since dawn and had slept less than four hours in the last two days. *Must be getting old,* he thought. *The hours come a lot longer than they used to.*

He pushed his chair back and stood. "Thanks again for your help, Jess." Jim walked to his deputy's side. "L.C.," he said, "I'm dog-tired, I'm hungry and I've still got a case of the yips. What say we call it a night? Kid Dobbs is still deputized. I stopped by the jail on the way over. Dobbs agreed to watch the prisoners until sunup."

L. C. Pierce flashed a wan and weary smile. "I think that's the best idea anybody's had today, Sheriff."

Jim strode from the saloon, L.C. a step behind, and paused to take a deep breath. The late afternoon air held a slight scent of dust, but to Jim East it was sweet as molasses and cornbread. *Any man who doesn't appreciate life has never come within an ace of losing it,* he thought.

He waved a casual good-night to L.C. as they parted at Main and McMasters, each headed for the comfort of his own home.

Fifteen minutes later he was in Hattie's arms, the smell of fresh sourdough biscuits and fried chicken blending with her scent of rose water and woman.

"Oh, Jim, I was so scared," Hattie said as she snuggled against his chest.

"It was time to be scared, Hattie," he said, "but it's over now."

"You look exhausted."

"I am. But some of that chicken I smell and a little nap—eight or ten hours, maybe—will take care of that."

A half hour later Jim pushed his empty plate away, waved off Hattie's offer to refill his coffee cup, motioned for her to sit beside him and reached for her hand.

"Hattie, I've decided something. Not just today, but over the past few months. There's a world of opportunity in Tascosa and the Panhandle, a lot of things a man can do to make a good living." He sighed and looked deep into her eyes. "I don't intend to run for sheriff again this fall."

Hattie's eyes misted. "I wouldn't have mentioned it for the world, but I'm glad you made that decision. I've worried so about you. In case you hadn't noticed, Jim East, being a sheriff isn't the safest line of work for a man."

"Or for a woman to have to worry through," Jim added, his tone tender. "I haven't spent nearly enough time with you over the past few years, girl. I plan to make that up to you. Until you get tired of having me underfoot and boot me out the door."

She squeezed his hand. "That'll be a while, Mister East," she said.

Tascosa
January 1887

Jim East handed his badge and the keys to the Oldham County jail to newly elected Sheriff Tobe Robinson, concluded the exchange with a handshake, and led Hattie from the courthouse into the blustery north wind that swept down McMasters and swirled onto Court Street. Neither spoke until the door of their home closed behind them and blocked the chill outside.

"Well, former sheriff East," Hattie said as she draped her coat on a peg and turned into his arms, "I guess I have you to myself for a while now."

Jim grinned at her. "For better or for worse. And maybe even sometimes for dinner."

"I've got a treat planned for you this morning, Jim," she said. "Chocolate. I've been saving it for weeks for a special occasion."

Jim pulled two chairs around to face the fireplace and placed a small table before them.

The two sipped at the rich, steamy delicacy in silence for a time, content with the moment and the simple pleasure of each other's company.

Finally, Hattie sighed and turned to her husband. Jim saw a mixture of relief and pride in the deep brown eyes.

"Any regrets, Jim? Over giving up the badge?"

"A few. There were so many crimes I never solved, people I never caught. One of the things that grates on me is that I never found proof Bill Moore was stealing LS cattle. Now he's fat and happy and has a hatful of money. I never could abide a man who would steal from the brand he rode for, Hattie. The old cowboy in me coming out again, I suppose." He fell silent and listened to the moan of the wind outside.

"Jim, you accomplished more than enough during your term," Hattie said. "People will remember what you did as sheriff of Tascosa."

Jim stared into the fire for a few heartbeats, then shrugged. "No, Hattie. They won't remember what I did. People remember things that happen. They'll remember the big gunfight on Main Street. They'll remember the dead men buried on Boot Hill. But they won't remember a thing that never happened."

He leaned back, stretched in contentment, and pulled Hattie closer to him. "They won't remember the big range war that tore the Texas Panhandle apart, Hattie. Because it didn't happen. I'll be more than happy to settle for that."

EPILOGUE

After he turned in his badge as sheriff of Oldham County, Jim East worked for a year as a ranch foreman, then bought the Equity Saloon on Tascosa's Main Street. It was in that establishment that he was involved in his last recorded gunfight when he killed gambler Tom Clark in a shootout in 1889. When Tascosa was in its death throes as a community, Jim East moved to Douglas, Arizona, in 1903, where he served as city marshal, chief of police, and police judge. He died there on May 12, 1930, at the age of 77.

Pat Garrett returned to New Mexico, lost a fortune in a vast irrigation scheme, and later served the state again as a special investigator and sheriff. In February 1908, near Alameda Arroyo, New Mexico, the famed lawman was killed by a gunshot to the back of his head. The identity of his killer was never established.

Dave Rudabaugh, the unwashed partner of Billy the Kid, made his escape into Mexico where he terrorized a village until the inhabitants finally became fed up and solved the problem by chopping off Rudabaugh's head and displaying it on a stake in the town square.

Lem Woodruff recovered from his severe gunshot wounds and was tried along with Luis Bausman, Charley Emory, Tom Emory and J. B. Gough (the Catfish Kid) for the murders of Ed King, Frank Valley, Jesse Sheets and Fred Chilton in the "Big Fight." The first trial resulted in a hung jury; in a second trial the defendants were acquitted.

No proof was ever established that Bill Moore, fired from the LX under a cloud of suspicion, had started his own ranching empire with the aid of a long rope and a running iron. He became a successful and respected ranch owner in New Mexico.

Jess Jenkins parlayed his earnings in Tascosa and Hogtown into a career as a successful businessman and entrepreneur in the Panhandle.

Tom Harris, leader of the cowboy strike, took his own life sometime in the late 1800s.

Tascosa, the one-time cow capital of the Texas Panhandle, did not survive the winds of politics, railroads and progress. The original site of Tascosa now is home to the famed Cal Farley's Boys Ranch, the land deeded to Farley by Julian Bivins, LX Ranch owner. Today there are only two tangible reminders of Tascosa's past. One is the old two-story courthouse which now serves as a museum on Boys Ranch. The other is Boot Hill.

About the Author

Gene Shelton is a lifelong Texas resident, raised on a ranch in the Panhandle. As a youth, he worked as a ranch hand and horse trainer, and rode the amateur rodeo circuit as a bull rider and calf roper.

He is the author of *Last Gun, Captain Jack,* and *Rawhider,* the first three books in the *Texas Legends* series, as well as two other acclaimed Western novels, *Track of the Snake* and *Day of the Scorpion.* He has been an active member of the Western Writers of America, Inc., since 1981.

A newspaperman by trade, he has been a reporter for the *Amarillo Globe-News* and the *Dallas Times Herald.* His most recent assignments were as managing editor of the *Sulphur Springs News-Telegram* and as copy editor for the *Tyler Courier-Times.* He has also written numerous magazine articles for *The Quarter Horse Journal, The Ranchman,* and *Black Belt Magazine.*

He has taught fiction-writing classes at several colleges and universities in the East Texas area.